THE NUMBERS

McCarter didn't feel they were any closer to eliminating the threat than the moment they stepped foot in this godforsaken desert. Sure, they had some idea of the terrorists' plans but they didn't really know where they would hit or how they would do it. And if Phoenix Force failed in their mission, it only increased the chances of the nuclear material getting to its final destination.

The fact remained that Able Team didn't have any more ability to wage war against the nuclear threat than Phoenix Force. At the end of the day, they had to succeed. Failure wasn't an option and neither was compromise. This time around, the stakes were high enough that there could only be one outcome for Phoenix Force: absolute victory! Because if David McCarter knew something with certainty, it was this.

Anything less would mean tragic defeat for America and her people.

DON PENDLETON'S

STONY

AMERICA'S ULTRA-COVERT INTELLIGENCE AGENCY

MAN®

WAR TIDES

A GOLD EAGLE BOOK FROM
WORLDWIDE®

TORONTO • NEW YORK • LONDON
AMSTERDAM • PARIS • SYDNEY • HAMBURG
STOCKHOLM • ATHENS • TOKYO • MILAN
MADRID • WARSAW • BUDAPEST • AUCKLAND

Recycling programs
for this product may
not exist in your area.

First edition June 2010

ISBN-13: 978-0-373-61991-7

WAR TIDES

Special thanks and acknowledgment to
Jon Guenther for his contribution to this work.

Printed in U.S.A.

WAR TIDES

Dedicated to the brave warriors of the
U.S. Navy SEAL team who rescued American
maritime captain Richard Phillips from
Somali pirates in April 2009.

CHAPTER ONE

Washington, D.C.

At just after 0400 hours on a cold Thursday morning, four FBI agents hustled Dr. Philip Stout from his offices at the U.S. Navy shipyard into a waiting government SUV.

The reason for Dr. Stout's visit to an emergency session of the Joint Chiefs of Staff was highly classified. None of the agents strayed beyond the polite conversation required by their jobs. Still, it didn't take an advanced science degree like one of several possessed by Stout to guess that his visit likely had to do with the contents of the briefcase handcuffed to his wrist. Inside the reinforced-aluminum box were secrets so classified not a single one of the agents escorting Stout to the Pentagon had a security clearance high enough to know even the nature of its contents.

Not that they needed to. Their job was simple: transport the doctor from the shipyard to the Pentagon and keep him alive in transit.

As far as Philip Stout was concerned, the four men assigned to protect him were better off not knowing the things he knew. Stout had spent the past eight years of his career developing a prototype for the U.S. Navy, and he was about to deliver all of its secrets to the Joint Chiefs. In some ways, it made Stout feel like the member of a transplant team who had to get a badly needed heart across town with only a small window of opportunity. In some respects, it wasn't that far from the truth. If the secrets he carried with him fell into enemy hands, it could well mean a whole new day of terror for America.

And while the FBI agents accompanying him may or may not have realized that, they *did* realize the importance of protecting him. Especially when their SUV stopped at an intersection a mere seven blocks from their destination and two black nondescript vans suddenly appeared in the deserted intersection.

It took only a moment for the agents and Stout to realize the intent of the passengers who poured from the backs of the two vans. They wore urban-camouflage fatigues, black hoods with red headbands, and toted SMGs. The agent riding shotgun rolled down his window as he ordered the driver to take evasive action. He reached into his jacket and withdrew a Glock pistol, leaned out the window and snapped off a few rounds. The resistance proved to be short-lived when the driver, while in the course of executing a J-turn, smashed into a massive garbage truck that had appeared out of nowhere. The truck was one of the front-loading types designed to pick up commercial Dumpsters, and one of its large steel bars punched through the SUV's rear door with the screech of wrenched, torn metal and cracked glass.

A low rumbling emanated from the truck a moment later, the droning sound of hydraulics reverberating through the SUV's cab. The thrumming sound hurt

Philip Stout's eardrums as the SUV began to tip forward and its rear wheels rose off the ground. Pandemonium erupted when the two agents seated on either side of him turned and began to fire their pistols at the truck. Unfortunately their efforts were in vain because the SUV continued to tip forward and soon they had to give up firing in favor of holding on to the rear seat.

Stout and the driver fared better than the rest of the occupants as they were still seat-belted in place. The two agents in back with Stout were soon clinging to their seats for dear life, their feet actually dangling in midair while they tried to hold on. Then the vehicle flipped off the steel bar of the garbage truck, the front end now providing a pivot point that dumped the SUV onto its roof.

The agent riding shotgun in the front seat screamed as his arm became pinned under the weight of the vehicle. The agents with Stout had ended up on their backs, and were trying to right themselves when the doors swung open to reveal a swarm of hooded gunmen. One of the agents reacted with incredible speed. He brought his pistol into view, snap-aimed at the closest gunman and squeezed the trigger. The report of the gunshot was deafening in the confined space, but it proved effective as the round struck the agent's target in the chest and knocked him off his feet.

A heartbeat passed and Stout's world suddenly came alive with the raucous, brutal cacophony of autofire. Stout shuddered amid the maelstrom of burned gunpowder, bright flashes and ear-shattering reports from a half dozen SMGs. But none of the rounds found his flesh. The firestorm of violence ended as suddenly as it had begun and left only ringing and dulled senses in its wake. Amid the searing odor of cordite, Stout detected just a whiff of blood. Lots of blood.

Before Stout could decide what to do next, rough hands cut free the seat belt and then dragged him from the SUV. Stout considered resisting but then realized it wouldn't do him any good. Well-trained and armed FBI agents had been unable to repel these aggressors, so to even attempt such an escapade, being unarmed and unprepared, wouldn't have been the act of either a wise or educated man.

And Philip Stout considered himself both above all else.

Stout looked into the eyes of the man he assumed to be the leader. They were dark eyes, eyes that burned with hatred and the fires of fanaticism. Stout had seen them before, eyes that belonged to men who were driven by something much deeper than mere political or religious conviction. That was a mistake so many Americans made. To think that terrorists were really interested in furthering the cause of any one group or religion bore inherent dangers. No, men like this were not driven by such trivial considerations. They considered the eradication or subjugation of those who did not subscribe to their same personal codes of belief as the paramount goal of their activities.

Before Stout could even inquire as to the man's intent, another one of the terrorists grabbed his arm and held it out in front of him. The shiny steel manacles dangled in the streetlights for only a moment. And then, oddly, they were no longer visible and the burning sensation that followed seemed to take a very long time to reach Stout's brain. That's when it registered that the reason he no longer saw the cuffs dangling was that they were no longer attached to his wrist.

And that was because he no longer *had* a wrist.

Stout looked down and saw his hand, still twitching

slightly, lying on the street directly in front of his shoes. He let out a scream even as he looked up and into the eyes of the terrorist one more time. His eyes had changed shape, crinkling at the corners, and Stout realized the man was smiling beneath that mask. Next to him, he held up a very long, sharp object—some kind of sword—coated with just a patina of sticky redness about midpoint along its length. Stout opened his mouth to scream again.

It would be his last scream.

CHAPTER TWO

The noonday sun had long cleared away the gray winter clouds by the time the three men of Able Team arrived on the scene.

Carl "Ironman" Lyons, Able Team's leader, stood with arms folded and studied the wrecked Ford Expedition with cold blue eyes. Lyons wore tan slacks and button-down shirt with tie beneath his brown leather jacket. On his belt he wore the badge of an FBI agent, visible to any of the real FBI personnel who might scrutinize him, but the .357 Magnum Colt Python revolver remained concealed in shoulder leather beneath his left armpit. Lyons gave the scene one more look and then ran his hand through his thin blond hair.

A shorter man with light brown hair, brown eyes and a mustache walked up and stopped beside him. Lyons glanced for a moment at the profile of Hermann Schwarz. Known among his colleagues as "Gadgets" for his wizardry in electronics, particularly countersurveillance technology, Schwarz had been friends with Lyons for more years than either of them could remember.

"Well?" Lyons inquired.

Schwarz shrugged. "I did an inspection of both the SUV and the surrounding area. Whatever did the damage to that vehicle wasn't any kind of an explosive device. There's all sorts of paint transfer along the back, like a neon orange color."

Lyons furrowed his brow. "Like maybe on a city truck?"

"Yeah, something like that."

Before Lyons could ask any more questions, a third man joined their huddle. He had gray-white hair, black eyes and a husky build, but it was a mistake to assume there was any flab in that physique. Rosario "Politician" Blancanales exchanged glances with his comrades, and Lyons could tell just by the look on his face he didn't have any better news. Given Blancanales's unique talents for diplomacy, Lyons had let his friend handle the inquiries with the other agents investigating the scene, as well as the forensics team. A half dozen agencies were represented, and neither Lyons nor Schwarz had the patience to deal with all the red tape. That left Blancanales as the optimal choice.

"What is it?" Lyons asked Blancanales.

"I'm afraid it isn't much is what it is," Blancanales said.

Schwarz chuckled. "Sounds a bit like a Buddhist riddle."

"Only not as easy to solve. I talked to everybody who's anybody on this case. Nobody has the first clue what's going on or why this happened."

Lyons shrugged and splayed his hands. "Well, we already know that much. Hal and Barb gave us the likely motive in this morning's briefing. Were you sleeping during that part?"

ABLE TEAM had been at Stony Man Farm for a training exercise when the call came from the Oval Office to activate them. It took only fifteen minutes to get from the training grounds to the War Room in the basement of the old farmhouse, where Hal Brognola opened the briefing with a chilling statement.

"It would seem that some unknown party has laid their hands on the plans for a new prototype submarine being developed for the United States Navy." Brognola then looked at Barbara Price and prompted her with a nod.

The Stony Man mission controller fingered a strand of her honey-blond hair behind her ear before saying, "Approximately three hours ago, four federal agents and a military scientist from the Washington Naval Yard were ambushed in downtown D.C. on their way to the Pentagon. Aaron?"

The other man in the room, a big and burly type despite being confined to a wheelchair, was Aaron "the Bear" Kurtzman. The Stony Man cybernetics genius tapped a key on the terminal board in front of him, and an overhead projector displayed the face of a young, wiry-haired man in a business suit.

Simultaneously the lights dimmed and Price continued her narrative. "That's Dr. Philip Stout, a specialist in the construction of nuclear-powered naval ships. Six years ago he graduated with his doctorate from MIT, an education he'd won on a scholarship after almost twenty-five years as a submarine officer. The vessel he designed was under a direct nod from the Secretary of the Navy and the Department of Defense."

Brognola interjected, "You should probably know that this vessel is more than just another submarine. It's a superweapon designed to carry a very small crew complement, penetrate enemy waters and deliver a first-strike nuclear payload."

"And according to the information we received from the President, Dr. Stout was on his way to a meeting with the Joint Chiefs of Staff at the Pentagon to present the plans for the prototype," Price said.

"Okay, question," Lyons said. "I thought America had entered into a strict policy of nuclear nonproliferation."

Price nodded. "They have, but with the continuing threat from nations like Iran and North Korea, not to mention the increased terrorist activity around the world since we first invaded Iraq and Afghanistan, there are certain elements within the DOD that insist on a backup plan. And apparently the President has agreed to this."

"But only as a backup plan," Brognola added.

"What about this attack?" Blancanales asked. "We have any suspects?"

Price shook her head. "Not yet, but we're working on it. It seems pretty obvious to us, though, that we're dealing with a terrorist organization of some kind."

"What makes you think so?" Lyons asked.

"First, the attack was extremely well organized. It was done very early in the morning in a place where there were no witnesses and no emergency services close enough to render timely help. Second, whoever coordinated this attack obviously knew a good number of details, not only about this meeting and the route the FBI had planned out, but also relative to Stout's work on this new prototype."

"When you say prototype, are we to assume that they've already built this thing?" Hermann Schwarz inquired.

"Not insofar as we know," Brognola answered.

"I don't get it," Lyons said. He shrugged and added, "I mean, what's so special about this particular submarine?"

Price said, "It's called a Fast-Attack Covert Operations Submarine, or FACOS. Its crew complement is only six men and it boasts an underwater speed nearly twice that of any conventional submarine currently in use around the world. It can deliver up to four nuclear warheads at ten megatons each. Its size makes it nearly impervious to any antisubmarine defenses and its footprint is generally too small to trigger most surveillance systems presently in use."

Blancanales let out a long, low whistle. "What'll they think of next?"

"Exactly," Brognola said. "This gives you some idea why we're concerned. If the plans for this prototype fall into the hands of any terrorist organization with significant resources, such as al Qaeda, the show is over for the free world."

Price continued, "Even if a terrorist organization *didn't* have the resources to build the FACOS, they could easily sell it to the highest bidder in trade for nuclear material. That would permit them to create dirty bombs or even begin exploring techniques for manufacturing nuclear fission devices. We can't let that happen."

"No argument there," Schwarz said.

"So what's the mission?" Lyons asked.

"You'll be posing as FBI agents attached to Homeland Security," Price answered. "You are to learn everything you can about the incident this morning, pick up the trail of its perpetrators and follow that wherever it leads you."

"And if we find out it is terrorists?" Lyons asked.

"Then you have carte blanche to do whatever needs

to be done to neutralize the threat," Brognola replied. "The only caveat is that if you can't recover the plans for the prototype, then you're to destroy them and anyone who's laid eyes on them."

THE THREE MEN of Able Team had understood that order, and the potential consequences that might come from having to execute it. While they weren't exactly keen on involving potentially innocent bystanders, they understood that the mission went well beyond the standard "terminate with extreme prejudice" clause. They were dealing with a critical threat: the potential of the design of a nuclear-powered and nuclear-armed warship that could be turned against the entire free world. So it didn't exactly come as a comfort when Lyons heard the news from Blanca-nales and Schwarz that they weren't any closer to identifying the enemy.

Before they could engage in any further discussion, a uniformed police officer approached them. "Are you guys with that Homeland Security task force?"

"Maybe," Lyons replied.

"Well, if you are, there's a guy from the D.C. traffic safety department in that big truck over there." The officer pointed to a large white panel truck parked just beyond the yellow police tape used to cordon the area. "Says he wants to talk to somebody from the FBI."

"That would be us," Blancanales said with a smile at his two cohorts.

Able Team accompanied the officer to the panel truck and ascended the makeshift steps leading into the back. As they crowded inside, one of the two technicians wearing headphones and seated in front of several small monitors took the earpieces from his head and smiled.

"Morning, boys," he said, extending a hand to shake each of theirs. "The name's Grant. I'm a technician with the TSD and I think I have something you can use."

With that, Grant turned in his seat and began to run some type of video on the monitor as the three men leaned closer. "Late last year," Grant said, "the city implemented a new traffic safety program. Basically, we had an increase of traffic accidents at intersections so we put in a camera system at those areas with the highest numbers of incidents. That intersection out there was one of them."

"Don't tell me," Lyons said. "You got all this on video?"

Grant shook his head. "No, not all of it but a small snippet—about twelve seconds to be exact. You see, the cameras are timed to take a picture any time a vehicle runs a red light or is detected speeding through an intersection. However, we also capture a video of the infraction because as soon as the light turns yellow, the system is set up to start performing a digital capture. It's not admissible in court, but it does help the officers reviewing the photographs to make a positive determination as to whether on infraction actually occurred."

"That's all fascinating, pal," Lyons said. "But we're not really interested in what is or isn't admissible in court."

Blancanales obviously saw the potential for conflict and immediately stepped in with a pleasant chuckle. "Pay no attention to him, Grant. He's always grumpy when he doesn't get breakfast. I think what you're trying to say is that you didn't get the entire incident but did get about twelve seconds of it."

Grant nodded enthusiastically, obviously not offended by Lyons's brusqueness. "Yeah, it looks like whoever made that mess out there was too occupied to realize they were getting caught on candid camera."

The Able Team warriors turned their focus to the video and watched with fascination as men in camouflage fatigues and black hoods with red bands burst from the back of a van. Fortunately, not only did they now have a description of the aggressors, but also the license plate shone clearly enough that they would likely be able to run a trace. After watching the twelve-second segment a couple of times, the trio exchanged knowing glances.

"Has anybody else seen this yet?" Lyons asked Grant.

The technician shook his head. "Nope, you're the first."

"Good. Let's keep it that way."

"Do you have a secure feed-transfer capability on this video?" Schwarz asked.

Grant smiled. "Of course!"

Schwarz then looked at his teammates and said, "Well, ain't that just dandy."

WITHIN AN HOUR of transferring the video segment to Aaron Kurtzman and his team of cybernetics wizards, Able Team was headed for an address on the south side of Washington, D.C. As Blancanales drove, Lyons and Schwarz rode in back of the specially equipped van that sported the latest technology in surveillance, electronic countermeasures and communications. They were engaged with Brognola and Price in a video conference facilitated by Stony Man's dedicated satellite uplink systems.

"We think we finally know who the assailants are," Price announced. "They call themselves the IUA, short for the Intiqam-ut-Allah."

"Never heard of them," Lyons replied.

"Loosely translated, the name means 'the Revenge of Allah,'" Brognola offered helpfully.

"They're a relatively new group, a radical cell that grew up from al Qaeda and finally split off when their numbers got large enough," Price continued.

Schwarz snorted. "Oh, as if al Qaeda wasn't radical enough."

"What's their angle, this IUA?" Lyons asked.

Price replied. "Murder, mayhem and terror wherever they can spread it."

"In other words, the usual."

"Yes. They are fundamentally an Islamic extremist group, interested only in the conversion of all peoples to their religion. Anyone not willing to convert ends up on the shortlist for termination and *especially* us heathen, capitalist dogs here in the United States."

"Any idea how many we could be dealing with?"

"Not yet," Brognola said. "This particular group hasn't taken a whole lot of credit for terrorist acts around the world, which is interesting only due to the fact there are some significant incidents recently attributed to them by world opinion. They were especially prolific in Pakistan, India and some African countries. But their biggest impact has been recent events in Iraq. They have even taken on those terrorist groups with very similar platforms."

"That's odd," Schwarz remarked.

"Yes, we thought so, too," Price said. "But our intelligence, while scant, is pretty accurate."

"Doesn't sound like they play well with others," Lyons said.

"Whatever the case, you're to proceed with all haste but extreme caution. Understood?"

"Gotcha," Lyons said.

"Jawohl!" Schwarz said.

"Muy bueno!" Blancanales added from the driver's seat.

Price pursed her lips and shook her head with resignation before signing off.

"I don't think she's much on our sense of humor," Schwarz said.

"Speak for yourself," Lyons replied.

With that, the Able Team leader turned toward the armory. There wasn't any reason *not* to take Stony Man's intelligence at face value. If Price and Brognola were convinced that the IUA was extremely dangerous, then that was good enough for Able Team. Lyons opened a slide-away panel that released by punching in a code on the keypad set in the face of the heavily armored weapons safe.

"What's your pleasure?" he asked Schwarz.

"I'll take the G-11."

A good choice indeed, Lyons noted. Manufactured by Heckler & Koch, the G-11 sported a fifty-round magazine positioned horizontally above the barrel. It chambered 4.7 x 33 mm DE11 caseless cartridges, which eliminated the need for any extraction or ejection mechanism and this minimized muzzle rise. This in turn provided a tremendous increase in first-hit probability, particularly in the hands of a marksman like Schwarz.

Blancanales called for the Beretta SCS-70/90. This weapon only differed from the assault rifle version by sporting a folding, tubular metal butt and slightly shorter barrel. Blancanales preferred it for these features in addition to the fact it fired 5.56 x 45 mm NATO rounds at a cyclic rate of six hundred rounds per minute with a muzzle velocity exceeding 900 meters per second.

Lyons decided a combat shotgun would not do this

time, and opted for a trusted M-16 A-3/M-203 combo. He'd grown accustomed to earlier variants of this weapon while serving on the LAPD, and come to appreciate it over the years for its reliability and accuracy. Not to mention that if they were going up against some terrorist hardasses, the Able Team leader wanted some extra oomph in his arsenal, which the M-203 grenade launcher promised to provide.

Each of the Able Team warriors also carried his preferred sidearm and plenty of extra ammo. They weren't expecting trouble—assuming the terrorists had done what they came to do and were probably long gone— but they were damn sure ready for it.

When they pulled up in front of the address where the vehicles had been registered, Lyons took shotgun position and looked out the window. The darkened structure loomed in the hazy afternoon light. The crumbling facade of the factory didn't surprise Lyons in the least since he'd already convinced himself and his colleagues that the place would probably be abandoned. Neither did it surprise him to see the many broken windows, with glass strewed across the rutted parking lot. What really frosted Lyons was the audacity of the terrorists to have parked their vans out front in broad daylight. It was as if they were saying, "You moronic Americans are too stupid to track us down, so we aren't even going to bother trying to hide our transportation."

Well, Able Team had a message for them.

"Ballsy of them to just park right out front," Blancanales said as if he could read his friend's mind.

"Think they're not expecting company?" Schwarz asked.

"No," Lyons said. "I can't buy that."

"I smell a trap," Blancanales offered.

"Me, too," Schwarz said.

"Well, we're not going to find out sitting around out here," Lyons said.

Blancanales grunted and then put the van in gear and turned into the parking lot. He increased speed when he passed between the once stately chain-link gates that now dangled uselessly from their fence poles. Immediately the air came alive with autofire, and muzzle-flashes issued from the darkened interior of windows on the second floor. Most of the rounds missed but those that did hit ricocheted off the reinforced Kevlar and stamped-steel body of Able Team's customized van—the latest in bulletproof technology being tested by Stony Man.

Lyons jacked the charging handle of his assault rifle and said, "Let's play ball."

CHAPTER THREE

Namibia, Africa

The road from Walvis Bay to Windhoek, national capital of Namibia, had seen its share of world history, and if the pain in David McCarter's backside was any indication, it had seen more history than repairs in certain parts.

Windhoek, on the other hand, sported all the conveniences of most modern cities. Not that this had been McCarter's first visit to the region. It had taken the South-West Africa People's Organization, aka SWAPO, twenty-two years to bring independence to this area and another two within the United Nations to convince South Africa to end its regional administration. Since 1990, the country had been governed under a democratic constitution headed by a president and national assembly. And while McCarter spoke a little Afrikaans, very little, the official language thankfully remained English.

"Dr. Brown, let me be the first to welcome you to the Republic of Namibia," said Dr. Justus Matombo, chief medical adviser to the national assembly.

"It's our pleasure, Doctor," McCarter replied, shaking Matombo's hand.

Matombo wasn't a terribly large man, although he had unusually thick forearms. The black skin of his forehead glistened only slightly with sweat in spite of the air-conditioned offices within the government building on Lossen Street in downtown Windhoek. His eyes were an unusual shade, almost slate blue, a testament to the mixed ethnicity that ran throughout the entire population. The ancestry in Namibia traced its roots to Dutch rule hundreds of years ago, so such ethnic mixes were the norm rather than the exception.

McCarter introduced the men accompanying him as his "medical colleagues" in turn; not all were physicians like himself. The only other "doctor" among them was a tall, lanky black man with a pencil-thin mustache who specialized in hematology. Calvin James nodded in greeting as he shook Matombo's hand. The remaining three men were "scientists" with varying specialties in different areas. "Biologist" Rafael Encizo, "nuclear radiation specialist" Thomas Jackson Hawkins and finally "geologist" Gary Manning rounded out the five-man team.

The cover and credentials for the Phoenix Force operatives implied they worked for the World Health Organization. Matombo didn't have a clue he faced five of the most dangerous combat veterans in the world. Dangerous to the thugs and criminals who terrorized nations and oppressed the innocent, that is. To those who could not protect themselves from the animals that preyed on the helpless, the five men of Phoenix Force were beacons of hope, justice and protection in a world filled with injustice and violence.

"I cannot tell you," Matombo continued, "how very grateful we are for your assistance."

"The details were sketchy," McCarter said as Matombo escorted them to a meeting room. "We sort of got just a small understanding of your problem as they rushed us onto a plane. Could you elaborate more on the current situation, mate?"

After Matombo had shown them into the room, arranged for refreshments and they were comfortably seated at a conference table, he related the story.

"About two weeks ago, a local medical facility in the city of Lüderitz received three patients with radiation sickness. All in the same day."

A weighty silence fell on the group as they briefly exchanged looks that ranged from surprise to genuine concern. The gravity of Matombo's tone got attention from every man at the table.

"The story was written off originally as some kind of accident with a medical device, but given the compelling nature of the radiation poisoning, the medical center alerted my office," Matombo continued.

"What did you do?" James asked.

"I sent a team down there immediately," Matombo replied in a matter-of-fact tone. "The data they began to send back gave me and the entire presidential cabinet cause for concern, not to mention the medical community of specialists. Then one of the members of the team mysteriously disappeared. He hasn't been heard from since. It was at that point I decided to recall them."

"Only they didn't make the return trip," McCarter interjected.

That much Stony Man had alerted Phoenix Force about when they diverted their return from another mission and sent them straight to Namibia. When a CIA officer working inside the country got wind of the incident, he made notification to his handler, who in turn notified the

South African section chief. Before long, the information had come before the eyes of the most powerful individual in the free world, and Harold Brognola had been ordered to send Phoenix Force to investigate.

"You said it was the *nature* of the radiation poisoning that compelled your investigation," Hawkins said. "Why is that?"

Matombo sighed. "Because their signs and symptoms were not those of the type of radiation exposure they claimed it to be. They had all been exposed to raw ore, U-92 ore to be specific, and that could only happen in one of two places."

"The Langer Heinrich or Rössing?" Manning inquired.

Matombo looked genuinely surprised. "You know your geography, sir."

"No more than any other geologist," Manning said easily.

In fact, Phoenix Force's chief explosives expert knew quite a bit that would have surprised Matombo. His background in fighting terrorism coupled with the knowledge gleaned of terrain while serving with the Royal Canadian Mounted Police had become areas of keen interest to Manning, much more as a hobby than profession. The Canadian had been over plenty of rugged country and he could read maps like nobody's business. His knowledge of explosives also implied a peculiar sense of what types of explosives would work on what types of topography.

"For those of you who may not be as familiar," Matombo said, "the Langer Heinrich calcrete uranium deposit and the Rössing Mining Properties are located in the Namib Desert, approximately twenty kilometers apart. They are both owned predominantly by the Rio Tinto Group out of Australia."

McCarter noticed Matombo had failed to mention that Iran also had a partial-ownership interest of fifteen percent in the Rössing. For a long time now, the Namibian government had sworn up and down to the world community that Iran had neither purchased nor absconded with any of the U-92 ore from the mine, the key ingredient required to make weapons-grade plutonium.

"These mines have grown to become the fifth largest producer of uranium ore in the world, gentlemen," Matombo continued. "And I can assure you that the operation is well secured. If individuals that far south are experiencing radiation sickness, it is *highly* unlikely they were exposed to either of those sources."

"You think that someone may have discovered a new source?" Rafael Encizo asked pointedly.

"I believe it is a strong possibility we must consider at this point."

"What about your team?" McCarter asked. "You said they didn't return."

Matombo nodded emphatically. "They sent me an e-mail advising they had completed all of the research they could there and they were going to leave Lüderitz the next morning. They never showed up and they were not found along any of the usual routes, even after a considerable search by our national rescue teams and a military detachment."

"Could you confirm they even left Lüderitz?" McCarter replied.

"We cannot confirm or deny anything at this point." Matombo's eyes narrowed. "And that is a very unusual question coming from a physician. You almost sound as if you're more interested in the disappearance of the team than in the medical situation. I thought you were sent here by the World Health Organization."

The Phoenix Force leader could see that Matombo was nobody's fool, and he knew if he tried to lie his way through it that the doctor might just challenge his medical knowledge. That wouldn't bode well for any of them, in spite of the fact they were there at the behest of Ombarta Nandago, the Namibian prime minister. Stony Man granted some leeway of judgment to McCarter in these matters and it was his discretion as to how far to take their cover.

"Look, guv," McCarter said, "you're obviously an educated man. Let me come to the point. We are here in a bit more of a capacity than your government led you to believe. But trust me when I say we're here to help."

"And we're interested in finding your people, yes," James said. "If you want our help."

Matombo's expression remained impassive during this time, but when James extended the offer, the physician visibly relaxed. "Finding my team and seeing them returned safely is my number-one priority. Of course, finding out how these citizens protracted radiation sickness is also of great concern to me. I appreciate your candor, gentlemen. You shall have my full cooperation and the resources of my office. No questions asked."

"Thank you," Encizo said.

"Yeah, the 'no questions asked' part will be especially nice," Hawkins added.

McCarter lent him a sour eye as he said, "We'll need to know everything you can tell us about your team, dossiers on its members...everything. It would also help if you could give us some idea of when someone last saw them."

"At least an eyewitness who can confirm or deny they left Lüderitz when they were supposed to," James added.

"You think one of my people could be involved in this?" Matombo asked with incredulity.

"Involved in what?" McCarter asked with a shrug. "We aren't even sure what's going on here yet, mate."

"We simply want to know whether or not they left so we know where to start looking," Encizo added.

"I don't understand."

"Well," McCarter explained, "it already seems obvious whoever grabbed up your chums are operating out of Lüderitz. Knowing whether they met their fate in the city before they left or if they were ambushed after leaving will give us a better idea of who to look for."

Matombo shook his head. "I trust what you tell me, Doc…er, I mean, *Mr.* Brown. But what I do not understand is how you can help just by knowing this."

"Simple. We'll know if those behind the team's disappearance are operating within the city or if they're being fed intelligence."

"In other words, we know the search needs to start in Lüderitz," James said. "We just need to be certain if it will end there."

Hawkins grinned broadly. "You see, we generally like to terminate problems at the source. Hitting lackeys isn't usually a permanent solution to a problem like yours."

"I understand now," Matombo said. "I will see what I can do to get this information for you."

McCarter nodded. "Right-o. In the meantime, we're going to head straight for Lüderitz."

"Would you like me to arrange an escort?"

"That won't be necessary. But some decent transportation would be helpful."

Matombo stood as he replied, "We have a fleet of various vehicles at our disposal. I believe we can find something appropriate."

DR. JUSTUS MATOMBO was true to his word, and before long Phoenix Force was headed southeast out of the city and bound for the port city of Lüderitz in a pair of matching, late-model Dodge Nitro SUVs. They split the equipment between the two vehicles. McCarter and Hawkins rode with Encizo behind the wheel in the lead vehicle, followed by James, Manning and Matombo in the second. McCarter had tried to discourage Matombo from tagging along but the man wouldn't hear of it, citing his required oversight of their transportation, as well as his cooperation as the official representative of his government. McCarter decided not to fight the guy about it. Matombo still had plenty of juice and could make it very difficult for them if he really wanted to, and McCarter figured it better to err on the side of cooperation.

That didn't stop them from having Matombo ride in the tail vehicle. That afforded the Phoenix Force leader some privacy when he contacted Stony Man with his update. Brognola and Price listened while McCarter gave his report, telling them everything including how he felt compelled to reveal they weren't exactly as the U.S. government had initially represented them.

"You think he's trustworthy enough to stay quiet?" Brognola asked.

"For now," McCarter said. "I think he'll keep still as long as we cooperate with him. I wouldn't put it past him to shoot off his mouth if he thought we were holding back."

"This complicates things," Price said.

"But we know you did what you thought was best," Brognola added. "I have complete confidence in your decision. It's probably for the better, anyway, since Able Team is stepping into the thick of it here."

"They're on a mission you think is related?"

"We don't have any doubts at this point," Price said. "What's happened there coupled with the events here in Washington is too proximal to be mere coincidence."

"Yeah, well, you've never been much for coincidence, either, love."

"Right." Price filled him in on their discovery of the traffic video and the IUA. She concluded with, "Able Team has a lead they're following up even as we speak."

"So this is a new terrorist cell."

"Pretty much," Brognola said. "They only recently were identified by Israeli MOSSAD as a group who has grown large enough that they could pose a significant threat to the security of the U.S. and her allies. You are to assume they are fully trained and equipped, and you are to deal with them by S.O.P."

McCarter didn't have to ask what that meant; a rookie could've figured it out. "Acknowledged. As soon as we know more, we'll get in touch."

After they signed off, McCarter lit a cigarette and groaned. He reached back toward Hawkins, who in turn responded by pressing a sweaty can of soda into his palm. McCarter yanked the top and took a long pull from it, draining nearly half the contents. The dry, dusty air and afternoon sun beating through the windshield had left him parched.

"What's the scoop, boss?" Hawkins finally asked.

"Either of you ever heard of the 'the Revenge of Allah'?"

They shook their heads.

"Me, either. Until Barb and Hal just told me about them. They're a new terrorist group, up-and-coming, and a case Able Team is working might just be related to what we're doing here."

"In what way?"

"Somebody lifted the plans to a nuclear-powered sub and left the designer and some federal agents dead. Took them out in bloody broad daylight, no less."

"Sounds lovely," Hawkins said.

"So plans go missing for a nuclear-powered device, and parties unknown suddenly show up here with radiation poisoning," Encizo said.

"Right," McCarter said. "Go figure."

They rode a couple more miles in silence and then something cast a shadow over their vehicle. McCarter leaned forward and strained his eyes to see beyond the limits of the roof. He caught the first glimpse of the helicopter before they actually heard the sound of the rotors chopping the air, felt their vibration through the vehicle. They were flying awfully low and McCarter felt something prick his sixth sense. Before he could react, the shortwave radio clipped to his belt squawked for attention. He removed the earpiece from the clip holder on the lapel of his shirt and inserted it into his right ear.

Keeping one eye on the chopper, he answered, "Go."

Manning's voice came back. "We just talked to Matombo and he said that bird above you has markings of the Namibian national guard. It looks like maybe someone let the cat out of the bag."

"What does he think they want?"

"Most likely they know about our little excursion here and they want us to stop. Apparently, official trips into Lüderitz have to be authorized."

"Funny how that slipped Matombo's mind."

"He started apologizing as soon as he saw the bird," Manning said in a quieter tone. "I don't think it was purposeful."

"Tell that to them?"

Before the Canadian could reply, the ground ahead of the lead vehicle churned with dust and the pattern that emerged could only have been produced by automatic weapons fire. Then the road erupted in a red-orange blast and left a crater three feet deep in its wake.

Encizo leaned on the brake pedal.

"Go off-road!" McCarter ordered. "Don't stop."

Encizo nodded and tromped the accelerator even as McCarter shouted at Manning to have James do the same. Both vehicles barely had all four wheels on the soft, sandy ground when heavy sparks followed by black smoke poured from the chopper hovering just above them. The whirlybird began to spin—lazily at first and then with increasing frenzy—before the pilot finally lost control and had to set it down. Hard. The smoke and dust left in its wake made it impossible to see in the mirrors of their SUV.

"There's some cover," Hawkins said as he gestured toward a rocky outcropping.

Encizo nodded and whipped the wheel to put the SUV in that direction while he expertly controlled the vehicle as it fishtailed in the loose sand of the Namibian wilderness. McCarter signaled Manning, who indicated they saw it, as well, and were right on their tail. Within a half minute they had reached the cover of the large rocks, although not without the cost of a few bullet holes in the frames of their SUVs.

As they bailed from the vehicle into the chill desert air, they could hear the reports of autofire, detect the whine of ricochets or the buzz of rounds burning the air just above their heads.

"Boy, oh boy," James said as they converged on the cover of the rocks. "We have walked right smack-dab into a stinger's nest."

"What is happening?" Matombo demanded, fear evident in his voice. "Who *are* these men?"

"They aren't friendly, whoever they are," McCarter stated. He exchanged glances with the faces of his teammates. "Options."

"I got us some heavy thunder, boss," Hawkins said, patting the M-203 grenade launcher mounted beneath his M-16 A-2.

Manning hefted the M-60 E-4 heavy-barreled machine gun. "And I can bring some."

"Good," McCarter said. "That should give us the covering fire we need."

"Need for what?" Matombo asked.

"To crash their bloody party," the Phoenix Force leader replied with a wicked grin.

CHAPTER FOUR

"Let me off here!" Lyons ordered.

Blancanales pumped the brakes and Lyons went EVA with the vehicle still moving at better than twenty miles per hour. The Able Team leader didn't lose stride as he touched the pavement and rushed the front doors of the broken-down factory. The terrorist gunners, firing from positions on the upper floor, tried to cut him down but they didn't have fields of fire that close to the building. Lyons made it through the rickety doorway unscathed and into the cold, dusty interior.

His breath was visible by the only light in the factory, shafts of sunbeams streaming through cracks and holes in the darkened windows. The shadows nearly obscured a pair of terrorist gunmen save for the light reflecting off their machine pistols. Lyons swung his M-16 A-3 into acquisition and triggered it from the hip. The weapon chattered a 3-round burst that took the first terrorist in the guts before it flipped him onto his back. Lyons had the second gunman targeted before the body of the first hit the stripped concrete floor. Lyons's rounds struck the terrorist even as the man fired his own weapon and sent bullets into the ground. The man dropped to his knees as blood poured from his chest wounds. The light faded from his eyes before he toppled face-first to the concrete.

Lyons tracked a 360-degree arc with the muzzle of the M-16 A-3 before rushing to a metal stairwell. The fact the enemy had only left a defense of two men on the lower level bothered the warrior enough to pause and consider that he might be walking into a trap. Then again, what did it matter? They had to stay on mission and make sure the terrorists didn't get away from them, irrespective of the risks. Springing the trap would accomplish the same thing as planning a stealth assault.

Lyons shot up the steps and made it about three-quarters of the way to the second floor before another pair of terrorists emerged from the darkness above. The men hadn't seen Lyons and he hadn't seen them, so they nearly collided save for the Able Team warrior's reflexes. Too close to engage with the business end of his assault rifle, Lyons spun the weapon so the butt came up and caught the terrorist to his right under the chin. He followed through and a crack echoed along the stairwell as the impact flipped the man over the metal railing. The shout of surprise died in the man's throat when he landed head-first on the concrete.

The other terrorist realized the proximity made any use of his rifle useless and he whipped out a combat knife. He leaped toward Lyons, knife blade pointed down and away from his body. Years of Shotokan training screamed at Lyons and he reacted by stepping inside the entry point of attack that would put the knife wielder's blade as far from its intended target as possible. As he leaped aside, Lyons delivered an elbow to the side of the terrorist's jaw while simultaneously checking the nerve in the forearm with the butt of his rifle. He followed with a hammer fist to the man that crushed his nose against his face. The swiftness and efficiency of the attack bought Lyons the time he needed to follow up with a disarm maneuver.

The knife clattered from numb fingers.

Lyons really went to work. He swung the rifle into the terrorist's solar plexus, and the air rushed from the man in a whoosh. Lyons followed with a stomp kick to the knee that crushed tissue and ripped tendons. The terrorist emitted a howl of anguish as he folded on himself, and Lyons finished his attack with another kick that smashed the man's head between the sole of Lyons's boot and the wall of the factory. The terrorist's body tumbled down the stairs.

Lyons turned and continued up the stairwell, undaunted in his mission to eradicate every last one of the IUA terrorists.

BLANCANALES AND SCHWARZ were pinned down.

The van provided their only saving grace, as venturing from the shelter of the vehicle would have meant the end for the pair of Able Team commandos. Bullets zinged off the pavement or slammed into the roof. There were no windows on the side of the van facing the terrorist assault line inside the second floor of the warehouse, so the specialized Kevlar body of the van easily repelled the firestorm without compromising structural integrity.

"It would seem they're not going to make this easy on us," Blancanales announced.

"No, it sure doesn't," Schwarz agreed.

"I wish to hell Ironman would have given one of us time to go with him."

Schwarz decided the moment had come to even the odds, and in way of response to his comrade he grunted as he flipped a switch on the control panel inside the specially equipped van. A small LCD screen set in the sensitive array flickered to life and a picture of several moving shapes materialized a moment later. The heat of the gun barrels firing on them obscured the targets somewhat, but not enough that Schwarz couldn't implement an effective firing solution.

"Let's see if we can't give Ironman some support in another fashion." Schwarz stabbed a button on the console and the van came alive with a steady, heavy vibration.

Blancanales gripped the arms of the driver's seat and looked around the van nervously. "What the hell is that?"

Schwarz apparently hadn't found time to fully brief his companions on every new on-board feature of the van, since they had taken possession of it only a few days ago. The roof-mounted, electronically controlled and fired .50-caliber machine gun happened to be one of those features.

Schwarz jerked a thumb toward the roof. "A top-ten hit by John Moses Browning and the Fifty Calibers."

"I've heard that tune before," Blancanales said with a grin. "An oldie but a goody."

"I do try."

Chips of concrete marked where the .50-caliber shells struck, raising clouds of dust and debris that obscured the van. Blancanales saw the opportunity to bail and cradled the Beretta SCS-70/90 in a ready position. He crossed the open space and managed to get clear of the front as he sprinted along the side of the building and came up on its rear. Once he reached a safe point, Blancanales stopped to catch his breath and put his back firmly to the wall. There were no terrorists shooting at the rear because there were no windows.

But Blancanales found what he'd hoped to find: a door.

The warrior took several more deep breaths of the chill midday air and then rushed to the door. He tried the handle first. Locked. Blancanales stepped back, held the SCS-70/90 tight and low and squeezed the trigger. The 5.56 mm rounds shredded the flimsy metal of the lock and the door popped from the lock and swung outward.

Blancanales smiled as he edged through the gap, thankful fate had gone easy on him so far. He'd never been the superstitious kind but right now was a time he could believe in it. Lyons had once again opted for the direct approach by charging the building in a frontal assault like a madman. Now Blancanales had to traipse after him, cover his six so he didn't get it shot off by a horde of well-armed terrorists.

Blancanales spotted a stairwell to his right. The body of a terrorist heaped at the bottom of the steps marked Lyons's trail. Blancanales hopped over the body and took the steps two at a time. The reports of autofire had faded with the onslaught delivered by the electronic heavy battery being poured out by Schwarz. Blancanales figured it was proving enough to keep terrorist heads down, and that would buy him the time he needed to find his friend.

Blancanales should have known it wouldn't be difficult. As he reached the top of the steps, he glimpsed Lyons hunkered behind a large steel drum for cover as at least a half dozen terrorists were angling for a clear shot. Blancanales took them by surprise when he rested his Beretta across the railing that lined the opening to the stairwell and, using it as a sort of bipod, strafed them with a sustained barrage of NATO rounds.

Lyons glanced at his friend and then with a wicked

smile he popped up from the cover of the steel drum and joined in the offensive. The terrorists were unprepared to have the tables turned on them in such a fashion, and it didn't take much to cut them to ribbons. Blancanales took out four of the six with bursts that struck heads, chests and stomachs. Lyons implemented a more methodical strategy, taking the time to draw close aim on his targets before squeezing off 3-round bursts in precise kill-zones. Their assault lasted only a matter of seconds and when the dust cleared the Able Team pair couldn't hear anything but ringing in their ears, didn't smell anything but spent gunpowder.

A squawk resounded in Blancanales's ear, a signal from the van com. "What's up, Gadgets?"

Schwarz's voice came back. "I got company here!"

Blancanales heard the autofire through the earpiece the same moment he and Lyons heard it echo through the cavernous second floor from outside. He tried to inform Lyons but the Able Team leader already seemed aware of it because he was on the move before Blancanales could utter a word. The two men descended the steps with all speed and made for the front door. They emerged from the semidarkness into the blazing sunlight, the effect nearly blinding them, but caught enough of the scene in front of them to understand.

Three terrorists had entered one of their vans and were trying to make a break for it, shooting at Schwarz as they attempted to flee. Before either Lyons or Blancanales could react, the unoccupied van suddenly exploded in a flaming gas ball. Metal shards rained near them and one missed Lyons by mere inches. The Able Team duo raced for their van as one of the terrorists who had taken advantage of the distraction got behind the wheel and fled with a squeal of tires.

Lyons and Blancanales reached the van, Lyons diving into the back and shutting the door behind him as Blancanales got behind the wheel.

"You all right?" Lyons asked, his eyes shooting to the splotch of blood soaked into Schwarz's shirt.

Schwarz had been gripping his forearm, and when he pulled his hand away it was slick with more blood. "Minor wing."

"Don't look minor." Lyons groused as he broke out the first-aid kit.

Blancanales put the van in motion and whipped it around with enough force to knock Lyons off balance. Lyons muttered curses under his breath but they weren't really at Blancanales; he knew the stakes were high here. A lot depended on them catching up to those IUA terror-mongers. If the terrorists escaped, it could mean serious consequences for the entire country.

Lyons finished bandaging Schwarz's arm and then moved to a spot between the front seats while Schwarz turned his attention to the console. The terrorists had put considerable distance between them but Blancanales managed to gain on them. Considering the head start they had, Lyons was impressed that Blancanales had enough foresight to figure their best direction, and he said as much.

"No sweatski," Blancanales said. "The highway was the most logical choice for escape."

"Still…" Lyons said, but he didn't press it. The warrior looked over his shoulder at Schwarz. "You got any electronic doodads that might be able to disable that thing?"

Schwarz shook his head. "Nothing comes to mind."

Lyons reached down and scooped up his M-16 A-3. He detached the M-203 from it as this model could perform in an attached or stand-alone capacity. The warrior reached into the bag and withdrew a 40 mm round. As he slammed it home and closed the breech with a pronounced movement he declared, "This should do the trick."

Schwarz expressed horror. "That van's our only remaining lead. You're going to blow it up?"

Lyons grinned and his eye took on a fearsome glint. "Watch and learn, my friend. Pol, get up beside that thing."

"Best possible speed. Aye-aye, skipper."

Blancanales put pedal to metal and shortly they were gaining on the terrorists' van. The thing the terrorists had forgotten was that most rental vans had governors on them—not that it would have been any competition against the 8-cylinder Hemi engine beneath the hood of Able Team's van, which was further enhanced by a Cummins turbocharger. When they rolled up parallel, Lyons opened the side door of the van, took careful aim and squeezed the trigger of the M-203. The shotgun-style pop of the weapon drowned out the sound of breaking glass.

The driver's compartment immediately began to fill with smoke, and the van quickly took on an erratic course. Lyons ordered Blancanales to steer to their right rear quarter even with the front bumper of the enemy van so that they could keep the van from swerving into oncoming traffic. The thick white smoke now permeated the van interior, and the driver had no choice but to pull to the side of the road. He went a little too far and ended up rolling down a shallow, grassy embankment. Fortunately, the van came to halt where it wouldn't pose any danger to bystanders.

As they came to a stop behind the van, Schwarz slapped Lyons on the shoulder. "Well played, Ironman!"

Lyons nodded acknowledgment before he bailed from the van with Blancanales and approached the enemy vehicle with weapons held at the ready. The rear doors opened and Lyons reached up and hauled out a pair of choking, gagging terrorists without giving them the chance to dismount. They hit the ground hard and Lyons held one down with his foot while he pointed the muzzle of his M-16 at the other.

Blancanales shouted for the driver to surrender, but the guy came out with SMG in hand and left Blancanales no choice. The terrorist triggered several rounds skyward as Blancanales tapped him with two rounds to the chest. The terrorist came off his feet and landed flat on his back in a muddy depression.

Blancanales returned to the prisoners and applied plastic riot cuffs on their wrists while Lyons covered him. He then took over watch duty while Lyons searched the van thoroughly.

The Able Team warrior finally emerged from the van several minutes later and Blancanales noted the puzzled look. "What is it?"

"Nothing."

"Uh, sorry, I don't get it. What do you mean nothing?"

"Just like I said. There are no plans, no papers, nothing… zip, nada. The thing's totally empty."

"You didn't actually think they were going to leave us the kitchen sink, did you?"

"That's just it," Lyons said. "If they didn't have the plans with them, then that means either they already got rid of them or—"

"They blew them up," Blancanales finished. "You're right, that doesn't make any sense."

Lyons turned his eyes on their prisoner. Like the

other IUA combatants they had encountered, Lyons noticed the burning fanaticism in the man's eyes.

"I don't suppose we'd have much chance of coercing this guy—" Lyons kicked the bottom of the terrorist's heel "—into telling us anything."

Blancanales studied him. "You're probably right. And we don't really have time anyway. If they—"

The roar of an engine and echo of autofire cut his words short. The pair looked in the direction of the van and saw Schwarz battling it out with another van full of IUA goons, this one similar to the others. The terrorists didn't seem very interested in negotiations. About a half dozen IUA gunners, automatic rifles clutched in their fists, erupted from the side of the van as it skidded to a halt on the loose gravel along the side of the road.

"So *that's* how they did it," Blancanales said.

Lyons nodded quickly as he took off in Schwarz's direction and called over his shoulder, "That's our missing link!"

The Able Team leader only got about a half dozen strides before he noticed one of the IUA terrorists lift a rocket launcher onto his shoulder and aim it in the direction of Able Team's new war wagon. Lyons glanced at Schwarz, who also saw the move, and felt a relief as Schwarz made haste to get clear. Lyons went prone and aligned his M-16 on the launcher-toting terrorist, but he was a moment too late. Milliseconds before his volley of 5.56 mm rounds struck flesh, the rocket left the launcher with a deafening roar. The terrorist's body fell to the pavement at the same moment Able Team's high-tech van burst into a fireball with enough force to lift it off the ground.

Flames roiled from the van and vapors shimmered in the air, distorting images surrounding it as heat consumed the combustible fuels. Lyons ignored the destruction, stealing a glance to make sure Schwarz made it away before he turned his rifle on the next terrorist. About the same time he heard Blancanales begin to open fire with the Beretta, and Schwarz joined moments later with another M-16.

The three Able Team warriors hammered the five remaining terrorist gunners with a fusillade of high-velocity rounds. The terrorists danced under the onslaught like marionettes controlled by puppeteers. One terrorist caught a number of slugs to the throat, and blood spurted from the gaping neck wounds as his body slammed against the wall. Two more fell under the unerring fire from Schwarz and tumbled down the slight incline.

The van lurched to life, tires squealing, but the trip came to an abrupt end when Lyons shot out both the front and rear tires on the passenger side, causing the driver to lose control. Seeing any attempt to operate the van as futile, the surviving terrorist bailed from the driver's seat and used the van to cover his escape. Lyons scrambled to his feet and sprinted off in pursuit.

It took Blancanales some time to figure out Lyons's intent. "Where the hell are you going, Ironman?"

But the blond warrior was already out of earshot.

CHAPTER FIVE

Namibia, Africa

The chopper crash hadn't seemed to produce any ill effects on the crew that emerged from her smoking fuselage. Oily clouds vented into a sky colored a dark hue by the desert sunset and initially obscured their numbers. David McCarter counted roughly a dozen men. They toted machine pistols and assault rifles, which meant they were probably trained to use them, but McCarter knew it would take more than that to intimidate the battle-hardened veterans of Phoenix Force.

Behind a nearby rock, Manning had set up his M-60 E-4, and he opened up on their enemies as soon as they broke from the chopper. The steady chug of the heavy-caliber weapon played like music to the Briton's ears as Manning poured on the heat. Manning wasn't trying to hit anyone as much as keep heads down and attention away from Encizo and Hawkins, who left McCarter's side as soon as Manning triggered the first salvo.

McCarter watched the two beat feet across the uneven and treacherous floor of this Namibian desert hellhole. At the moment, the Phoenix Force leader wished to be anywhere but here. He concentrated his thoughts and put all his energies into raising the muzzle of his Fabrique Nationale FAL battle rifle and triggering short bursts on sure targets in support of Manning's efforts. The plan they put together was almost too simple. Encizo and Hawkins would try to gain a flanking position on the enemy and take them out with ordnance from Hawkins's M-203 when they had a clear field of fire.

McCarter had ordered Calvin James to take one of the vehicles and escort Dr. Justus Matombo in the opposite direction from their position, not to stop until they hit Lüderitz and could notify the Namibian militia. At first, they had thought they were up against the militia, which served as the country's national guard, but that seemed unlikely now. Matombo swore the military would never have fired on civilian vehicles—and especially not those with government markings—without ample warning. McCarter tended to believe that from his own experiences, even in a country that had experienced as much strife as Namibia. That left terrorists. Whether they were IUA didn't matter at that point—staying alive was what counted right now.

McCarter made that point loud and clear as two enemy gunmen fell under his marksmanship. Years in the British SAS and training as a pistol champion had made McCarter a sharpshooter with few equals. The first terrorist he hit took a double-tap to the chest that flipped the man onto his back. The second gunman caught a slug that took out his knee and tripped him up so he landed hands and knees on the ground, sparing him the next shot. McCarter didn't miss a second time and he finished the terrorist with a burst to the left flank.

McCarter paused to assess the results of Manning's handiwork, who was no more a stranger to small arms than him. The M-60 E-4 sported a swivel bipod that operated smoothly and featured built-in recoil dampeners that prevented slippage even on smooth surfaces. The heavy weapon boomed a ceaseless, ear-busting tune as Manning swept the firing zone with steady side-to-side motions. The 7.62 x 49 mm NATO rounds pummeled the enemy gunners who were angling for any cover they could find, without much avail. Phoenix Force had claimed the only real protection among these rocks, and the area around the road where the chopper had put down was sparse, affording their adversaries little protection from Manning's onslaught.

McCarter watched another moment and then took up position and continued firing.

T. J. HAWKINS and Rafael Encizo didn't waste any time picking their way across the uneven terrain to gain a flanking position.

Not that their enemies weren't mindful of that fact, as several of them charged the Phoenix Force pair while they were still on the move. Whether an accidental rendezvous or simply dumb luck on the part of the terrorists, Encizo didn't wait to ponder the point. The Cuban raised his Heckler & Koch MP-5 subgun and triggered a 3-round burst that struck the first man in the upper chest and sent him reeling as the weapon he'd been toting flew from lifeless fingers.

The second terrorist didn't fare any better as Hawkins fired his M-16 A-3 from the hip. A pair of 5.56 mm zingers punched through the target's face and blew out most of the back of his skull. The gunner's body stiffened a moment, the arms and legs making herky-jerky movements, and then he toppled to ground and left a cloud of dust in his wake.

The last of the trio realized the odds were no longer in his favor and smartly decided to find cover. Unfortunately for him, the thought came a moment too late. Encizo caught the man with a well-aimed trio of shots to the midsection. The bullets perforated the stomach and one lung. A crimson geyser erupted from the terrorist's mouth. He stopped in his tracks a moment, dropped his weapon and then slowly collapsed in a heap.

Encizo shook his head. "That was close."

"As a razor," Hawkins added with a nod.

The pair continued toward their destination and in less than a minute they had come around on the enemy's right flank. Hawkins went prone behind the base of a large tree while Encizo took up a firing position between two branches that would allow him to cover his friend from most any angle. As some of the chopper smoke cleared, Hawkins could see the terrorists were completely preoccupied with McCarter and Manning, and he and Encizo had reached their position undetected. Time to act before their luck changed for the worse.

Hawkins flipped up the leaf sight on the M-203 and quickly figured his range. They couldn't have been more than half a football field from where the terrorists were cloistered together behind a couple of small boulders about ten yards apart. Hawkins sighted down the rails at his target and squeezed the trigger. The 40 mm HE grenade arced silently across the sky and landed dead-on. The explosion blew apart several of the closest men and disoriented the remaining terrorists.

Hawkins immediately loaded a second grenade, this one a red smoker, and let fly just forward of their position. As soon as it went, he and Encizo were up and moving. Hawkins loaded a third grenade on the run as Encizo sprayed the area ahead with repeated bursts from the MP-5. A couple of the terrorists tried to use the smoke to retreat from McCarter and Manning, completely oblivious to the fact they were trapped between the Phoenix Force warriors. In whatever direction they ventured, Phoenix Force had them covered and they wasted no time taking advantage of that fact.

Encizo dropped two terrorists with the subgun he triggered from the hip, holding low and steady on the run. The Cuban had honed his skills on hell-grounds around the globe, and the first terrorist fell with blood spurting from his side where twin 9 mm rounds had punctured his heart. Encizo's shots caught the second man through the breastbone with enough force to flip him off his feet. Hawkins and Encizo were careful to keep some distance from the wall of red smoke because they could still hear the steady chop-chop-chop of Manning's M-60.

It wouldn't do to get caught up in the Canadian's fire zone.

Not that it made any difference because a few more seconds elapsed before the machine gun fell silent and the echoes of small-arms fire utterly died away.

The Phoenix warriors converged and met at the center of the battle zone, which for all intents and purposes had become little more than a graveyard. Broken and bleeding bodies were strewed across the rocky desert floor. The odors of spilled blood and spent cordite, the smells of war, pelted their nostrils like the little bits of sand and gravel from a sudden swirl of dust devils around their fatigues.

"Well," McCarter said, waving at a cluster of gnats buzzing around his nose as he inspected the devastation. "I'd say that's the bloody lot of them."

Encizo looked at the carnage and then toward the sky, which had completely reddened. "We've got maybe another twenty minutes of daylight before it's totally dark. What time is it?"

Hawkins glanced at his field watch. "It's going on 2100 hours."

"We should do a quick recon on that chopper," Manning suggested.

"You think it's safe?" Hawkins said.

McCarter shrugged. "Guess we won't find that out until we take a look-see."

The warriors agreed on their approach and moved toward the chopper in a sweep-and-cover maneuver they had practiced hundreds of times before. Much of the smoke had dissipated and they could see the crumpled shape of the chopper clearly as they approached. When they were close enough, Hawkins could make out the emblem of the Namibian flag on the side, a red stripe running diagonally from the left bottom corner, bordered by white with a green triangle in the lower right and blue triangle in the upper left. Within the blue field was the image of a sun.

Encizo checked a pulse at the neck of the pilot, who sat motionless in the cockpit, and then shook his head at McCarter.

Manning made a quick inspection of the chopper, and after a time said, "Sikorsky CH-53G. I remember these babies when I trained with the GSG-9. Probably surplus purchased from the German Bundeswehr after the Cold War ended."

"That pilot," McCarter said to Encizo. "What nationality?"

"Hard to tell for sure but he looks Middle Eastern."

McCarter nodded. "Yeah, they're bloody IUA, all

right. Only question is, how did they get hold of military equipment?"

"Maybe they stole it," Hawkins offered.

"Would've been some kind of report on that, don't you think?"

"Maybe there was," Manning said. "Maybe we just didn't know about it."

McCarter frowned. "Well, whatever the explanation is, we better head out to see if we can catch up to James and Matombo. They ought to have at least a half hour on us."

And with that, they headed for the remaining SUV.

CALVIN JAMES HADN'T LIKED the idea of separating from his unit, and he especially despised trading combat action for this baby-sitting detail on Matombo. But like every professional in Phoenix Force, James did his job and he knew how to follow orders. Whether he liked it or not, he had a responsibility to pick up his share of the risk but he also had a responsibility to work as part of a team. That team took its orders from leader David McCarter, and there was no room for negotiation in that sense.

Fortunately, the attack had come when they weren't too far from Lüderitz, and it took less than a half hour before they found themselves entering the eastern fringes of the city. Lights twinkled and a chill south Atlantic breeze blew across the Namib Desert coast. Like most seaports, Lüderitz had known prosperity greater than the less hospitable cities inland. Its origins as a trading post and fishing village lacked fanfare, but the discovery of diamonds in 1909 changed the fortunes of its citizenry. The one stigma had been the rocky and shallow floor of the harbor, effectively preventing the entry of larger seacraft. However, this had increased the appeal of the port for historical tourist value and its prime, seaside real estate in both the commercial and residential sectors.

"Would you like me to show you to the waterfront district?" Matombo asked.

"What's there?" James asked.

"This is where the medical center is located."

James thought it over and shook his head. "I'd rather not until my team's reassembled."

"You do not operate alone." Matombo's voice implied it was merely an observation.

"Sort of," James replied, keeping his eyes on the winding, narrow road glowing in the headlights. "We take individual paths when mission parameters dictate it." James cast a glance at Matombo. "Like keeping you alive. But as a habit, no, we don't like to operate independently. Our teamwork is what makes us most effective."

Matombo cleared his throat. "I will say that while I disagree with your deception, your friends seem to be men of good character. Such a trait is considered admirable and honorable in my country."

James nodded appreciatively. "Thanks. We like to think so, too."

They rode the remaining distance to their hotel in silence. The Lüderitz Seaport Hotel occupied a prime seaside location with a stunning view of the Atlantic. In other circumstances it would have been a paradise for the getaway vacationer, but James somehow had trouble getting comfortable. Matombo had arranged for an entire block of rooms adjoining one another where the doors separated three two-room suites. Fortunately, Lüderitz was in its off-season and the hotel was all but completely vacant.

Once James had unloaded the gear from the vehicle, he attempted to contact McCarter by secured satellite phone.

The Phoenix Force leader answered midway through the third ring. "Yeah?"

"You're clear?" James said with an audible sigh.

"Right-o and no casualties. At least, nobody friendly. You're at the hotel?"

"Roger that." James looked over his shoulder at Matombo, who was digging busily through the portable refrigerator for a complimentary drink. "Our digs are pretty nice, although I don't think we'll be here much to enjoy them."

"All the best vacation spots seem to get taken up by mission-minded blokes like us," McCarter joked.

James chuckled. "It's our lot in life."

"That it is, mate."

"Instructions?"

"Hold tight until we get there. I'd say we're no more than ten minutes out."

"Understood. Dr. Matombo wanted to show me straight to the medical clinic but I figured I'd wait up for you. Didn't feel right going it alone."

"That's a good call. And, James?"

"Yeah, chief."

"I didn't give that to you with the idea of a shit detail in mind. You were the best man for the job under the circumstances."

"Aw, shucks, you say the sweetest things, boss."

"Just keep your eyes open. Matombo's our only decent connection right now and his credentials should go a long way to getting cooperation from the locals. He's a key asset and that's why I want you watching his back."

"Got it."

"Stay frosty and we'll see you shortly."

The click of the call disconnecting wasn't as loud as the one James heard coming from the slightly open window. The curtain billowed inward and James caught the flicker of light on metal. The Phoenix Force warrior shouted a warning at Matombo even as he dived for the doctor, who stood at a nearby table with a pocket-size bottle of liquor in one hand and a tumbler filled with ice cubes in the other.

The sudden chatter of autofire was followed a heart-beat later by the shattering of that tumbler in Matombo's grip. James caught just a glimpse of Matombo's surprised expression before he tackled the physician, saving him from a maelstrom of hot lead buzzing the space they occupied a millisecond earlier.

James felt one round tear through his shirt and the burn of a graze. The Phoenix pro landed on top of Matombo, and then rolled them both together until they were behind the moderate cover of the bed. James ordered Matombo to stay down as he reached beneath his shirt on his right flank and produced a Colt M-1911 A-1 pistol. James didn't like the thought of firing blindly without confirming his backstop but the tattered curtain and continuous weapons fire offered a viable target. The firing ceased just a moment before James triggered three rounds, aiming for what he estimated as center mass.

The curtain barely wisped with the passage of the 185-grain .45-caliber slugs, but the tormented squeal outside the window left little doubt to their effect. James got to his feet and pressed the attack by sprinting across the room and diving out a second window he'd noticed open on check-in. James landed catlike, crouched and aimed his pistol down the walkway. The gunman he'd shot lay on the ground, body still twitching. James heard footfalls behind him and spun in time to see a second attacker level a machine pistol at his hip and spray the area with rounds. James rolled into the cover of a rocky outcropping, the beginning of massive rocks bordering the sea.

The rounds ricocheted off the surrounding rocks with buzz-whines and then the firing stopped. James poked his head up long enough to watch the retreating gunner as he rounded the corner of the hotel. James gave it only a moment of thought before he jumped from the rocks and sprinted after his attacker. If he could take the guy alive, Phoenix Force might be able to obtain critical mission intelligence. He hated disobeying orders but he knew McCarter would understand given the circumstances. Nobody posed a threat to Matombo at that point.

The chase covered the distance of the parking lot and continued over a waist-high wrought-iron railing, through a decorative hedgerow and then across an open oceanside square overlooking a harbor filled with sailboats and fishing trawlers scattered at anchor. The antique lamps cast eerie shadows across the decorative square that sported benches and massive, decorative slabs of concrete underfoot. James's lanky form and long strides propelled him across the distance and before long he was on his quarry's heels.

They crossed a street and entered a shopping district before James overtook the gunman. He delivered a trip-kick maneuver that toppled the man and sent him rolling along the sidewalk head over heels. The gunman lost his weapon somewhere and came to his feet gracefully only to find himself facing down James's gun barrel.

The guy delivered a spin kick with greased lightning behind it that took James utterly by surprise. He didn't drop his pistol but the kick deflected the barrel long enough to provide the distraction his enemy needed to follow with a front kick directed toward James's groin. Reflexes honed from years of training and experience in hand-to-hand combat saved James from a crippling injury. James took the brunt on his thigh and ignored the shooting, numbing pain that lanced up his leg.

James pivoted and delivered a left haymaker that landed on the man's jaw and snapped his head sideways. James immediately followed with a back-fist to the exposed temple and then delivered a smash kick that took out a knee. The guy dropped like a stone and howled in agony. James cut the outburst short by sticking the barrel of his .45 into the gaping maw.

"So much as try anything else and you're dead," James said.

Wisely, the man whimpered around the barrel and nodded once to signal his compliance.

CHAPTER SIX

A gathering of onlookers along a sidewalk in the shopping district near their hotel drew McCarter's curiosity as the remaining members of Phoenix Force rode into Lüderitz. He couldn't see what the crowd was staring at so he shook it off. None of their concern—he had other things to worry about, like pulling the team back together and locating the missing medical team.

Under other circumstances, the United States didn't commit their sensitive operations groups or paramilitary units to domestic events in sovereign countries. Most of that work was clandestine and best left to the CIA or military intelligence. Whenever nuclear materials were involved, though, that rightly got the brass nervous and always prompted the President to make it Stony Man's business.

"Rafe, stop."

Encizo's eyes darted to the rearview mirror, where he caught the surprised expression in Manning's profile. Without another word, he pumped the brakes and brought the SUV to the curb.

"What's up?" McCarter asked.

"I just saw Calvin," Manning said. "Or at least I think I just saw him."

T. J. Hawkins, who was seated in the rear seat next to Manning, said, "Well, which is it, partner? You saw him or you didn't see him."

"There."

Manning pointed to a place where the crowd had parted and watched as James proceeded down the sidewalk with a fistful of an unknown, young male held by his jacket in one hand and in the other hand his pistol held in a discreet fashion at his side. Being on the passenger side of the vehicle, Manning and McCarter immediately bailed from the SUV and rushed to assist.

James nodded at the pair when they were close enough to recognize. "About time you guys get here."

McCarter noticed the blood-soaked sleeve of James's jacket. "You hit?"

"Graze. I'll be okay."

"Who's your new friend?" Manning asked as he jerked a thumb at James's prisoner.

The sudden wail of an approaching siren reached their ears.

"No time for chitchat, boys," McCarter said. "Let's get going before the law arrives. Last thing we need is a firefight with the bobbies."

As they made for the SUV, James said, "They have bobbies here?"

"I don't think so," Manning said.

McCarter made no reply.

IT TOOK JUSTUS MATOMBO more than an hour of interviews and several phone calls to the capital city before he could dispel any further inquiries from local police constables. Whatever he'd said, Matombo somehow managed to protect the five members of Phoenix Force from being questioned, so McCarter had cause to rejoice about that. The team didn't need that kind of attention right now. Matombo had even arranged for a room to replace the one with shattered glass and bullet-riddled walls.

Sometimes the backing of the Oval Office had its advantages.

Matombo stepped into the hotel room, closed the door and sauntered over to the prisoner Phoenix Force had bound to a chair. To everyone's surprise, he hauled off and slugged the Arab male in the chin, snapping his top and bottom teeth against each other and damn near knocking him out cold. James and Manning rushed forward to haul Matombo out of reach even as the doctor was winding up for a second shot.

"You bastard!" Matombo's face had taken on a visibly reddened hue even given his dark skin. "Were it not a violation of my oath, I would *kill* you."

"Yo, yo…easy there, Doc," Hawkins said as he inserted himself between Matombo and the prisoner. "We need this one alive to talk to us."

As James and Manning released Matombo after making sure he wasn't going to try again, the physician straightened his rumpled clothes from the tussle and reverted to his more dignified persona before speaking. "That animal is responsible for the disappearance of my people. I am sure of it. For that, he must pay."

"And he will—you can count on it, guv," McCarter said. "But right now you need to get hold of yourself and let us do our jobs."

Matombo appeared to think that over and then in one final gesture of defiance told the prisoner, "I will make it my personal mission to see that my government hangs you for your crimes."

The Arab male stared hatefully at Matombo but remained silent.

McCarter, who had been seated with his arms draped over the back of a chair, kicked himself to his feet and rapped a knuckle against the side of the prisoner's head. "Listen up, junior. We know you and your friends are up to no good in this country and we expect you to talk. So let's not be making it difficult on us."

Encizo nodded. "Yes. Otherwise we might have to make it difficult on you."

"You work for the Revenge of Allah," McCarter said.

The prisoner sat stony-faced and quiet.

McCarter rapped him again. "I'm sorry, but you bloody well are going to have to speak up because I couldn't hear you. Now, are you working for the Revenge of Allah?"

Still nothing.

McCarter stepped back, folded his arms and scratched his chin with a sigh. Finally he looked at James with a nod. The medic took his cue and went to the bed where he'd stored his medical bag. In addition to the combat medical equipment contained within it, enough to treat any of them for even serious injuries, James always carried several doses of a variety of barbiturates designed to reduce the inhibitions of resolute prisoners and get their tongues wagging. While the concept of "truth serums" belonged in books and movies, many studies had proved beyond any doubt that certain combinations of these drugs were sufficient to the task when coupled with effective interrogation techniques.

McCarter never liked to resort to this sort of thing except in special circumstances and, as head of Phoenix Force, he had sole approval or veto authority for the use of such methods. Of course, he also absorbed responsibility if it resulted in the death of a prisoner. To his recollection, a subject had never died in the care of Phoenix Force when such methods were employed, and he meant to keep it that way.

Within twenty minutes they had broken the prisoner's will and had the guy chatting away amiably, in almost flawless English, no less, about their plans in the country and the whereabouts of the missing medical team. As soon as the interrogation finished, McCarter ordered James to give the prisoner a sedative that would keep him docile and under wraps long enough for a military detachment to arrive from Windhoek and take custody of him. He then went into an adjoining room for privacy and contacted Stony Man Farm.

When Price and Brognola got on the line, McCarter briefed them on the events of the past few hours.

"At least you managed to get Matombo's cooperation," Price said when McCarter had finished.

"That bloke's been a real godsend, for sure," McCarter replied.

"What did you have in mind for your next move?"

"Well, naturally we'll have to mount a rescue operation for the medical team. We can't be effective going against the IUA presence here until we're certain all innocent parties are accounted for and not going to get in our line of fire."

"That should make things go over better in the international-relations department," Brognola said. "Then what?"

"It looks like we were right about another source being discovered near the two yellow-cake mines, although we aren't really sure of the exact location. The prisoner we questioned told us the IUA has sent a detachment of miners smuggled in through Lüderitz to perform the extraction, get it back here and transport it out. They weren't taking very good precautions and so when they got sick it just happened to be the dumb luck of medical staff that they discovered it when they did."

"It makes sense," Price said. "Lüderitz is really the picture-postcard version of a small German folk town since that's its roots. Since it's off-season for tourists, they could probably get the U-92 out of there without anyone noticing."

"Except somebody did notice," Brognola pointed out. "So you plan to rescue the medical team, which is being held at an old diamond mine just outside of town, and then go after the mining operation itself."

"That's the plan," McCarter said. "We'll still have to pinpoint the exact location of the yellow-cake mine. We're hoping someone on the medical team can tell us more. We think it's probably somewhere south of Langerheinz. The terrorists have the medical crew holed up in a place called the Kohlmanskop Ghost Town. It's about fourteen klicks outside of the city. As Barb's already pointed out, nobody's been there recently while tourism is down so the place is perfect since it's virtually deserted year-round."

"That means you should be able to confine casualties to our terrorist friends, too."

"That's how we figured it. Looks like the luck of the draw was with us this time, Hal."

"All right, sounds like you have things well in hand. Contact us again when you have more to report. There's a call coming in now from Able Team so I'm sure I'll have something more to tell you about their progress on this end."

"Right," McCarter said. "Out here."

BARBARA PRICE FROWNED as she stared at the conference phone receiver in the center of the table. She signaled Brognola—still on the phone with McCarter—
through the glass enclosure of the massive briefing
room in the Annex that he should join her as soon as he
wrapped it up.

"You want to say that again?"

"I said the IUA totaled our van," Lyons replied. "And
nearly totaled Gadgets with it. But we did manage to take
two prisoners, which are proving to be most cooperative."

"How did you get them to talk?"

"You *really* want to know, Barb?"

"No…not really," Price said.

Although the spunky and beautiful mission controller for Stony Man didn't micromanage, Price still expected the teams to operate with some semblance of
military decorum. It didn't mean she called every shot,
though. Sometimes it was best to leave certain details
to the team leaders and not get too cozy with the minute-
by-minute operations. Occasionally Lyons or McCarter
pulled a doozy of a stunt, and in those times she had no
trouble coming down hard on them. But those times
were so few and far between that Price usually tried to
look the other way. Give them too much and they'd take
advantage; don't give them enough, though, and they
would become ineffective. And that latter one could
easily get every member of the team killed during an operation.

Price never wanted that on her conscience. Beside the
fact, Brognola did enough worrying about that for both
of them, and at least one of the two had to remain clear
and levelheaded at all times.

"What did you find out?" Price asked.

"Well, we recovered the plans to the FACOS prototype," Lyons said. "But I don't think we're out of the woods."

"Ironman, I just got off the horn with McCarter," Brognola interjected. He took a seat across from Price at the table. "He says they're close to rescuing the hostages, but that they also discovered the IUA is running some kind of rogue mining operation for U-92. And apparently they're hell-bent on protecting their assets because the team's already been ambushed twice. What's happening there?"

Lyons recounted the events of their assault on the warehouse, as well as their encounter with the terrorists along the highway.

"It sounds like you've achieved the mission objectives," Brognola said. "What makes you think there may still be a threat?"

"The two prisoners we took here have told us their superiors set up some kind of secret construction facility in Charleston."

"South Carolina?" Price asked.

"That's the one," Lyons said.

"What in the devil could the IUA be cooking up there?"

"A project to build these submarines and a bunch of them," Lyons said. "Neither of these turkeys admits they know exactly where it's located, only that it exists."

"And you believe them?" Brognola asked.

"Yep."

"But if they never had the plans, how could they possibly build the prototypes?" Price said.

This time, it was Rosario Blancanales who answered. "Apparently, the design specifications for this sub were leaked long ago, Barb. The terrorists have been ongoing in their construction efforts for months. There are at least four prototype submarines ready, and another two that should be completed in short-order.

"You see, they only needed the plans in order to figure out how the nuclear reaction chamber was constructed, since that serves as the primary means of ship-wide power. Everything else is apparently active and they are only waiting for the raw materials."

"Well, I just got off the horn with David," Brognola said. "Phoenix Force has their hands full in Namibia, but I have his assurances they'll put this one to bed in less than twelve hours. There is a possibility, however, that the terrorists managed to get at least one shipment of ore out of the country."

"If they have and that U-92 ore reaches American shores, it's a good bet the terrorists could still get these submarines active," Lyons said.

"Even without the plans?"

"Well, not from the sense of nuclear propulsion," Blancanales answered, "but Gadgets has a theory about that. Hold on, I'll put him on because there are only two extensions here at the motel."

A moment passed and then Schwarz's voice came on the line. "Hey, gang."

"Politician says you have a theory about these terrorist subs," Brognola said.

"You betcha," Schwarz replied. "Our canaries here told us in the event this didn't go off, the head honcho of their outfit had a contingency plan."

"Which was?" Price said.

"Apparently they arranged to have a buyer procure about half a dozen specialized diesel motors from a local firm in Charleston. These motors are unique in that they're used by diving outfits and underwater salvage companies to power equipment and the like. I'm betting the terrorists plan to drop these in as substitutes if they can't get their hands on the original design specifications for the nuclear power plants."

"So you think they could still make these things active?" Brognola asked.

"Well, at least enough to put out to sea and launch a series of nuclear warheads at specified targets, yeah."

"I can't understand how this would've gotten past our initial screenings," Price said, looking directly at Brognola. "We thoroughly questioned everyone with a security access to this program from the Oval Office to the Pentagon. They all swore that if any information had been leaked it would have to be by Dr. Stout."

Brognola nodded and directed his voice toward the speaker. "That's true. Stout was the only one to possess the technical knowledge to create this sub. And he was under constant watch."

"What about information and data security on his equipment? Could it have been compromised?" Schwarz asked.

"Members of our own team assisted the NSA with security and counterbreach implementations."

"In fact, nearly line for line of the security programs was written by Akira himself," Price added.

That spoke volumes. Aaron Kurtzman oversaw the team of cyber wizards that included Carmen Delahunt, Akira Tokaido and Huntington Wethers. Schwarz's experience in electronic surveillance and counterintelligence paled in comparison to the combined efforts of that brilliant crew, and he said as much. "Well, Akira's kung fu is strong. If our own people were working on it, it's *highly* unlikely the IUA would have acquired the resources necessary to penetrate Stout's systems."

"Then that can only mean one of two things," Lyons

said. "Either someone on the inside knew more than they let on or the IUA's managed to plant a mole *real* high up. I'm betting the latter."

"Based on what?" Price asked.

"A few things are glaring. First, they had to have known the exact time and route the escort team planned to use when they transported Stout to the Pentagon. Second, they were ready and waiting for us at the factory, because the ambush they set up had been too elaborate for them to craft on the fly. And finally, Hal said that Phoenix has been ambushed twice since they got into Namibia and they've only been there what, three or four hours? The IUA seems to be one step ahead of us on every mark up until now. That's more than coincidence or tactical foresight."

"And while I hate to ever admit Ironman's right, seems to me they could have just as easily split with the plans and not given us another thought," Schwarz said. "Instead, they chose to stick it out and try to put us down for good, which means someone told them we were too great a threat to be ignored. Not likely they came to that conclusion all by their lonesome."

Price looked sideways at Brognola. "Those are awfully good points, Hal."

Brognola nodded. "As much as I wished otherwise, I think you're right on the money with this. And since it's your theory, I'm open to hearing suggested tactics."

"I say we get to Charleston and find this base before the terrorists go live. If even one of those subs gets loose, we could have a disaster on our hands."

"Agreed," Brognola replied. "You have my authorization to proceed directly to South Carolina and learn whatever you can."

"That's almost five hundred miles, which means a driving time of at least seven hours."

"Yeah," Schwarz said, "but that's only if we let Politician behind the wheel."

As Price picked up another line she said, "We'll arrange transport to Dulles. You can pick up one of the commercial flights that leave nearly every hour on the hour for South Carolina. Leave your weapons with whatever crew picks you up at the hotel. We'll arrange for a fresh arsenal to be equipped in your vehicle when you arrive."

"Understood," Lyons replied.

"Take care," Brognola said.

"We'll take it any way we can, boss," Lyons said.

And then he was gone.

Brognola looked at Price with a grave expression. "We're running out of time."

CHAPTER SEVEN

Latif al-Din tried to hide his rising anger as he listened to the reports from his cell leaders.

The news could have been better, much better, but boiling himself into a fury wouldn't change the situation. Somehow the Americans had figured out what they were up to and had managed to ruin his plans for the project they called FACOS. Now he would have to fall back to his secondary plan, and while that remained a viable option, it wasn't his preferred course of action.

No good could ever come in letting the enemy dictate a response, no matter how foolproof the contingency plans. It gave them entirely too much power.

Al-Din now considered his options and after a time he ordered the chief project overseer to begin installing the diesel engines.

"And what of the men from whom we bought them?" al-Din's second-in-command asked.

"I'm led to understand they live above their shop."

"That is correct, sir."

"Send a small force late tonight to eliminate them

and destroy their building. That should erase any evidence of their dealings with us."

"Of course."

After the aide bowed and left the room to relay al-Din's orders, the chief tactician in charge of their Namib Desert operations signaled for permission to speak. Al-Din nodded.

"Sir, were it in my power I would wish to be the one to carry better tidings."

"Your news isn't good, either?"

"Unfortunately not. The team you ordered me to send to destroy the American strike force utterly failed. We believe it may have been caused by mechanical failure of the chopper we stole from their maintenance yard."

"Sounds more like a failure in your training methods," al-Din interjected. "But we shall deal with that later. What else have you to report?"

The tactician cleared his throat before saying, "As soon as I received word of what had transpired, I sent our two lookouts in Lüderitz to dispatch one of the Americans and a government representative working with this commando team."

"This representative… Who is he? Some kind of intelligence operative?"

"No, sir, we do not believe so. We think he is a doctor."

"A doctor? You mean to tell me that two of our trained assassins were overcome by one scum-sucking American agent and an unarmed physician?"

"The doctor is a man named Matombo. He is the chief medical adviser to the Namibian government and his circle of influence is large. And the American—"

"Enough!" Al-Din could feel his face flushing now. "I have had all I might stand of your insolence and ineptitude."

The man fell silent and lowered his head in a demonstration of shame. Under the circumstances, al-Din considered it fitting the man acknowledge his shame. Such a gesture was humbling, putting inferiors in their proper place and making a public show of the fact they considered themselves beneath al-Din. Such things were more tradition among the former glory of the Algerian freedom fighters. Before the Americans invaded Iraq, and before the war killed every living member of al-Din's family.

"I bow to your advice, sir."

"And you do well in that," al-Din told the tactician. "It is time we turn this over to our European associates."

This announcement stunned the tactician so much he raised his head enough to glance into al-Din's eyes.

"You look surprised, Hezrai, although I can't imagine why such a move would shock you. After all, we built our alliance with that mercenary group for a very good reason. Our security and secrecy has been compromised."

"But is it the right time?"

Al-Din produced a scoffing laugh. "It is the perfect time. In fact, I cannot think of a better time to exploit this opportunity. Certainly we have paid them enough money to do nothing up to this point. We must find a way to divert the Americans from our plans, to confuse their intelligence network. The Europeans would provide a perfect ruse."

Al-Din paused to reflect on his own ingenuity, the chair beneath him creaking as he put his weight on the rear legs and stroked his beard.

He was glad to have it back. Upon first entering the United States he'd shaved it off, leaving only the wisp of a mustache. He'd then dyed his mustache and hair a striking blond, and with glasses and several months of

proper training he managed to enter the country posing
as a Dutch investment broker. They had stolen the
identity from a real man, whose name al-Din no longer
even recalled, after kidnapping him and killing his
family. Once inside the country, they let it slip to
Interpol and Dutch authorities that the man was responsible for killing his own family and then released him
inside the United States.

It didn't take American law enforcement long to find
the man, but by then al-Din no longer even moderately
resembled the man he'd managed to impersonate. Now
almost a year had passed and their construction reno-
vations beneath the American port city of Charleston
were complete.

"I want you to contact the Europeans in Walvis Bay.
Tell them we need them to draw the Americans away
from the mine until our team is safely away from
Namibia with the U-92."

"And what of the shipment currently en route?"

"What of it?" al-Din asked with a shrug. "It is being
processed into weapons-grade plutonium during transport, but it will not be enough for all of the missiles. We
must hit every target. Not just some of them. Otherwise
our efforts here will be utterly in vain."

"As you wish, al-Din. I shall contact them immediately."

When he hesitated to leave al-Din looked at him with
irritation. "Something else?"

"Yes, sir, but I hesitate to bring it up at this time."

"Stop wasting my time, Hezrai," al-Din rumbled
dangerously.

"The small contingent of Americans in Washington, D.C."

"What of them?"

"They managed to capture two of our own."

"Can't your informants help us with that little problem?"

"I suppose but…"

"What, fool? What?"

"Sir, they will expect additional payment."

"They can expect whatever they wish. Were I in your predicament, I might remind them that they have been compensated more than enough and we expect their services to continue until we've achieved our mission objectives. Now get out of here, I have work to do."

"I shall pass on your, em, sentiments, sir."

When Hezrai had left him alone—finally, blessedly alone—al-Din reached into the drawer of his desk and withdrew a bottle of French cognac. His countrymen didn't drink alcohol as a matter of religious principle. Some even considered it a mortal sin, but al-Din had never been a religious man—something that proved to be a disappointment to his superiors back in Algiers. It was their intolerance of his lifestyle and confounded interference in his plans for revenge that had finally driven al-Din from his home country. One day he hoped to go back but for now he was content to proceed with his plans.

His father had left him well enough off that he didn't need money. His connections had provided all the necessary resources for this particular operation. Finding members sympathetic to his cause with the expertise in ship-building he required had proved the most difficult task. But al-Din didn't know the meaning of the word *cannot,* never mind the fact he didn't even believe in the impossible. His father had taught him there wasn't anything he could not do that he put his mind to do and it was a lesson al-Din had clasped close to his heart for these years. After enjoying a couple of drinks in silence, al-Din stowed the bottle and rose from his seat. He proceeded out of the office in the back of the waterfront shop they were using for cover. Proceeding down the hallway to the back of the shop, al-Din pressed a lever disguised as a light fixture and a part of the wall suddenly gave way to reveal a set of narrow winding steps. Al-Din descended the stairwell and emerged onto a grated catwalk that overlooked the construction facility.

It wasn't terribly large at a span of only one hundred yards, but they didn't require a lot of room. The thing that amused al-Din most had to be the fact the infrastructure had already been put in place courtesy of the U.S. government. The facility was originally designed to provide a sea-based post of operations and secondary hiding location for high-ranking members of government, but the Department of Defense had eventually abandoned the project due to budget constraints. The original contractor, suddenly finding itself without funds, pulled out quickly and the place had been abandoned.

Some money in the right hands revealed its location, and aside from some corrosion and dust from years of disuse, al-Din found the place relatively well preserved.

The restoration project began immediately and in just three short months al-Din had an infrastructure suited to the task of constructing the FACOS prototypes. Now he watched with admiration as the crews of fifty welders, riveters, shipbuilders and metalworkers were tasked by engineers educated in the finest Middle Eastern universities.

As he watched them work harmoniously, a sense of pride swelled in his chest and a smile played at his lips. Over the past months he'd watched the ominous forms take shape, six in all. They sat like sharks hovering just above the water in their dry docks of the frames, their rear-mounted sails rising ominously above the sleek, knifelike bodies. The sails were equipped with full sensor suite packages, each one costing about a third of their value on the black market. These had been secondary stock produced by a Japanese electronics firm with a DOD contract.

The submarines were marvels of engineering; al-Din had no trouble admitting that fact. Each sub was eleven meters in length and three meters from the keel to the top deck. The deck in the bow was currently open to reveal the launching systems for the missiles, each one capable of delivering a payload of one, but during submersion they were covered. They could hold up to eight men but their standard complement was only six.

They had only two weaknesses. First, because of their compact size they could not exceed a maximum depth of 110 feet, although al-Din didn't consider this a flaw since they could easily match the speed of most U.S. submarines in service and easily outrun all but the swiftest high-performance surface vessels. Second, they were not able to fire their missiles while submerged because the pumps weren't big enough to provide the ballast required to move the water through. Still, al-Din knew they would be able to deliver the missiles and still have time to make their escape in the end.

Yes, once the Americans realized the threat, it would be far too late. There would be no effective response to the missiles launched against the cities all along the prime real estate they called the East Coast, and although the yields of these missiles would not be that of ICBMs or aerial deployed bombs, the death toll would still be in the millions.

Soon, Latif al-Din would show America the price of his flesh and blood.

Namibia, Africa

SYLVAN FACCIO HUNG up the phone, spit into a waste-basket at his feet and swore.

"Don't be a slob, Sylvie," a voice behind him admonished.

Faccio turned to face his blond partner, who sat on the bed. The big and muscular German was named Weisgaden. "My sinuses are fucked up. And for chrissake stop calling me 'Sylvie.'"

"All right, *sheisse.*" Weisgaden threw up his hands. "Why be so squirrelly, *freund?*"

That was Weisgaden's other habit that irritated Faccio. Not only was the guy unable to take just about anything seriously, but Weisgaden also had a tendency to speak half in English and half in German. Just certain words, really. Nothing specific that Faccio could put his finger on, but more like a random annoyance. Enough of an annoyance that there were moments Faccio felt like carving out the German's eyes with the red-hot tip of the combat knife he took everywhere with him.

A third man emerged from the bathroom, the sound of a flushing toilet announcing his entrance. He stood there tall and lanky, attired in hiking boots, khaki pants, a military-cut shirt and OD-green vest. Just like a great hunter on an African safari, the man known as Norm Hellerman said, "I think both you mates ought to just move past all the foreplay and get married already. I mean, why be coy about how you truly feel for each other?"

Weisgaden expressed something between a grimace and a grin. "Fuck you, you kangaroo bush-hopper."

Hellerman looked at Weisgaden a moment longer

and then exchanged a grin with Faccio. "See there? He's already talking dirty. What more could a guy ask for, mate?"

Faccio only gave the Australian mercenary the finger. He couldn't figure how he'd been so lucky getting on a detail with these two clowns. Things had been fine doing local work back on Sicily. How he'd ever let a former client talk him into working with the likes of Hellerman and Weisgaden, Faccio would never understand. But at the moment, it didn't really matter because they finally had some action on the horizon, and he would be able to find comfort in doing what he did best.

"You two want to stow that shit long enough to listen up?"

Hellerman looked surprised. "That's kind of funny, 'cause I don't remember anybody dying and leaving you in charge."

"I ain't saying I'm in charge. But I just got off the phone with our client. Seems they've run into some trouble in Lüderitz."

Weisgaden put down the pistol he'd been rubbing with a gun cloth, and his eyes flashed with a new alertness. "Lüderitz? Why should they have any trouble in that ghost town?"

"They say there are five Americans and one local, some kind of doctor, causing trouble for their operations."

"Five Americans? Military? Maybe Delta Force?"

Faccio shrugged. "Don't know—they didn't say. Could be U.S. black ops, maybe even independent contractors. Whoever they are, our contact wants us to shag our asses down there and take care of business."

"Well, I for one am ready to get the hell out of this shithole," Hellerman said as he gathered up his gear. "Sitting around here's putting corns on my bum."

"Too much information, bush-hopper," Weisgaden replied.

Without further banter, the three men gathered their equipment and prepared to depart the hotel. They decided not to check out of their rooms since they were paid up through the week and the drive from Walvis Bay to Lüderitz wasn't that far. With any luck, they could get down there, do the job and be back by morning. Five Americans wouldn't be much of a problem if they weren't expecting trouble—especially the kind of trouble at which the three mercenaries excelled.

Faccio hadn't worked with Hellerman or Weisgaden before—and he fervently hoped he wouldn't ever have to again—but word in his circle of influence was they each possessed considerable skills and were respected soldiers of fortune in their own right. So they weren't a class act and personable types. So what? They knew how to do the job and that's all Faccio really cared about. He only had to work with them, not be their bosom buddy.

They loaded their equipment in the SUV and Hellerman took the wheel. He'd operated in South Africa many times before and knew the terrain better than either Faccio or Hellerman. He maneuvered through the cold, rain-washed streets of Walvis Bay like an expert and soon they were on the B-4 bound for Lüderitz.

Movement throughout the country was surprisingly simple. Namibia didn't have the legal resources of other countries and frankly didn't need them. Crime wasn't particularly high in the sparsely populated areas, and what zones might be more dangerous—such as highly concentrated areas of workers around diamond mines and the like—were highly restricted. Vehicles caught anywhere near forbidden zones were immediately stopped, occupants searched and all possessions seized. Random death and destruction occurred regularly in those parts, and unless one had a death wish they were best avoided altogether.

In some respects, Faccio had to admit he liked it that way. It made things much easier for operations like this one, and they could pretty much assume the role of dumb tourists if they did come in contact with authorities. Tourism provided most of the economic staple in this part of the world, and police hassling visitors was generally frowned upon by the majority of citizens. There was a sort of live-and-let-live policy in force and only the most serious crimes got any attention from the law.

The trip to Lüderitz didn't take long and soon they were cruising the streets, bound for the hotel where their targets were supposedly registered with the Namibian government doctor.

When they were within a few blocks, Faccio retrieved his pistol, checked the action and then replaced it in shoulder leather. He reached into the nylon bag next to him on the backseat and withdrew a Steyr subgun. He put the weapon in battery before laying it across his lap where he could readily access it.

Hellerman, seated in the front passenger seat, had begun similar preparations. When Weisgaden came to a stop beneath the overhang, he put the selector lever into park and then reached inside his jacket. He withdrew a piece of paper and held it into the lights of the dash.

"The guy we're looking for is named Matombo. He's the local helping this American team."

"Got it," Hellerman said before he and Faccio went EVA.

The two men stepped inside the warm, dry vestibule and proceeded through to where the front desk clerk sat at the counter reading a book. They stepped up to the man, who looked up and greeted them with a studious but not unfriendly gaze.

"May I help you, gentlemen?" He had a heavy German accent.

"We'd like a room," Hellerman said.

"Yes, of course." The clerk went about the perfunctory task of putting a registration sheet on the counter and turning his attention to a computer terminal. "We have no more suites, I do apologize. But there is one room with a king—"

Hellerman slapped his hand down over the registration sheet and favored the clerk with a death's head smile. "Perhaps I wasn't clear, mate. I meant to say that we need a room number."

The clerk jumped at the thunderclap sound of Hellerman's hand striking the counter. "I—I beg—" the clerk stammered.

"Dr. Matombo, of the Namibian government," Hellerman said. "He is here with five men, Americans. What rooms are they occupying?"

Faccio thought carefully about something and leaned forward and whispered in Hellerman's ear. "The clerk said they had no more suites available. This is a big place. They're probably in the suites."

Hellerman seemed put off at first but then appeared to consider Faccio's point. "You know, friend, you might just be on to something." Hellerman turned his attention back to the clerk. "The suites you say you don't have available. Where might they be?"

"But…you, eh, I don't—"

Hellerman produced a very large stainless pistol that

Faccio recognized as a .44-caliber Ruger Redhawk with a six-and-three-quarter-inch barrel. "Quit your bloody stammering, man, and tell me where the fuck they are."

CHAPTER EIGHT

Even this far inland, the breezes blowing off the Atlantic Ocean sent a biting chill through David McCarter. The Phoenix Force leader peered through the greenish haze of the infrared binoculars and studied the layout of the deserted town in front of him. Most of the buildings were dilapidated—run down from years of neglect and misuse—which created not only a hazard to him and his men but also made the mission more difficult.

This meant they were going to have to perform a building-by-building search to locate the hostage medical team.

"It'll take a lot of time," Rafael Encizo pointed out as he lay next to McCarter.

"We don't have a choice," McCarter said.

"Guess we'll just have to do it real quiet like," Hawkins stated.

That would be easier said than done, and everybody on the team knew it. What they didn't have time to do was to debate the issue. This was the only way they stood a chance of getting inside the town, finding the hostages and getting out without giving themselves away and getting the hostages killed. It wouldn't have been McCarter's first choice to do it this way, but he'd been in the business long enough to know it was the only way.

McCarter was about to lower the binoculars when he spotted the first sign of movement. He made a minute adjustment to the focus knob to get a better look. Yeah, definitely a sentry wearing a hooded parka and carrying a slung assault rifle. So it looked as if the information they had obtained from the prisoner was going to pay off after all. But McCarter had to admit he couldn't complain about that. At least now there were no doubts left in his mind. They had come to the right place. The only information they hadn't been able to obtain was an enemy head count. Getting intelligence on the hostages had been easy. There were five people in all: two male doctors, two nurses—one male, one female—and one female lab tech.

"Looks like maybe the Kohlmanskop Ghost Town is going to live up to its name," McCarter said as he lowered the binoculars. "Let's do this."

Without another word the men of Phoenix Force scrambled to their feet and took up a skirmish line with about twenty-five feet between them. Crossing the rocky desert terrain in pitch darkness would likely prove to be more treacherous than a head-on confrontation with the guards. McCarter counted it unlikely the resistance wouldn't be significant, since it made sense the majority of the IUA's personnel would be attached to the mining operation secreted somewhere in the Namib Desert.

They would need to take at least one of the terrorists alive if possible, if for no other reason than to confirm the information they had received about the mining location. When Matombo first heard that bit of news he'd suggested they contact the Namibia Militia to penetrate the mine and shut it down. But McCarter disagreed, citing the militia was ill-equipped to deal with a trained terrorist force. This was Phoenix Force's specialty, and it was in the best interests of the Namibian government to let them handle it. Matombo had no recourse but to agree when the senior authorities told him much the same thing over the phone.

In some respects, Matombo could see their point. Namibia was a country that had suffered its share of internal strife and factions were embroiled in the civil strife that had affected most of the continent. To use military resources in such an overt fashion would have made the citizenry nervous enough to consider taking up arms once more to defend their country. Indeed, there were still areas of Namibia—areas where the new concepts of law and order didn't apply—best avoided by those not equipped to combat them. These were the areas even the militia avoided, because the government didn't wish to undermine the established rule of democracy that resided in the more populated areas.

But David McCarter had neither the time nor the inclination to get involved with internal politics in Namibia. They had one job and only one job as he saw it: rescue the hostages and destroy the IUA terrorist threat to America. All other concerns at that point were either unimportant or not his concern. He would gladly leave the politicking to the bureaucrats.

As they drew closer to the perimeter of Kohlmanskop, the jagged, broken outlines of its neglected architecture began to take form. In reality the place didn't look all that much different from the rocky terrain of the desert that surrounded it. But McCarter had a bit of trouble understanding how such an ugly and foreboding and isolated place like Kohlmanskop could be even remotely interesting to tourists. Not only that, the place more than likely sported a number of potential hazards to visitors, which was probably why most tourists who came to see it were restricted to certain areas.

When they were within thirty yards or so, McCarter knelt and keyed up the throat mic of the tactical radio set utilized by Phoenix Force. He ordered each man to report in and once they were accounted for, he gave the order to move. The plan was to strike hard and fast, not giving their targets a chance to respond. The more confusion and chaos they created, the less likely it was the terrorists would have time to kill the hostages. The most natural response would be to locate their attackers and defend their positions. Also, with it being very close to dawn, the enemy would be tired and less alert than in the evening or in the middle of the day.

McCarter encountered his first sentry within a minute of giving the order to converge on the town. The sentry tried to unsling his weapon and bring it to bear on McCarter, but the Briton beat him to the punch with a short burst from an MP-5. For this particular mission, all of the Phoenix Force warriors had chosen to carry MP5s with the exception of T. J. Hawkins, who had chosen to hold on to his M-16 A-3/M-203. The 9 mm slugs punched through the sentry's chest and he collapsed onto the cold sand of the desert floor.

An immediate cacophony of autofire greeted their ears as somewhere nearby a machine gun opened up on their area. McCarter threw himself to the ground immediately and began to low crawl. It was still dark—although dawn wasn't far away—so McCarter's only guide as he crawled was the hand he kept in front of him searching for a solid object like a boulder or tree. Even one of the broken-down buildings of Kohlmanskop would have been a welcome relief right at that moment.

While the Phoenix Force warriors didn't know what kind of weapon the terrorists had turned on them, they knew the bullets that streaked overhead were more than capable of inflicting severe damage to flesh. Once every third or fourth shot, a standard round was replaced by a tracer, which gave the terrorists a distinct advantage in determining where the fire needed to be adjusted. Whatever the situation, McCarter realized they would have to take up the machine gun emplacement and do it quickly if they expected to survive until morning broke.

McCarter keyed up the throat mic. "Green Leader to Green Four."

Hawkins's voice came back immediately: "Green Four here, boss."

"Find the chatterbox and shut it down."

A moment of silence passed, then Hawkins replied, "Roger, wilco."

Almost as if on cue, the steady thumping of the machine gun stopped and an eerie silence fell over the battleground.

AS THE MACHINE GUN STOPPED, T. J. Hawkins froze and squinted into the semidarkness ahead. His eyes had adjusted somewhat to the gloom, but the machine gun hadn't been going long enough for him to pinpoint an exact location. In all likelihood, they had stopped firing long enough to either reload or change barrels. In either case, Hawkins didn't really plan to give them another opportunity. The numbers were running down and Phoenix Force was running out of time in locating the hostages. They had expected some resistance, but certainly nothing of this magnitude; for the terrorists to have the foresight to emplace a machine gun nest belied some forethought in their tactical planning capabilities.

In most cases, it had been Hawkins's experience—not to mention the experience of most of the Phoenix Force team—that terrorists didn't really plan in a military fashion. The general ideology and tactical foundations of terrorism centered on striking selected targets either unaware or incapable of fighting back. But this particular bunch acted almost as if they had planned for this kind of eventuality, and the machine gun opening up on the approaching Phoenix Force warriors only reinforced that idea.

No more than fifteen seconds passed before the machine gun started up again. And this time Hawkins was ready. The former Delta Force commando scanned the perimeter of the Kohlmanskop Ghost Town until he spotted the muzzle-flash and tracers spitting from an old window in one of the dilapidated buildings. Hawkins searched immediately ahead of him with diligence until he spotted the irregular outline of a protruding rock large enough to steady the M-203 grenade launcher. Hawkins crawled to the rock and positioned the over-and-under in such a way it would provide him an unobstructed view of the area ahead without interfering with the operation of the rangefinder sight. Hawkins raised the rangefinder into position, closed one eye and acquired the muzzle-flash, which put it between the four diagonal lines protruding from the circular ring of the sight.

Hawkins took a deep breath as he allowed his finger to curl around the trigger of the M-203. He let off half, steadied the stock against his shoulder and waited another second or so before squeezing off a shot. The M-203 popped loudly with the ejection of the 40 mm high explosive grenade, but the 12-gauge kick was negligible as Hawkins had the stock so tight against his body he barely felt it. The grenade arced into an acquisitions trajectory and landed square on target, decimating the building wall immediately in front of the machine gun emplacement, as well as the two men who had been manning the weapon.

Hawkins scrambled to his feet and moved toward the perimeter without hesitation, confident that his teammates were already moving toward their respective objectives, as well.

"GREEN LEADER to Green Four," David McCarter's voice squawked over the tactical radio. "That was a bloody nice shot, mate."

Gary Manning had to agree with those sentiments. Over the years, T. J. Hawkins had become an invaluable part of the Phoenix Force team. The loss of their leader, Yakov Katzenelenbogen, had been a blow to every single man on the team in a different way. The promotion of McCarter to team leader and selection of Hawkins as their new member had restored their spirit, as well as their numbers. While this might have seemed unimportant to the outsider, it had proved very important to the morale of the well-oiled machine called Phoenix Force.

As soon as the high-explosive round hit the machine gun emplacement, Manning was on his feet and moving toward the perimeter as fast as his legs would carry him. He wasn't quite as lanky as Calvin James, but years working in the outdoors had forged a solid build on him, and granted him with an endurance few men his age enjoyed. Manning also did regular training and exercises to keep his body in top physical condition, as did

all the members of Stony Man. A soldier who could not
endure the physical stressors of combat was even more
unlikely to endure the emotional ones.

As Manning neared the perimeter of the town, a terrorist peered from behind a building with an assault
rifle held at the ready. Manning saw him milliseconds
before the guy opened fire and the Canadian jumped
behind a natural defilade just in time to avoid being cut
down by a volley of high-velocity slugs. Manning
swung the muzzle of his MP-5 into acquisition and
snapped off a pair of short bursts. The first one went
high and right, but the second was closer even though
the terrorist ducked behind cover.

One round managed to graze the terrorist's hand,
and he yelped with pain as he disappeared behind the
building. Manning couldn't actually see the injury but
he knew from the outcry his shots had some sort of
effect. Manning didn't wait for the terrorist to regain his
senses; rather, he jumped from the defilade and rushed
the position. It was a tactic he had used many times
before with great success. The idea behind it was to take
the enemy off guard by doing something completely unpredictable. Some viewed it as recklessness, but it was
quite effective when implemented under the correct circumstances. This turned out to be one of those times,
only because Manning had wounded the terrorist and so
taken him somewhat off guard already.

The terrorist had squatted with his back against the
wall and was holding his injured limb as Manning
rounded the corner. He looked up with surprise and
tried to shoot Manning, but the effort proved fruitless,
given his injury coupled with the proximity of his
enemy. The 3-round burst Manning triggered from the
MP-5 literally blew the terrorist's skull apart like a

grapefruit exploding under the pressure of a sledgehammer. Blood and brain matter splattered the crumbling wall of the building as the headless body tumbled to the ground and twitched a few times before going still.

Manning jumped over the corpse and negotiated the unsure footing while keeping his back to the wall of the building. A flutter of movement caught Manning's attention, and he turned in time to see a terrorist emerge from a building across the makeshift thoroughfare that had once served as a main artery through the Kohlmanskop Ghost Town. The terrorist didn't apparently notice Manning, but the Phoenix Force warrior certainly noticed the terrorist. Manning raised his MP-5 and triggered a sustained burst as he swept the muzzle of the weapon in a corkscrew fashion. The terrorist dropped his assault rifle and danced like a marionette under the impact of the rounds.

Confident he had neutralized the terrorist threat in this section, Gary Manning moved on.

CALVIN JAMES LEAPED to his feet and charged the town building in front of him as soon as Hawkins's grenade exploded.

The ex-SEAL had performed more assault operations like this than he could remember. But no matter how many times he did it, James always kept it in his mind that he was neither faster than a bullet nor immune to making a tactical mistake. The one he made as he approached the town very nearly cost him his life. Had it not been for the rock that tripped him, James would've surely fallen victim to the hailstorm of lead fired by a terrorist concealed behind a broken piece of wall in one of the buildings

James rolled with the fall, came to rest on his back and

yanked a Diehl DM-51 grenade from the load-bearing equipment harness he wore. The DM-51 had become a popular ordnance item with the Stony Man commandos for both its effectiveness and versatility in the battle zone. The grenade body itself was a thin cylinder filled with a dense mixture of PETN explosive. The exterior of the body was then covered with a removable sleeve that contained thousands of steel balls, each about 2 mm in size, that acted in an antipersonnel role.

James yanked the pin, rolled onto his left side and threw the grenade overhand with all the force he could muster. The warrior then buried his face in the sand and covered his ears a moment before the blast. He couldn't hear the scream of the terrorists over the concussive force of the explosion and the secondary vibrations that rolled through his head as the grenade did its grisly work. The shower of dust and debris, however, coupled with the leg that had detached from his enemy landing near him, told the story well enough.

James scrambled to his feet and leveled his MP-5 in the direction of the explosion. A much larger part of the wall had been blown away, leaving only a gaping maw with charred edges. James took a few hesitant steps, sweeping the area ahead of him and on both flanks with his eyes before he edged one foot over the broken wall and ducked into the building. As he maneuvered his way through what remained of the framing, James could see the evidence of the building's age. The wood had practically rotted away to nothing in some areas, and there were bits of garbage and broken glass strewed haphazardly throughout the entire structure. To his surprise, some of the walls were still intact, although there were large holes in many of them and even some evidence of graffiti.

He recalled the conversation between McCarter and Matombo relative to the condition of the area once they had learned the terrorists were holding the medical team hostage here. It surprised James in some respects that the Namibian government would consider this area anything other than a place that should have been condemned and demolished long ago. It didn't make much sense to the Phoenix Force warrior that someone would have actually paid real money to come look at a bunch of broken-down structures like these. Oh, well, he supposed everybody needed a hobby.

James picked his way through the obstacles left by the failing structure and eventually found a point of egress on the far side. He emerged through a half-collapsed doorway and onto the area that faced a group of buildings immediately across the way. James heard a staccato burst of autofire but recognized it as belonging to one of the MP-5s. He held his weapon in the ready position and knelt, but he quickly saw he wasn't in the line of fire as he watched Gary Manning take down a terrorist who had appeared from a building across the street.

As soon as James confirmed his area was devoid of further threats, he keyed the mic of his radio.

"Green Three to Green Leader. Charlie sector secure."

Before McCarter could reply, Encizo's voice broke through. "Green One here. I've got *big* trouble!"

Somewhere in the near distance, heavy small-arms fire ensued.

CHAPTER NINE

The four terrorists armed with heavy assault rifles didn't surprise Rafael Encizo, mostly because he'd been expecting them.

The very fact they were watching this particular building and clustered together made it pretty obvious to Encizo that he'd struck pay dirt. There was a better than off-chance the five hostages—assuming they were alive and well—were being held somewhere beyond this point where he'd stumbled upon the guards. What Encizo hadn't expected was to find them quite this alert or organized.

The Cuban warrior dived behind a wall in the nick of time. As he keyed his tactical radio and called for help, a hailstorm of 7.62 mm rounds chopped the air around him and punched through the flimsy, paper-thin wall behind which he'd sought protection. Encizo rolled from his position and gained additional cover behind a thick pillar. The condition of this building seemed considerably better than the others, and given its location on the far side of Kohlmanskop Ghost Town, Encizo could only assume it was newer than the rest.

As the echoes of the autofire died away, Encizo heard the excited patter of footfalls rushing his position.

Encizo took a knee, steadied his body against the pillar and raised the MP-5 to his shoulder. As soon as the first terrorist came into view, Encizo squeezed the trigger in a sustained burst that caught the man utterly off guard. A half dozen 9 mm Parabellums punched through the terrorist's stomach and lifted him off the ground. His body slammed into another pillar positioned across from Encizo's.

The other terrorist accompanying his now-deceased partner responded with admirable moves as he rolled away from Encizo's fire zone and came up in a shallow flanking position. In other circumstances, the Cuban would have been cut down instantly by the terrorist. Unfortunately for the IUA gunner, Encizo had plenty of backup in the form of a fusillade produced by the weapons of Gary Manning and David McCarter. The terrorist's weapon clattered to the ground as he danced and twitched under the punishing stream of autofire. As Manning and McCarter let off the triggers, the terrorist's body impacted the wall and he slid to the ground leaving a bloody streak in his wake.

Manning and McCarter ducked into the building and took up firing positions behind the nearest available cover.

"Nice of you to join me," Encizo said.

"Don't mind if we do," McCarter replied.

Manning nodded and Encizo took up an advance position that afforded him a view into the next room. The remaining two terrorists were no longer in sight, and Encizo had to wonder where they had taken cover. There was always a strong possibility they intended to kill the hostages before Phoenix Force could rescue them, although it wouldn't have made much sense. The hostages were no longer valuable to the terrorists since Phoenix Force had discovered their hiding place. To kill them now would surely make the surviving terrorists' lives forfeit, and it was entirely probable the terrorists knew that.

When he was sure they weren't waiting to ambush him, Encizo broke cover and pushed into the adjoining room. He found a new vantage point from where he could cover the entire area ahead and then shouted an all clear for McCarter and Manning to proceed. It only took them a minute to clear the first floor. The three stood at the base of the winding metal steps and looked into the encroaching darkness above. They had no way of being sure the terrorists weren't lying in wait for them, but they wouldn't get very far if they stood there and debated the issue. This was one of those times where they would just have to follow Carl Lyons's advice: "Just nut up and do it."

McCarter radioed that James and Hawkins should hold position, and then the three men proceeded up the winding stairwell.

They stepped onto the second-floor landing, and noted that the long hallway branched in opposite directions. Several closed doors lined the hallway, and while sky above them had begun to lighten, it was still dark enough outside that they could not see far ahead.

"Oh, bloody hell," McCarter muttered.

"Looks like we'll have to perform a room-by-room search," Encizo whispered.

Manning frowned. "I don't suppose anybody could suggest a less risky option?"

"I wish I had one," McCarter said. "But the bloke's right. We're going to have to do it one room at a time."

"I was sort of afraid you'd say that," Manning replied.

"On with it," McCarter said.

The threesome fanned out, keeping distance between them and their backs to the wall to present minimal targets for the terrorists who might be waiting in the shadows. They reached the first two rooms unchallenged and found them empty. As they arrived at the third closed door, Encizo felt hairs stand on the back of his neck—his built-in sixth sense from years of experience as a professional combatant—so he signaled McCarter to proceed with extra caution.

McCarter kicked the door in and dropped flat to his stomach. The reaction saved his life as the air above him swarmed with bullets from the terrorists' weapons. McCarter rolled out of the line of fire before either of the terrorists could adjust their sights. Their second volley ripped large gashes in the wooden floor, and wood chips and plaster from the surrounding doorway. Manning stuck his weapon in the opening during a lull in the firing and swept the room blindly with a steady stream of 9 mm rounds. He wasn't too concerned with hitting any of the hostages, since it didn't seem likely the terrorists would have taken up positions that someone could have given away simply by shouting a warning.

As Manning swept the room with autofire, McCarter and Encizo nodded to each other and simultaneously removed Diehl DM-51 grenades from their suspension harnesses. They pulled the pins, let the spoons fly and then tossed the grenades into the room in concert.

Manning then lowered his MP-5, which he'd emptied on the room with zeal, and pulled a different grenade from his own load-bearing equipment strap. This grenade had markings quite different from those of the DM-51. Its gray body and purple lettering betrayed the intended purpose. Designated by the U.S. Army with the nomenclature AN M-14 TH3, the grenade contained a thermate mixture that burned in excess of four thousand degrees Fahrenheit for nearly a minute, and could penetrate a half inch of homogenous armor.

Although it probably hadn't been necessary, seeing as the DM-51s likely did the trick, Manning yanked the pin and tossed the incendiary grenade into the fray. The trio then vacated the immediate area as quickly as possible to avoid the searing and agonizing effects of molten iron. Within a minute of the grenade exploding the better part of the room was engulfed in flame.

The trio continued to exercise caution as they searched the remaining rooms and eventually found the hostages. All five were bound and gagged—with bruises and other markings, including cigarette burns and what looked like remnants from being whipped with thick leather straps—but were breathing and awake. Encizo and Manning went about the process of freeing the five hostages from their bonds while McCarter covered the door with his MP-5. Phoenix Force had more than likely eliminated all of the terrorists, but there seemed little reason to take a chance they had missed one or two along the way.

Once the hostages were freed, the Phoenix Force commandos escorted them to the first floor and away from the building where they had been held captive for nearly seventy-two hours straight. Encizo could see the look in McCarter's eyes, the strain of holding back the urge to ask them a flurry of questions. He had to admire the Phoenix Force leader's restraint and compassion. These were medical people, not soldiers, and they were not trained to undergo debriefing so soon after a traumatic experience.

McCarter ordered Manning to relieve Calvin James so that he could attend to the wounds of the hostages who needed immediate attention. When James arrived, he got right to work and enlisted Encizo's help with the bandaging and basic triage. Fortunately, they had brought plenty of water and McCarter busied himself with returning to one of the SUVs they had concealed beyond the rise and driving it down to where the hostages were gathered. McCarter took temporary guard duty and ordered Hawkins to get the other vehicle.

By the time Hawkins returned with the second SUV, the hostages were in pretty good shape and seemed in much better spirits than when Phoenix Force had found them. James had treated their wounds, applied special salve to the burns and even had the two females laughing a little in the charming way for which he was known.

McCarter pulled him aside and grinned. "You're pretty good with the ladies."

"What can I say? A brother's got to have some serious mojo if he wants to get a woman's attention. Especially in a place like Chicago."

"Just don't let it go to your head, Romeo," Encizo quipped.

James grinned at his friend and countered with, "You just mad 'cause you ain't got game."

McCarter shook his head and then went to sit on the waist-high wall where the hostages were seated. He knew from Matombo's description that the fair-haired man was the leader of the group and immunologist by the name of Devon Sheinberg. Although he had dark circles under his eyes, Sheinberg looked in surprisingly good shape and his blue eyes hadn't seemed to lose any of their luster as they twinkled in the morning sunlight.

"Dr. Sheinberg, my name is Brown. While I can't specifically tell you who I work for or why I'm even in Namibia, suffice it to say that I represent the combined interests of your government and those of the United States. If you're up to it, I'd like to ask you some questions."

Sheinberg shook McCarter's hand firmly. "Oh, I'm up to it." He looked over his team and then locked eyes with McCarter. "And even if I wasn't, I'd find the strength to answer them anyway. I'm sure I speak for all of my people when I say that today we became indebted to you for our very lives. Personally, I wasn't sure we'd come out of this at all. And seeing you come into that room like you did, well—"

Sheinberg choked up and McCarter could see the moisture collect in the corners of the man's eyes. He understood that kind of emotion, because he'd experienced it a number of times himself, although he'd never openly show it. McCarter came from a background where men were allowed to cry. They just did their crying alone, and they never showed weakness to an ally or foe under any circumstances. To do so usually meant a death sentence in McCarter's line of work, and only other men like him would have been able to understand that. Still, the Briton was not without compassion and he gripped Sheinberg's shoulder as a signal it was all right.

Sheinberg quickly regained his composure. "Sorry. Been kind of a long week."

"No need to be sorry, sir. Maybe we should do this later."

Sheinberg shook his head with an emphatic expression. "Absolutely not. I'm okay now, really. I'm ready to talk to you, to answer your questions. Ready to talk to anybody just as long as I can keep my mind off what's happened."

McCarter nodded. "Good enough. What can you tell me about the men who took you?"

"I'm afraid I don't follow. What specifically would you like to know?"

"Did they ever speak to one another in front of you?"

Sheinberg nodded. "On a number of occasions, actually. Unfortunately, I don't speak Arabic so I can't tell you what they were saying."

McCarter nodded and pressed his lips together for a moment and thought. "How did you know it was Arabic?"

"I did a year of my residency along the Gaza Strip."

"Seems like a strange place for an internship, bloke."

"Not really," Sheinberg said, shaking his head. "That part of the Middle East is one of the best places for an immunologist to work. You see all kinds of diseases. Most of those diseases only come because of bad drinking water, poor sanitary conditions or lack of adequate medical attention. The area is replete with malaria, typhoid and other diseases that result from the bacteria carried by insects and poor personal hygiene, which makes people in impoverished areas most susceptible to the high rate of traumatic injury and malnutrition."

Well, McCarter sure as hell couldn't argue with that logic. Between the lack of technical advancements in the area coupled with violent outbreaks—due primarily to the continuing war between the PLO, Hamas and the Israeli government—there was also no shortage of misery. Such conditions provided doctors with a test bed of subjects for which they could find better ways of treating diseases around the world. A guy like Sheinberg, a man dedicated to preserving life and alleviating suffering, would find such a place a valuable environment in which to learn his trade. His expertise would be valuable, too, to the Namibian government.

"Did they take you anywhere else before bringing you here?"

Sheinberg shook his head. "No, I don't think so."

"Forgive me for saying this, but you don't sound overly sure."

"I'm not. You see, they attacked us on the road between Lüderitz and Windhoek. I'm not even really sure what happened other than the fact that they must've done something to the road, because we put the nose of our small bus down into a ditch. When we all got out to inspect the damage, they came from out of nowhere and jumped us. I remember them putting something over my mouth, something that burned at first but then eventually things began to get foggy. The next thing I know, I wake up and I'm blindfolded, and the inside of my mouth is really dry, which tells me that they drugged us with something."

McCarter nodded in understanding now. "So you were unconscious. There was no possible way for you to know if they had taken you somewhere else before they brought you here."

"Exactly. I cannot even tell you for certain how long I was unconscious. I assume none of us can."

"I understand. Thanks for taking the time to talk to me, Doc. As soon as you guys have had a chance to rest and get something in your stomachs, we'll be on our way out of here. You're in the Kohlmanskop Ghost Town in case you haven't figured it out by now. So we're not real far from Lüderitz."

"My thanks to you once again, Mr. Brown," Sheinberg said, sticking out his hand.

McCarter shook it and then had the Phoenix Force warriors gather around him in an area just out of earshot of the hostages.

"What did you manage to find out?" T. J. Hawkins asked.

McCarter shook his head and tried to keep the discouragement from his voice. "Not a whole lot. Sheinberg says he doesn't remember much of anything. The IUA ambushed them while they were en route back to Windhoek. They used some type of inhalant to subdue them. My guess would be ether or something similar, maybe something mixed with turpentine."

Manning shook his head. "It's crude but it's effective."

"It just doesn't make a whole lot of sense," McCarter said.

"What's that?" Encizo said.

"Snatching up this medical team at all. I mean, what did the IUA have to gain by that? They didn't grab them because of their expertise in radiation poisoning, and they sure as hell didn't snatch them for ransom. Just doesn't seem like this was anything in their best interests. In fact, it looks to me like they almost exposed themselves unnecessarily, and that's not something you see in a terrorist organization."

Manning nodded. "David's right. Not a bit of this makes sense. While the Revenge of Allah may be a new group and we don't have a lot of intelligence on them, there are more basic operating parameters within Islamic terrorist groups. So far, the IUA has not behaved in either a logical or a predictable manner. They went out of their way to snatch up this medical team, a move that they should've known would draw immediate attention. Then they ambushed us on the road using stolen military equipment. And if that wasn't enough, they then tried to assassinate Matombo while he was under our protection."

"And let's not forget the fact that they've twice made attempts to take down Able Team in broad daylight," Encizo added.

"They're one bold bunch, I'll give them that," James said.

"Well, whatever's happening here," McCarter concluded, "it seems clear Sheinberg's team doesn't have any information about this uranium ore mine or what we can expect to find. I guess that means we'll have to take whatever precautions are necessary to limit our exposure, and take out the trash. For now, we had best get going because we have a long day ahead of us yet."

The Phoenix Force members grunted their assent and then turned and made their way back to the hostages. The return ride to Lüderitz would be cramped, but that didn't negate the success of their mission. For the moment, the men of Phoenix Force were content with the fact they had saved the lives of five bystanders and taken a few of the IUA terrorist bastards along the way.

To McCarter, though, it felt like a bit of a hollow victory. For all they knew, the terrorists had managed to get enough of the uranium ore mined that they could use it to make weapons-grade plutonium. The numbers were running down and McCarter didn't feel they were any closer to eliminating the terrorist threat than the moment they stepped foot in this godforsaken desert icebox. Sure, they had some idea of the IUA's plans but they didn't really know where the terrorists would hit or how they would do it. And if Phoenix Force failed in their mission here, it only increased the IUA's chances of getting the nuclear material to its final destination.

The fact remained that Able Team didn't have any

more ability to wage war against the nuclear threat than Phoenix Force. At the end of the day, they had to succeed. Failure wasn't an option and neither was compromise. This time around, the stakes were high enough that there could only be one outcome for Phoenix Force: absolute victory! Because if David McCarter knew something with certainty, it was this.

Anything less would mean tragic defeat for America and her people.

CHAPTER TEN

Phoenix Force had barely traveled a mile when Mc-Carter, positioned in the front passenger seat of the lead SUV, spotted a cloud of dust on the road ahead at the peak of a slow, gentle hill. At first, the Phoenix Force leader didn't think too much of it but after a time he realized it was a little too early and a little too coincidental that another vehicle would be in this area. Especially at this particular time of morning. That meant one of two things: either they were additional terrorists—perhaps reinforcements sent to investigate a missed check-in—or something else.

"Well, whoever they are," Calvin James said in response to McCarter, pointing out the trail of dust that could have only been left by a motor vehicle, "there's a good chance they aren't friendly."

"They could be bandits, possibly thieves even," Sheinberg commented from the backseat.

McCarter's brow furrowed as he glanced back at the doctor. "Bandits? What makes you think that?"

"They've been known to operate out here on more than one occasion," Sheinberg said. "During the tourist season, they pretty much keep to themselves. Too many witnesses, you know. But in this case, this is the time of year where they can pretty much operate freely with little interference. A lot of people come out this way, local citizens and natives from the surrounding towns. Scavengers, mostly, looking for anything they can find to make a quick buck. You're dealing with an economically depressed country, a place where even the criminals are left with slim pickings. Don't tell me it would surprise men of your experience to learn that such things existed in our country."

As McCarter jacked the slide of his MP-5, he replied, "Nothing surprises me anymore, friend."

"Green Leader, you read me?" Manning's voice echoed over the radio.

McCarter replied, "I read you and I see them. Assessment?"

There was a brief pause and McCarter assumed that Manning was talking it over with Encizo and Hawkins, who were accompanying him in the other SUV. The ride back had proved to be as cramped, hot and uncomfortable as they surmised it would. At first, Encizo had come up with the idea of putting all the hostages in one vehicle save for one member of Phoenix Force and the rest of the team in the other. This way, if they encountered any sort of trouble, most of Phoenix Force would be together and able to run interference while the other vehicle escaped. It was a good idea except that it would have left one of the vehicles poorly armed and light on trained combatants in the event they had to set up a defensive perimeter.

Encizo had to admit he hadn't thought of that.

Manning's reply finally came through. "We can't be sure, but we've agreed that it's likely not an IUA welcoming party. Could be hunters or poachers, or even a group on safari, although that doesn't seem probable being as it's not really the season. And we've been told on more than one occasion the tourist crowd is bleak this time of year."

McCarter briefly explained Sheinberg's theory about criminals or bandits.

"It's possible," Manning said. "It certainly sounds a hell of a lot more plausible than terrorists. If you ask me, bandits would be the lesser of two evils."

"Well, we've got less than a minute to decide how we want to handle this," McCarter said. "Any ideas?"

"I'd suggest you guys continue on your path. It's a good bet that they can't see us given all the dust you're leaving and the fact it's still pretty early in the morning. When we get close enough we'll break off and cut a flanking maneuver... Say we'll come in on their five o'clock. That'll be your ten o'clock, so watch your fire zone on that side. You copy?"

"Understood and acknowledged. See you on the other side."

"So what's the plan?" James asked.

"You ever play chicken?"

"Not since I was a kid," James said with a wicked smile.

"Well, then, you're about to feel young again. As soon as you see the whites of their eyes, you bear hard right. And don't slow down."

"Roger that," James said.

As they drew close to the vehicle, McCarter looked for any distinguishing marks but didn't see any. It was just a plain SUV—not too dissimilar to their own—with four occupants inside. James kept the path of their SUV straight and steady until the last possible moment, and only by sheer luck did they choose to turn to the right as James broke off to their right, thereby avoiding a head-on collision from which neither group would have survived at those speeds.

James kept the accelerator to the floor but expertly controlled the SUV when on several occasions it fish-tailed. In the hands of a less experienced driver, they could have easily gone out of control and probably flipped the vehicle several times, killing everyone aboard. In this case, the skill and quick reflexes of the Chicago badass, reflexes born from years perfecting his expertise as a street fighter and Navy SEAL, proved the saving grace for everyone aboard.

James regained the road about a half mile from where he had broken off and steadily brought their vehicle to a halt. There were excited voices chattering in the back-seat, the two women, but Sheinberg did his best to keep them quiet. Apparently, this hadn't been his first time in such circumstances and for a moment McCarter had to wonder just exactly what kind of background he had. Then again, he couldn't say that he wasn't glad to have someone like Sheinberg along for the ride. Obviously the guy had some experience with these types of things; McCarter couldn't see how he could have avoided it having served in a place like the Gaza Strip.

"Turn us around!"

James jammed the stick into Reverse, popped the clutch and tromped the accelerator. He picked up enough speed as he watched the area behind him through the rearview mirror. When the moment was right, he swung the nose around in a perfect J-turn.

Such a maneuver wasn't an easy one to perfect and McCarter had to admit he was impressed with his friend's hidden talent behind the wheel. As James completed the turn and dropped the stick into second,

McCarter said, "One of these times you'll have to show me how to do that."

"Be my pleasure," James said, eyes locked on the road.

By the time they caught up to the vehicle that had nearly collided head-on with them, McCarter could see it had already taken some significant punishment from his comrades. Encizo, who was behind the wheel of that SUV, rode on their tail at the five-o'clock position just as Manning had said they would. The Canadian and Hawkins were leaning out opposite windows in the backseat and triggering a steady stream of 9 mm Parabellums from their MP-5s. Two occupants in the SUV they chased were also leaning out their windows and returning fire, but the angle made it difficult for them to actually hit anything. McCarter didn't recognize either of the men shooting at them, but one thing was certain: they were members of the IUA. In fact, McCarter had been asked to venture a guess he would have said that these men were European.

In either case, one thing remained obvious. These men were hostile, and they would be dealt with in the same fashion for which Phoenix Force was known to deal with its other aggressors. McCarter ordered James to hold position at about seven o'clock as he rolled down the window. He braced the MP-5 against the side of the SUV and stuck his head into the chill desert air. The sand and other debris blasted his face and made it difficult to aim at his target. McCarter wished for some goggles right about then but he knew such a nicety was unavailable.

Little point in wishing now, McCarter told himself.

The Briton took a shallow breath, keeping his mouth closed to prevent from choking on the cloud of dust churned by the wheels of the fleeing vehicle and triggered his MP-5. The back window of the SUV spider-webbed some more before finally shattering under the ceaseless punishment of autofire. Both of the gunners had been firing from the passenger side, but the man in the back ducked inside as soon as he spotted McCarter shooting at them. For a moment, the Briton could see some sort of tumbled happening inside in the backseat, but the man now poked his head out of the driver's-side rear window.

"Watch out!" James warned him.

"I see him!"

McCarter could see the man's face a little better, make out a few more distinguishing features. He had dark hair and eyes, swarthy skin; he looked almost Italian or Spanish, certainly not Arab. The man firing from the front passenger seat was big and blond, looked almost like Lyons. No, these were Europeans or Americans—no doubt about it. But what was their interest in Phoenix Force? For a moment, McCarter didn't have a solid answer to that question. He supposed there was a remote possibility they had engaged the enemy too soon, not gathered enough intelligence first, which simply would've meant that these men were defending themselves. Somehow that theory just didn't hold water for McCarter; there had to be another explanation.

At the moment, however, McCarter knew he wasn't going to give any explanations except in the form of bullets. The steady chatter from the gunman's SMG, a 9 mm Uzi, chopped up the road in front of them or punched holes in the flimsy fiberglass body of their SUV. McCarter knew the situation was going to get out of hand very quickly with possibly injuries to the hostages and Phoenix Force before they could neutralize the enemy. These weren't first-year cadets they were up against and those weren't pop guns they were shooting.

McCarter ducked inside. A heartbeat before, several rounds smashed the passenger-side rear door window. The Briton whipped his head around at the sound of a scream and Sheinberg shook his head as he tried to cover both of the nurses with his arms. "We're okay!"

McCarter nodded, blew a sigh of relief through clenched teeth and then stuck his head out the window again. "Time to end this bloody mess," he muttered.

McCarter sighted down the MP-5 and triggered a pair of controlled bursts at the tires of the enemy vehicle. The rounds landed on-target and the rubber of one tire immediately shredded, flying away in pieces. The driver tried to keep the vehicle under control, and had he been driving on sand it might've worked, but in this case the rough road constructed from makeshift composite and gravel added to the punishment. The wheel couldn't take it. Within a moment, they were riding on the rim and the speed was such they couldn't maintain any sort of distance. The driver had no choice but to bring the SUV to a halt.

"WHAT THE FUCK are you doing?" Hellerman demanded.

"What do you think I'm doing?" Weisgaden snapped. "They took out our tire and we sure as hell aren't going too far on the remaining three and one rim."

From the backseat, Faccio shouted, "Quit bickering like a couple of girls and start shooting!"

The two mercenaries in the front seat realized the wisdom of putting aside their differences for the moment as the SUVs that had been chasing them shot past their position. It wouldn't take them long to turn around and come back for a second pass. Weisgaden reached down and withdrew his Heckler & Koch HK-53 from where he'd stowed it between the console and the floorboards. The German mercenary leaped out of the SUV and took up a firing position behind the door. He wedged the stock of the weapon between the door and the A-post and aligned his sights on the nearest enemy vehicle.

"Commen zie here, bitte, mitt ohns," the German whispered. "I have something for you."

Hellerman didn't hear him, obviously lost in his own thoughts as he took up a similar position behind his door. In fact, neither of the mercenaries really paid much attention to the fact that the hostage they had brought along with them, the Negro doctor known as Matombo, was kicking and screaming and trying to pry himself loose from Faccio's grip.

The Italian had just about put up with all he could take from this man. They had brought him along as part insurance policy, part information source. Unfortunately he'd become more trouble than he was worth and Faccio's patience was quickly running out. In fact, he saw no reason why they needed the man anymore. They had found the five Americans, and as soon as they dealt with them Matombo would no longer be a consequence, only a liability. It seemed reasonable they take care of that liability now rather than wait until later.

As Matombo shouted another flurry of absurdities, Faccio leveled his Uzi at the man and triggered a short burst that went through his mouth and blew out the top of his skull. Matombo's head, or rather what was left of it, made a sickly crack as it smashed against the door now washed with his brains. Even a few bone chips were visible where they had embedded themselves in the leather.

Faccio stepped from the SUV, totally unmoved by the heinous act he had just committed against another human being, and dashed for the cover of a large boulder. As he ran he triggered his Uzi at the group of armed combatants bearing down on their position. They might have been outgunned by a man or two, but Faccio knew there was little chance they could be outclassed.

Whatever happened now, at least they would be doing what they were paid to do.

GARY MANNING COULDN'T SEE what had occurred inside the vehicle, but the sound of gunfire followed by a wash of red against the passenger window told him all he needed to know. Whoever these men were they had apparently been carrying a prisoner with them, or someone they considered certainly expendable within their group. Perhaps someone who would've been able to tell Phoenix Force who these newcomers were and why they were here at this time.

"I wonder if these boys know they just bought themselves a whole gaggle of trouble," Hawkins said.

"Whether they do or not," Manning replied, "it's quite obvious they don't care."

Without another word, all three members of the Phoenix team bailed from the SUV as soon as Encizo brought it to a halt. One of the men, the one who had just shot someone inside his own vehicle, bolted across the desert floor in the direction of a large boulder. He triggered his weapon on the run, and the Phoenix Force trio raised the muzzles of their MP-5s and responded in kind.

The man never made it to his intended haven. Thanks to the unerring marksmanship of the Phoenix Force commandos, a storm of lead punched through his body, tearing flesh from bone and blowing out exit holes the size of baseballs. The man's weapon clattered from his fingers and he tumbled into the dust, rolling with the momentum of his fall. He continued for several yards and came to rest just an arm's length from the boulder.

McCarter and James emerged from their vehicle. A heartbeat later they opened up in concert with a full-auto salvo on the remaining two gunmen. They were joined by Manning, Encizo and Hawkins within seconds. The thin skin of the enemy SUV proved no match for the metal storm of 9 mm slugs slamming into it at a combined rate of 3,500 rounds per minute. It was a matter of sheer numbers in this case, and the gunners with their SMGs were no match for firepower of that magnitude.

The pair died on their feet, screaming as rounds shattered the glass and body of the SUV, sending hundreds of jagged shards into their exposed flesh. The driver managed to retreat a distance of about twenty yards before looking down and realizing that one of the rounds had caught an artery in his belly. Red, hot blood squirted between his fingers as his brain registered he'd suffered a mortal wound. The next steps he took were unsteady, hesitant, and it seemed as if he was waiting for the final rounds in the back. To his surprise, they never came and he found it ironic that these men he didn't know had actually possessed enough honor not to cut him down like a dog. He wished he could have said the same for himself as he dropped to his knees, lost consciousness and fell onto his face.

He would never return from the blackness that overtook him.

McCarter gestured toward the dead Italian and ordered James to check him for identification. Hawkins remained with the two SUVs, keeping watch on the hostages while Manning and Encizo approached the enemy vehicle with caution. Once they had cleared it, McCarter watched Encizo as he looked into the back-seat. There was a long silence, and when Encizo's face reappeared, McCarter immediately realized the news wasn't good. McCarter walked stiffly and steadily toward where Encizo waited.

"What is it, Rafe?"

"I'm sorry, David," Encizo said. "But it's not pretty and you're not going to like it."

McCarter took a deep breath and then looked into the back of the SUV, bracing himself for the worst. And worst it was, something that no words could have prepared him for. For a long time, McCarter didn't say anything. He just stared in complete shock at the mangled head that had belonged to Dr. Justus Matombo. Once more, an innocent bystander had suffered at the hands of brutal animals who had the unmitigated gall to call themselves human beings.

"Oh, bloody hell," McCarter said, slamming his fist into the side of the SUV. "This is all my damn fault. I should've left somebody with him."

"David, there was no way you could have known. We thought the threat to Matombo had been neutralized. We all agreed that he wasn't at risk. It's not your fault."

McCarter realized the wisdom of his friend's words, but that didn't make it any easier to swallow. To this point, both Phoenix Force and Able Team had been on the defensive—warding off every attack the IUA threw at them—no matter what cost. But now this had gotten out of control. Sure, they had rescued the five hostages, but that had resulted in the death of an innocent man, a man who had died only because he'd chosen to help them instead of going through official channels. This would not go over well with the Namibian government, never mind the fact that Matombo had a wife and about half a dozen children.

"We need to get these bastards, Rafe," McCarter said quietly. "You mark my bloody words we'll get these bastards where they live and breed. And we're going to do it today."

Encizo knew even when he heard it that it was an oath McCarter meant to keep.

CHAPTER ELEVEN

David McCarter couldn't remember the last time he had experienced mixed emotions like these on a mission.

Under normal circumstances, the Phoenix Force leader didn't let such things bother him because he knew the impact it could have on his leadership, impairing his judgment to such a degree that it would have dire consequences for his team members. Indeed, a leader who couldn't put aside his emotions and maintain his objectivity was no leader at all. It was the kind of leader who generally got his people killed in a combat situation.

They had made the trip back to Lüderitz in silence, and McCarter's thoughts were filled with the body that rode in the very back of their SUV wrapped in a blanket lined with plastic. In a lot of ways, McCarter felt as if he'd lost a member of his own team today. While Dr. Justus Matombo hadn't been a part of Phoenix Force, he had stepped out on a limb to support the team in his belief that they could make a difference for his country. Unfortunately that belief had cost him his life—not that it was the first time that someone's convictions and doing what was right had invited a similar fate.

The one thing that McCarter could feel most grateful about was the fact that Sheinberg and his team didn't seem to blame Phoenix Force for Matombo's death. The loss of the man would be felt for a long time to come—no doubt about that—but at least from their perspective Phoenix Force had done everything they could to prevent such a tragedy. Even Sheinberg at one moment actually took the time to tell McCarter that he realized Matombo's death wasn't their fault, and that he planned to inform the Namibian government that this would've happened no matter what.

It was a nice sentiment, and the Briton appreciated it, but on the other side it didn't make McCarter feel much better. When they returned to the hotel, they got the rest of the story from the desk clerk and this time Phoenix Force didn't have Matombo to shield them from an inquiry by the local police. The bottom had utterly fallen out of their cover, and now the government was questioning their presence and their activities in a more official capacity. This would not only draw attention from officials in Windhoek, but it also put the President of the United States in a very precarious position. How could they justify allowing armed men, serving only the interests of the American government, to participate in armed conflict against unknown parties while putting citizens at risk?

The Namibian government had spent many years trying to quell the bad taste that had been left in its mouth from years of civil war. In fact, southern Africa was doing everything it could to recover from the reputation it had with the rest of the world as being a cold, violent and inhospitable place. The Namibian government, just like most of those countries in southern Africa, had taken one political black eye after another.

In the court of world opinion, southern Africa was a region that could not manage its affairs, feed its citizens or maintain any sort of law and order.

The incidents over the past eighteen hours had not helped that case, and to learn that it was Americans in the center of that fray wouldn't help the President's position much. Still, the Oval Office understood the importance of Phoenix Force's mission inside Namibia, and somehow, some way, the President would manage to convince government officials that their presence remained a critical necessity to the security of both Namibia and America until such time as the terrorists' mining operation could be located.

This was particularly good news when Harold Brognola told McCarter that very thing.

"Up to this point, the only innocent bystander has been Dr. Matombo," Brognola said. "Your rescue of the medical team went a long way toward smoothing over his death. The President wanted to let you know that both he and the Namibian government are quite aware that Matombo wasn't killed by any negligence or action on your part. It was an indirect consequence of being in the wrong place at the wrong time."

"I appreciate the sentiment," McCarter replied. "Doesn't make it any easier to swallow."

"Understood."

Brognola decided to change the subject in the interest of letting the uncomfortable moment pass. The Stony Man chief had learned a long time ago that the men in the field had to come to their own terms when things like this happened. It was the only way that they could find peace; each one of them found it in his own way. Stony Man had a program that required the regular evaluation of every member by a psychiatrist, but the tests were fairly standardized and the men of Able Team in Phoenix Force had learned how to play the game.

Brognola didn't worry too much about those kinds of details. Barbara Price had always had a pretty good finger on the pulse of the men. It was she who usually made the determination when they needed to take a leave of absence or vacation, or simply get away from things for a while by taking on individual missions suited to their particular talents. Brognola was confident that if there were any signs of a crack-up by any team member, or more ominous symptoms of post-traumatic stress disorder following combat missions, Price would alert him immediately and that individual would be suspended from active duty and ordered to participate in mandatory respite.

Brognola had been required to give that order maybe a dozen times in all the years the teams had been working with them. The worst thing he knew that they could do was to yank a member of the field prematurely. These were men of action who thrived on their ability to take that action when something or someone, terrorists or criminals, enemies foreign or domestic, threatened America or her way of life. These men were committed totally without mental or physical reservation to the security and peace of the nation. And they were willing to do whatever had to be done to ensure the longevity of the country and its ideals.

"Aaron's team has been working around the clock to try to get you a better line on the location of the mining operation," Brognola told McCarter.

"Any progress?"

"None so far, but we are remaining very hopeful at this stage. They're reviewing satellite photographs that were taken of the area six months ago in comparison to the present topography. Aaron thinks this might give us enough information to pinpoint the location of the mining operation. Yellow-cake mining happens close to the surface, so there's very little underground activity. That would make it extremely difficult for the terrorists to hide the exact location. The equipment required to safely mine it is also fairly large so they would have to be able to hide it when it wasn't in use."

"Which they probably wouldn't have bothered to do if they didn't think anybody was observing them," McCarter concluded.

"Exactly."

"Sounds like a pretty good plan. We've been talking with Dr. Sheinberg here about what steps we have to take to protect ourselves from radiation poisoning. He's arranged to have some equipment shipped from Walvis Bay. According to what he described to us, it's going to make fighting extremely difficult, but I think we've had enough training in this area that we can still be effective."

"We have complete confidence in you back here, David."

Brognola then began to fill him in on what information Able Team had been able to pick up so far. While it might've seemed bleak to the men in the field, Brognola remained as optimistic as he could and tried to pass on that optimism in both word and deed. Morale was already low right now, and he didn't want to give McCarter any more to worry about. The Phoenix Force leader felt badly enough about not being able to protect Matombo. Brognola saw no point in adding fuel to the fire.

"Your first and foremost mission at this point is to make sure that you come out of this alive. You take whatever precautions you think you need to. The IUA terrorists have already demonstrated they are willing to take extraordinary measures to protect their interests in this plot. I know we've handed you a tall order this time, but you've had tough ones like this before. We're rooting for you, and I know you'll come through." Brognola paused a moment and then with a laugh added, "Here ends the pep talk."

McCarter took the infectious humor in the way Brognola intended. "And boy am I glad it's ended. I was getting downright teary-eyed there for a second, Hal. It wouldn't do good to cry in front of my team."

"We'll be in touch as soon as we have an exact location on the mine. In the meantime, get some rest."

"Acknowledged. Out here."

McCarter hung up the phone and sighed. He wished he could have told Brognola something more, giving them some other information or another angle to check out. They had decided to use Hawkins's cell phone to take pictures of the trio that had attacked them near Kohlmanskop and transmit that information back to Stony Man for Barbara Price to evaluate. It didn't make any sense that a bunch of Europeans were looking for Matombo or Phoenix Force, unless they'd been hired by the IUA. And then another more ominous possibility had been suggested by Rafael Encizo. It wasn't too crazy an idea that some other organization was behind this entire plot, and the IUA was being used as the front for it. It wouldn't have been the first time that an organization with no ties whatsoever to the Islamic terrorist jihad would manipulate al Qaeda into being the scapegoat for their own plans.

To be sure, foreign governments had done this, and they weren't the only ones. Corporations, conglomerations, business interests and other radical groups such as neo-Nazis and militias—even political subversives in former Eastern Bloc countries—had attempted this sort of convoluted deception. It actually made for a good way of doing things, since countries like America and her allies were so bent on crushing the Arab-based terrorist hydra. Unfortunately for them, Stony Man had played that game enough times before that they wouldn't be fooled by it again. Still, McCarter knew that they needed to check it out thoroughly before making a determination. To assume that this was just another deception on the part of the IUA would have been tantamount to suicide, and David McCarter wasn't willing to play that game with the lives of his friends.

When McCarter joined the rest of the team in the room adjoining the suite from which he'd placed his call, the casual chatter died out and they all gave him their undivided attention. The weapons they had used in their assault on the Kohlmanskop Ghost Town were strewed over newspaper in various stages of disassembly for cleaning. No matter how tough things got, these four men were at the top of their game, disciplined and utterly professional. They kept their equipment in working order because they knew if they didn't, it might very well cost them the lives of themselves or one of their teammates. And David McCarter admired every damn one of them for it.

"What's the story, boss?" Gary Manning asked.

McCarter shook his head. "I'm afraid we don't know much more than we knew before, but Hal did sound as if we shouldn't give up hope yet. Aaron's team has been working to try to get us an exact location of the yellowcake mine. For now, we can take a break. As soon as the equipment is cleaned and back in service, I want all of you to get some shut-eye. Since we don't know what we're going to come up against, and we had a little surprise this morning, I think a watch is in order. I'll take the first one."

"You sure about that?" James asked. "Maybe one of us should take the first one, David. You've been pushing yourself pretty hard."

McCarter had to bite his tongue not to lash out at his teammate. He knew James was just trying to be considerate of the fact that McCarter had taken Matombo's death pretty hard. Not to mention that James knew, as did every member of the team, a tired leader was not an effective leader, and in this current climate of unpredictability and hostility, Phoenix Force couldn't afford that kind of management.

McCarter expressed a half grin. "Thanks for the offer, but no thanks, Cal. I'll be just fine and I'll wake you for the next watch in two hours."

James just nodded in way of reply.

As the men went about their tasks, Encizo asked, "Were they able to identify any of the three who attacked us?"

"No information came through immediately from the photos we transmitted, but Barb's plugging away at it. They think they'll have something more for us soon."

"You know, it occurred to me that those guys might've been mercenaries," Manning said.

McCarter arched an eyebrow, but it was Hawkins who said, "What makes you think that?"

"I don't know…it just seems to me that if the IUA wanted to throw us off the trail, give their people time to get away with the U-92 ore, they might have contracted with an outside group."

McCarter considered that a moment. "You mean, a decoy?"

"Why not?" Manning asked with a shrug. "Those

guys didn't have any reason to stop at the hotel and pick up Matombo first, unless it was important for them to find out what he knew."

"You think they questioned him, maybe even tortured him until he told them where to find us."

"That's exactly what I think," Manning said. "Which would explain some things on a number of levels."

"Such as?"

"Well, for one, it tells us that they knew we were going to Kohlmanskop Ghost Town to rescue the hostages. It also means that whoever they were, they were privy to the fact that the kidnapping of this medical team was of importance to us, since Dr. Sheinberg and his people would be the only ones who could actually tell us what they'd witnessed as far as people being poisoned by radiation. That information would be pretty inflammatory in the hands of the Namibian government, and it would certainly raise eyebrows in the international community. If anyone were to find out that terrorists might possibly have a mining operation going on for U-92 ore within this country, every U.S. ally would go looking for them."

"I'll be damned," Hawkins said as he looked up at McCarter. "He's got an awfully good point there, David."

"Assuming that Gary's right about these three, and the fact that the IUA had sent them to try to throw us off track, that would mean there was some significant purpose to the distraction," Encizo said.

"In other words, it wouldn't be enough that they just distract us. They would also need to stall us for a time," James said.

Encizo nodded. "Right. So now I have to ask myself why in the world was that important? Why would independent contractors, if that's what they were, since I don't think they are members of the IUA, risk exposing themselves like that? There was a tactical reason for their actions. I can't believe for a minute that those actions were driven solely by money."

"That's assuming Gary's theory about them being mercenaries or a hired hit team is correct," McCarter pointed out. He looked at Manning and said, "Not that I'm dismissing your idea, understand."

Manning nodded. "I understand. I know it's only a theory."

"So let's assume the theory is true," Encizo continued. "What would be so important that they would need to stall for time? What is it they need time to do?"

James scratched his chin and slowly his expression changed from perplexity to realization. "Maybe they needed time to get the U-92 out of Namibia. We know they plan to use those materials to power the FACOS prototypes, right? But to do that, they would have to convert the U-92 into U-238. It's the U-238 that can then be converted to weapons-grade plutonium, not the raw ore itself. There's no way they could set up a facility inside Namibia to do that, which means it would have to be either transported to some other location where they could convert it, or convert it en route to America."

"So you're saying that this whole thing might've been their attempt to distract us while their agents got the stuff out of the country?" McCarter asked.

"Why not?" Encizo said. "I can't think of a better place to hide such an operation than on a ship."

"So let me get this straight," Hawkins said. "You're proposing that the IUA terrorists brought people into Namibia to mine the U-92, which is the raw ore. They then use outsiders to keep any official inquiries or other threatening parties at bay while they get the ore transferred out of the country via ship. Then during transport, they have a floating lab to convert the U-92 into weapons-grade plutonium so the material is ready for use by the time they get it to the prototype submarines."

"Which we know they're building somewhere on the QT within the United States," James finished.

"*¡Madre Dios!*" Encizo whispered.

For a long moment nobody said anything. Each of the men looked among the others for some sign of doubt, some small glimmer in the eyes of their teammates that would imply the theory seemed too preposterous to be plausible. Nobody came up with that look—in fact quite the opposite—and at the end of it all McCarter had to admit that it sounded awfully close to as viable an explanation as they had at that moment. Especially given the available facts.

"If we're right, if we're even bloody close," he said, "and if they have managed to somehow get the raw material out of Namibia, this whole trip could be for nothing."

Very quietly and evenly, Gary Manning said, "You'd better call Hal back."

McCarter nodded slowly. "Yeah."

CHAPTER TWELVE

Carl Lyons stared out the window of the hotel room and kept what vigil he could on the rain-washed parking lot.

"Where the hell are they?" he mumbled as he looked at his watch.

Nearly 2000 hours and still no sign of the FBI detachment assigned to oversee the prisoner transfer.

Blancanales and Schwarz were hunkered over a miniature traveling chess set Schwarz purchased from a novelty store across the street from their hotel, along with a bucket of takeout chicken from next door. The two IUA prisoners were prone on the bed, bound at hands and feet and wearing gags. At one point, Blancanales had offered to give them something to drink and eat but the resolute terrorists refused any hospitality.

Schwarz looked at Lyons with a catty grin. "What's up with you, Ironman? You got plans with a hot date?"

"I got plans to ream these assholes when and if they ever get here," Lyons stormed. "We ain't got time for this."

"Relax, my friend," Blancanales said without taking his eyes off the chess pieces. He extended the half-empty bucket in Lyons's direction. "Have more chicken."

"Yeah, Ironman, have more chicken," Schwarz cracked.

Lyons, who was taking a long pull from his water, prepared to deliver a wisecrack to his friends when headlights swept into view. As it passed under the lights of the parking lot, Lyons could see it was a dark SUV. A moment later a second vehicle—this one a brown four-door sedan—followed the lead vehicle.

"They're here—"

Lyons never finished the sentence as he saw the first flashes of light from one side of the SUV. He shouted for Blancanales and Schwarz to hit the floor even as he drew the Colt Python from his shoulder holster and ate the carpet himself.

Blancanales and Schwarz rolled out of their chairs simultaneously, moving just in time to avoid a flurry of hot lead that ripped through the walls and shredded their chess board and bucket of chicken. Only milliseconds after the rounds buzzed past them, Schwarz jumped to his feet and shoved the panicked terrorists off the bed. The two were anxious to help him by rolling without even so much as a prompting from their captors.

"Gadgets, stay down!" Lyons roared.

Before the Able Team warrior could reply, Lyons shot to his feet, stuck his Colt Python out the window and triggered two rounds. Blancanales low-crawled to the closet where they had stowed their heavy weapons. For security reasons, they didn't want them so easily accessible while they had prisoners in their charge. Trying to open the door while on his belly proved difficult but Blancanales was equal to the task, and a moment later he had the heavy firepower in hand.

He slid the M-16 A-3 to Schwarz, who lay at the foot of the bed near him, and then whistled for Lyons's attention. The Able Team leader stopped shooting long enough to snatch out of midair the M-16 A-3/M-203 combo tossed to him. Blancanales then took up the Beretta SC-70/90 and inched back toward the door.

Lyons wasted no time pushing the muzzle of the M-16 A-3 between the curtain and window and triggering a sustained burst. He snapped off several rounds before watching in shock as two agents emerged from the sedan, pistols drawn, and took aim on the SUV. The driver was cut down instantly by a burst from a rifle-toting man in the SUV. The second agent nearly lost his head under a steady stream of lead from another gunner, but he managed to duck behind the moderate protection of his door at the last moment.

"Agents in the sedan are friendlies!" Lyons shouted to his comrades as he sighted on the shooter trying to kill the surviving agent and squeezed the trigger. A trio of 5.56 mm slugs landed on target and punched through the gunman's upper body. The impact pitched him onto the pavement.

Lyons's marksmanship drew the attention of the other three gunners in the SUV. Obviously they figured they had more to fear from Able Team than from a lone, scared agent with a semiautomatic pistol. While that made them smart, it didn't make them particularly effective. They aligned their weapons on the motel room but the delay in shooting it out with the occupants of the sedan bought Blancanales and Schwarz the time they needed to gain firing positions while Lyons covered them.

With a vengeful fury for being duped and nearly getting killed, all three Able Team warriors opened up simultaneously and flooded the area with a maelstrom of high-velocity rounds. The steady stream of firepower made short work of the SUV. Several rounds caught one of the enemy gunners in the skull and blew off the top of his head. He dropped his weapon as his headless corpse staggered around, a grisly sight under the circumstances, before it toppled to the pavement. Another man met a similar fate seconds later.

The remaining gunner obviously realized the odds were no longer in his favor and in the interest of self-preservation he turned and rushed toward the sedan. He jumped behind the wheel, and the surviving FBI agent barely managed to get out of the way in time to keep from being run over by the madman behind the wheel.

"Oh no, you don't," Lyons muttered as he aligned the range-finder sight of the M-203 on the target. Hitting a moving object with the 40 mm grenade launcher was a skill few men possessed. Carl Lyons happened to be one of them. When the 40 mm HE grenade landed, it struck the engine compartment just forward of the driver-side A-post. The vehicle exploded into a fiery red-orange gas ball, immolating the driver in the blink of an eye. The vehicle swerved and caromed off the curb of the parking lot before slamming into the concrete stanchion of a light pole. Secondary explosions followed a moment later.

Lyons and Blancanales were out the door in a moment.

"Guess I'll stay here and watch our prisoners," Schwarz muttered.

Lyons dashed to the SUV and scanned it quickly to make sure no survivors were concealed inside and waiting to ambush them while Blancanales rushed toward the FBI agent to ascertain possible injuries and render aid, if necessary.

Within a few minutes Blancanales and the FBI agent joined Lyons in the hotel room.

Schwarz had managed to get the two terrorists back on the bed and had them at gunpoint while cradling the phone against his ear. He handed the phone to Lyons with a look that said it was Hal Brognola.

"What in the blue blazes is going on there?" the Stony Man chief demanded.

"That's what I'd like to know," Lyons said. "Our little detachment turned out to be more of a welcoming party."

"You were engaged?" Price's voice echoed with complete astonishment.

"That would be an understatement."

"Well, there's no doubt you've been compromised," Brognola replied. "I think we ought to bring you in for the moment and get our bearings before committing to this plan of sending you into Charleston."

"With all due respect, boss, I think that's a bad idea."

"How so?"

"Well, you already said it yourself. The IUA knows about us. Pulling out now isn't going to make them let down their guard any."

"No, but a sudden lapse of silence might get them jittery, even possibly nervous enough to make a critical mistake and reveal themselves."

"No, I don't think so. Whoever's in charge of this outfit has shown himself to be intelligent and resourceful. I think a ruse at this point would be the better option."

"What kind of ruse?"

Lyons smiled at Blancanales and Schwarz, who were now hanging on every word. "Well, the guys I saw weren't Arabs. They were Americans. Maybe even real FBI agents who'd been paid off to make a simple hit."

"You think the IUA's reach is that far?"

"No, but I think they have some significant funding sources at their disposal. Deep pockets have always been critical to a terrorist group's survival."

"So what are you getting at?"

"I'm betting they sent this team here to shut up our two prisoners. It wouldn't take much to get Americans to kill Arabs these days. They'd see it as their patriotic duty."

"Still not sure I follow," Brognola said.

"They wanted two bodies," Lyons said.

"I'm listening."

"Well, then, let's give 'em what they wanted," Carl Lyons replied.

ROSARIO BLANCANALES STARED at the airport runway lights that streaked by as their commercial flight touched down in Charleston. He sighed with contentment that at last they were on the ground. It wasn't that flying bothered him, but he'd always suffered from a sense of claustrophobia whenever he flew. In some regards, the man known affectionately as Politician preferred open spaces, a chance to regularly stretch his legs. He surmised that was the chief reason he so much enjoyed the outdoors.

Lyons's idea to publicize the "demise" of the two terrorist prisoners through a number of national news agencies had been nothing short of brilliant. Lyons had been right that Brognola's idea to pull them wouldn't cause the IUA to let down their guard so easily. But if the IUA's still unnamed leader received the word his little killing team had succeeded in their mission to silence the prisoners—assuming he believed the story— it might get him to think they were killed before they could be interrogated. And while it might not put the terrorist leader completely at ease, the thought of anonymity might at least make him less cautious.

Still, Blancanales knew it remained an unknown and that their plan was based solely on assumptions. So far, the enemy had proved resourceful and unpredictable, a very dangerous combination. And that fact just plain made Blancanales nervous.

"You been awfully quiet, Pol," Schwarz said. Blancanales turned to look at his friend. "I'd offer a penny for your thoughts but I don't make that much."

That produced a small laugh. Hermann Schwarz's wit had always been something Blancanales admired. "Just thinking about Ironman's plan."

"Don't think on it too hard," Schwarz said with a wink. "You might do irreparable damage. Don't forget, we are talking about Ironman now."

The Able Team leader ignored the banter, or at least tried to make a show of it, as they taxied to the terminal. None of the men even bothered to wait for the plane to stop. They weren't toting any bags so by the time the plane had stopped at the gate they were out of their seats and making their way up the aisle.

The flight attendant, a pretty young thing with green eyes and dirty-blond hair done up in a taut bun, eyed them with an almost disapproving glance. The cold blue eyes of Lyons seemed to deflect any verbal protests and within a minute they were up the boarding ramp and making their way out of the terminal.

The airport in Charleston wasn't that big so it took only a short time to reach the rental facility. Their rental vehicle, a late-model Ford Expedition, sported all the extra features: pistols, submachine guns, an RS-202 M-4 shotgun and plenty of spare ammunition for all. They also found two long bags filled with fresh clothes, holsters and specialized communications gear. The trio checked into a prearranged hotel not far from the airport where they cleaned up, changed and armed themselves with pistols.

Once they were fresh, the men clustered around the table to plan their next move.

"Okay," Lyons began, spreading out a map on the table. "We only have a few hours left until sunrise. I say we make the most of it."

"What'd you have in mind?" Blancanales said.

"We're here, and the underwater equipment supplier is here."

Schwarz nodded. "That's about a thirty-minute drive."

"You want to check out that place tonight?" Blancanales asked. "I'm sure they're probably closed this time of the morning."

Lyons gave him a short nod. "Right, which makes this the perfect time to stake them out, see what kind of activity goes on down there after hours."

"Oh, I get it," Schwarz interjected. "And maybe do a little looking around while we're there?"

"Perhaps," Lyons said with a shrug. "We might just find something that'll help us track down the IUA. We know the kind of equipment they purchased. I'm sure you could use one of those electronic doodads to put into their computer and search their records."

"That's a good point," Blancanales agreed. "And while he works on that, we can search any paper files they might have kept on those transactions."

"Problem is, we still don't exactly know what we're looking for," Schwarz said. "Could take time to interpret whatever information we do acquire. Do we have that kind of time?"

"Maybe, maybe not," Lyons said. "I'm hoping, though, that Phoenix Force can buy us enough time to find this secret facility."

"You know I've been giving that a lot of thought, guys," Blancanales said. "It seems to me that it would have been difficult for the IUA to build such a facility from the ground up in this short amount of time."

"Well, according to one of the prisoners we took, they've been operating in the U.S. for almost a year."

"Exactly my point. Look, a year isn't much time to build a construction facility and recruit the expertise necessary to construct submarine prototypes of this complexity. You guys saw the same plans I did. This mysterious leader of the IUA may have resources, but there's no amount of money I can think of that could buy the raw materials needed for such an undertaking without drawing attention."

"Well, I've learned to trust your hunches, Pol," Lyons said. "But whatever the explanation, and I'm sure there is one, we aren't going to find answers sitting around here."

"Now that I agree with," Blancanales said.

"Then what are we waiting for?" Schwarz asked. "Let's go."

The men gathered their equipment, climbed into the SUV and soon they were bound for the seaside salvage yard on which the equipment shop was located. The trip didn't prove short of things to see and Able Team got their fill of the sights, even at night. Charleston was steeped in history that dated back to the origins of the nation. Statues, memorials and the like dotted the very urban landscape and proclaimed that history with native pride. Their destination didn't look too different from any of the other buildings in that area. This part of Charleston was older than others, but Able Team didn't note anything about the shop that stood out.

Blancanales brought the SUV to a stop and killed the engine.

For a long time the three men just sat and studied the building's exterior. The only lights were those in the parking lot and the security lamp mounted directly above a metal entry door painted dark orange. Lights twinkled across the water from the constant influx and departure of ships. All three of the men had been here at one time or another but none remembered it quite the same way.

After about a half hour, Schwarz yawned as he looked at the luminous hands on his watch. "Well, doesn't look like there's much exciting going on here."

"We should—"

"Wait," Lyons said, holding up his hand and gesturing for silence. He pointed at a sedan that rounded a turn up the street they parked on and killed its lights.

"Gee, that's not suspicious," Schwarz said.

"Tenants, maybe?" Blancanales asked.

"Maybe," Lyons said. "But if they belong here then why were they so anxious to turn off their lights?"

"Check it out," Schwarz said.

The vehicle rolled to a stop and four men emerged with various weapons silhouetted in their hands.

"Uh-oh," Blancanales said. "I'm betting those aren't Super Soakers they're carrying. Should we move on them?"

"Not yet," Lyons said through clenched teeth, almost afraid to move. He worried that if the new arrivals spotted them they'd die before they could get out of the SUV.

The men of Able Team fell silent and watched the gunmen fan out and approach the salvage equipment shop.

What didn't make sense to Lyons at this point was why they were here. If these were IUA terrorists, what were they doing here at this time of night? If they were coming for equipment, there wouldn't be any need for the weapons. It didn't seem reasonable they'd come back to the place to steal equipment they could just as easily purchase without the risk of drawing attention. On the other side of the coin, he had no idea if the men were even part of the IUA. Maybe they were gang members. It was just too dark to determine nationality or positively ID the kinds of weapons they carried.

"Whoever they are, they're up to no good," Lyons finally said.

"We have an obligation to do *something,* Ironman," Blancanales said.

Lyons scowled. "Our only obligation is to stay on mission. But since we can't be sure these subjects aren't part of that mission, we should probably check it out."

The threesome quickly checked their pistols, made sure the weapons were in battery and then waited a moment longer until the shapes faded into the darkness.

"I think we ought to hold off a little longer. It looks like they're interested in the same place we are, and it's lit well enough there the dark should obscure our approach nicely," Blancanales said.

Lyons and Schwarz grunted their assent.

And when the time was right, Able Team went EVA—prepared for the hell sure to follow.

CHAPTER THIRTEEN

Able Team converged on the armed quartet from three directions, cautious to space themselves enough they couldn't be cut down by any one gunman if their approach was detected. Not that it mattered. The gunmen seemed more interested in the door they had gathered around than in their surroundings.

Lyons was surprised when one of the men rapped on the door with enough force that the echo from his insistent beating could have raised the dead. Lyon slowed his pace and raised a hand toward his two companions to indicate they should do the same. Blancanales took note of the gesture and slowed, but kept his pistol raised and pointed in the direction of the enemy. Apparently his friend had decided he wanted to see how this panned out. Blancanales couldn't say he blamed Lyons. The primary purpose for which they had come to Charleston was to gain intelligence about where the IUA was operating. Destroying the terrorists became a secondary consideration.

Without good intelligence, they would be ineffective in permanently neutralizing the terrorist threat.

As Able Team got closer, one of the men beat on the door a second time. Lyons signaled his two companions again and all three stopped where they were, keeping their weapons trained on the four armed men clustered near the door to the shop. Another full minute elapsed before the door opened and light from the interior spilled out and silhouetted a human shape in the doorway.

Blancanales was close enough that he could hear the conversation between them.

"Ya? What the hell do you want this time of morning?" the guy in the door asked.

"We need some additional equipment," one of the men replied.

"At this time? You guys out of your minds or something?"

"Just let us in," another man said.

The man nodded at their hands. "What's with the guns?"

"No need to get nervous," the man who had been on the doors replied. "It's just for security reasons."

"Oh, for the love of… Just come in, I guess."

The men filed inside and for a long, uncomfortable moment the three Able Team warriors didn't move a muscle. Then the muffled chatter of autofire sent the trio into high gear. Lyons was the first to reach the door and he put all of his weight behind the kick at a point just six inches below the brass handle. Even though it was a commercial-grade metal door, it proved no match for the speed and strength of Lyons. The door whipped open with enough force to nearly dislodge it from its hinges.

Even as he came through the doorway, Lyons got low and moved off to the left—a signal that Blancanales should take the right side. Schwarz came through last, heading straight up the middle with his Beretta 93-R held in front of him in a Weaver's grip. They took in the scene within milliseconds. The man who had answered the door lay against the wall, his blood smeared across parts of it and his body crumpled against a baseboard in a heap.

The gunman who shot him, muzzle still smoking, whirled at the noise of Able Team's entrance and leveled his SMG on Schwarz's midsection. Schwarz didn't give the guy an opportunity to follow through. He triggered the Beretta 93-R, which was set for 3-round bursts. A trio of 9 mm Parabellums struck the gunman in the chest with a grouping so tight it created a single hole. The impact lifted the young man off his feet and dumped him into a pile on top of his own victim.

Carl Lyons got off the second volley, a double tap to the head of his opponent. The back of the man's skull disappeared in a grisly display of blood, bone and gray that washed the wall behind him. His machine gun sprang from lifeless fingers, and his corpse stood there a moment—stiff and erect—before collapsing to the dusty, cracked linoleum.

The third gunner had found cover behind a long granite countertop supported by a heavy metal base, using the top of the counter to steady his aim as he aligned his sights on Blancanales. Fortunately, the Able Team warrior saw the attack coming and managed to evade a maelstrom of hot lead by diving behind an island display of a large diesel-powered generator. Blancanales shoulder-rolled to a new position, leveled his SIG-Sauer P-229 and squeezed the trigger. Over long sessions at the range, the pistol had a tendency to create fatigue due to its recoil, but in this short-term scenario the P-229 was regarded as one of the most accurate pistols ever made. A pair of .40 S&W slugs skinned the countertop and literally shot the SMG from the man's hands. Blancanales followed with a third round that punched through the gunman's upper lip and sent his body reeling into a freestanding cabinet of machine parts. The cabinet teetered a moment or two, and then unbalanced and collapsed, dumping hundreds of pounds of machine parts onto the deceased.

All three men of Able Team spotted the movement at the same time. The fourth gunner was headed up the stairwell in the back of the massive shop, triggering a burst in their general direction to discourage thoughts of pursuit. Unfortunately for him, the trio of combatants was not the kind to let that stop them. Lyons kept the Colt Python leveled in the direction the man had disappeared and gestured for Schwarz to take point. Schwarz flashed him a thumbs-up and then dashed off in pursuit.

Blancanales took a moment to gather his thoughts, pushing aside the brief realization he'd come very close to getting his head blown off. In moments like this, there wasn't any point in giving such things consideration; that could get a guy killed faster than any terrorist.

Lyons followed after Schwarz a moment later, and Blancanales took the signal he was to hold rear-guard. He directed a silent nod of thanks at his friend and the warrior returned the gesture with a quick smile. They had been here too many times before to let just another close encounter shake their resolve. Blancanales had always done his job and the situation was no different this time; he'd hold the lower floor to prevent any reinforcements from gaining the upper hand while the minds of his comrades focused on the final target.

Hermann Schwarz felt as if his legs might come off

as he took the steps two at a time in pursuit of the final gunman. He knew the importance of taking the guy alive to be sure, but he also didn't plan to die in this place unnecessarily. Even as he chased after the man, Carl Lyons on his heels, Schwarz wondered why their quarry had chosen higher ground instead of making a clean escape out back where he'd have running room. It was almost as if the guy had some mission, something he needed to accomplish no matter what, even if it cost him everything.

Only a few seconds elapsed before Schwarz emerged onto the second-floor landing and got his answer to that very question. Before he could bring his pistol to bear, Schwarz watched helplessly as the enemy gunner cut loose with a sustained burst from his SMG. A dozen or better rounds reduced the unarmed man to ribbons and dumped his bleeding body to the floor. The terrorist swung the muzzle of his SMG in Schwarz's direction, but the Able Team commando beat him to the punch. Schwarz aimed low and squeezed the trigger—three rounds left the muzzle of his Beretta and cracked on their way through the target's left thigh. The gunner triggered a reflexive volley high and right of Schwarz's position but then discarded the weapon and reached for his severely damaged leg.

He dropped like a stone, screaming in agony as blood spurted from an artery.

Schwarz rushed the man's position, crossing the length of the open loft-style floor in under three seconds. Schwarz holstered his pistol and then reached to the cargo pocket of his Dockers. Lyons followed immediately behind him, kicking the SMG out of reach as Schwarz produced a thick plastic bag. Schwarz ripped it apart at the center and a bulky white field dressing flowered from the package with a pop of the air released from the hermetically sealed bag. Schwarz slapped the package onto the terrorist's wounded leg and then stripped off his belt.

"What the hell are you doing?" Lyons asked.

"Hit an artery," Schwarz said. "We don't stop the bleeding, he'll check out before they get him under a knife. And right now he's our only solid lead to the IUA's presence here. Check the bystander. He might still be alive."

Lyons felt skeptical but knew Schwarz was right. Obviously, the two men the terrorists had come to kill possessed enough information that they might be able to reveal the location of the IUA secret base. That made them a liability in the eyes of the terrorists and their savvy leader. It would have been worth the risk to ensure they remained quiet.

Lyons crossed over to the motionless form lying near a table covered with newspaper. A small outboard engine of some kind lay scattered in at least a couple hundred pieces across the table. They had probably been overhauling it when the knock came, which seemed like a strange thing to do at that time of the morning. Lyons knelt next to the body and felt for a pulse. To his surprise, he felt one—not strong and not steady, but a pulse all the same.

Lyons looked at Schwarz. "Well, he's alive. I don't know how, but he's alive."

CARL LYONS WASN'T accustomed to the hustle and bustle of a big-city emergency room.

Behind a big room surrounded by glass enclosures with steel mesh, and a desk occupied by a triage nurse wearing a uniform, a couple dozen patients sat cloistered in their seats. Many of them suffered from their ailments more quietly than others as they awaited treatment. Beyond the enclosure were rooms of various sizes, some separated by doors and walls and others by curtains, where the men and women of the medical profession darted around the emergency ward and did their best to conserve the frailty of life.

At the moment Lyons's thoughts went to the one life that possibly held secrets important enough to save the lives of millions of Americans. While it wouldn't be the first time Lyons had seen anything like this, he sure couldn't admit he'd ever gotten used to it. In fact, he could remember a couple of times waiting to see the outcome of his own friends and family. These days he had to admit that those lines of separation were gray, and the two men he called comrades-in-arms and friends, he also called family.

But that thought seemed too gruesome for the moment and he pushed it from his mind. He was standing outside of the emergency room on the far side of the ambulance entrance, one hand hanging loosely off the chain-link fence that bordered the wide driveway reserved for emergency vehicles. The wind that had buffeted them earlier that morning began to subside as the first vestiges of sunlight broke the otherwise dark horizon. City lights twinkled as most of Charleston was still sleeping soundly, and Lyons had to admit that he didn't mind the few moments of peace he could drink in.

The reverie passed as Lyons detected the opening of the emergency room doors. He turned to see Schwarz and Blancanales exit on the heels of a young emergency room doctor wearing the same blue-green pair of surgical scrubs he'd worn on their arrival. The difference now were the patches of blood, and who knew what other substances, spotting his chest and stomach areas. Lyons watched with feigned interest as the doctor snatched a matching cap off his head while fishing a pack of cigarettes from his pocket. He lit one even as Schwarz and Blancanales continued pressing the urgent matter at hand.

"But what can you tell us?" Blancanales said.

The doctor took a deep drag and exhaled. "I'm afraid I can't tell you anything at the moment. That man's injuries are severe…*very* severe. He'll be lucky if he makes it, let alone regains consciousness any time soon. I can't tell you anything more than that. It's in the hands of the surgeons now, and I don't have anymore information I can give you. Sorry if that's not good enough, pal, but I've been on my feet the last fifteen goddamn hours and all I want is a cigarette, a cup of coffee and a few minutes to myself. Am I asking too much?"

Lyons could see Blancanales—normally a man known for his saintlike patience and people skills—becoming angrier by the moment. The almost plaintive look from Schwarz keyed Lyons on to the fact that things were about to get out of control if he didn't step in. It wasn't often Lyons interfered in these kinds of things, since usually it was Blancanales's cool head that kept the Able Team leader grounded and not the other way around. However, it seemed that this was one of those rare moments where Lyons would have to play the part of "he who walks softly and carries a big stick."

"Pol," Lyons said in a calm, no-nonsense tone.

Blancanales looked in his direction and Lyons jerked his head to indicate they should leave the doctor be. Blancanales gave the man another hard look before he and Schwarz joined their companion at the fence.

"Let's give the doc a break for right now," Lyons said.

"We can talk to him more later, but there probably isn't much he can tell us. Like he said, it's in the hands of the surgeons now."

Blancanales stopped and seemed to seriously consider the point before he finally nodded. "Yeah, I suppose you're right, Ironman."

Schwarz saw his opportunity and said, "Boy, I'm not sure if I even heard that correctly. It almost sounded like he just admitted you were right about something. Wish I had my calendar book with me."

"Oh, you're just a riot today," Lyons said.

"Yep, that's a real knee slapper," Blancanales said. He looked at Lyons. "What about the terrorist?"

Lyons took a deep breath and sighed. "At the moment, he's cooling his heels with an army of FBI agents. After we arrived here at the ER, I could barely keep them away. The guy in charge is a real prick, goes by Shanahan I think. I called Hal and tried to get him to back them off, but he didn't feel it was a good idea at the moment. He thinks we're better off fading into obscurity."

Gadgets furrowed his brow. "Really? That doesn't sound like Hal."

Blancanales waved it away. "Looks like he's concerned about drawing too much attention, and after what we've encountered just in the past few hours, I can say I hardly blame him. We've caused quite a ruckus."

"Well, whatever he's got in mind, it sounds as if he thinks we're best leaving our one pipeline to the terrorists in official hands and not rocking the boat too much."

"He has a point," Schwarz said. "I mean, Politician's right. We *have* been drawing a lot of attention."

"Maybe," Lyons said. "But we're not going to find the IUA base by osmosis, and unless either one of you knows a really good tarot card reader here in Charleston we're no further along than we were when we got here."

For a moment the men remained silent, each one lost in his own thoughts and trying to come up with a better idea.

Then Blancanales seemed to brighten. "Maybe not."

"Uh-oh," Schwarz said. "I've seen that look before."

This time Lyons ignored the quip. "What is it, Pol?"

"What about that van they showed up in?"

Lyons shrugged. "What about it?"

"Well, first of all, nobody knows anything about it…including the FBI. Second, it might contain some information that would at least point us in the right direction." Blancanales waved in the doctor's general direction. "We have nothing better to do and as he's already indicated, our one witness isn't going to be out of surgery for quite a few hours yet. We have to take this opportunity to do a little more digging."

Lyons considered it and finally nodded. "You're right. Let's take a drive."

The Able Team warriors walked to their SUV and climbed in. Blancanales insisted he was okay to drive, but Lyons wasn't buying it. He'd seen his friend enough times to know when the guy was overtired. This was one of those times when Blancanales didn't argue the point. Wouldn't have done him any good anyway, and it would only put all of them in a foul mood. They had worked together for so long that each of them knew the others' weaknesses and strengths, things that they wouldn't have dared tell anyone else because it would make them vulnerable. It was this trust in the friendship that made them the most effective covert-operations team ever to hit the streets of America.

Able Team had operated in their capacity for many

years. In some sectors, they were nothing short of an urban legend, a group of three able-bodied men who fought hard and stood for justice and freedom. Now they were going to take it to the next level. They didn't have any guarantees that the van would contain information; in fact, it seemed pretty unlikely. The terrorists wouldn't be sloppy enough to carry something with them. But maybe Able Team would find something in the van, and that something coupled with clues at the shop would provide enough information for them to advance their objectives.

"Sounds like a long shot, but I certainly don't have any objections to you taking a look," Brognola told them.

"Just do us a favor and keep us informed of the situation at the hospital," Lyons said. "Especially if there's any change in the condition of that victim."

"We will most definitely do that."

"By the way, you hear anything else from Phoenix Force?"

"Nothing yet, but I'm expecting we'll hear something soon. I have complete confidence that we'll soon learn if they heard or saw anything that might give us a clue as to the IUA's plans."

"Sounds good. We'll let you know if we find anything more here. Out."

"Well, what's he say?" Schwarz asked.

Lyons smiled. "Just that he sends his love."

CHAPTER FOURTEEN

In nearly twenty years with the Federal Bureau of Investigation, Special Agent Tom Shanahan had never experienced a situation quite like this one.

Shanahan had wanted to question the three men involved in the gunplay that took place near the wharf, but somebody from on high had told him to back off. These men were operating under a certain set of special parameters and were not to be challenged. The only clarification was that these orders were coming straight from the top. When Tom Shanahan asked the special agent in charge of his unit exactly what the top meant, the SAIC had told him it meant higher than the director of the FBI. That in turn led Shanahan to understand that either the President or other members of the Oval Office were involved.

So Shanahan took the information as it was given to him, kept his mouth shut as he always did and focused on obtaining whatever intelligence he could from the guy in the interview room. With the latest closures of places like the Abu Ghraib and the detention facility at Guantánamo Bay, the questioning of all American citizens in the United States suspected of terrorism—in fact all those who weren't American citizens even—had been taken from the Central Intelligence Agency and placed in the hands of the most famous law-enforcement agency the world had ever known.

Shanahan couldn't say that he necessarily disagreed with that decision, although he did feel that there were some things that were better handled by the unique talents of those in the CIA. Still, he was expected to do his job and he had a reputation for doing it well.

Shanahan stepped into the six-by-eight room that contained a metal table, two metal chairs covered by a rubber padding and a water dispenser encased in heavy aluminum. The chairs featured no moving parts that could be used to create a makeshift weapon. Thick bolts secured the water cooler to the wall, bolts that could only have been removed by a special wrench with significant torque.

After Shanahan had closed the door behind him, he stared at the dark-skinned man seated in one of the chairs. The man had close-cropped brown hair and dark eyes. Shanahan wouldn't have described him as swarthy. No, this man had a complexion more like a California tan, almost natural. According to the young man's South Carolina driver's license, he was twenty-seven years old. His file stated he was unemployed and a divorced father of two whose wife had walked out on him some years earlier.

Shanahan folded his arms and made his best attempt at a smile. The room could have been nicer but it was the best the hospital could do on short notice. The doctor had indicated they generally used the room for psych evaluations, but as there wasn't anybody in need of it at the moment it turned out to be a good place for them to question their suspect. It would be at least four days before he could actually leave the hospital. They had secured his leg in a cast following surgical repair of his femoral artery. He sat with his leg propped on the table, and a wheelchair that had brought him to the room was positioned just outside the door.

"Are you comfortable, sir?" Shanahan asked.

"I want my attorney."

"Well, I'm afraid under the U.S. Patriot Act that you are presently not entitled to an attorney."

"Don't try to bullshit me, man," he said, jerking a thumb in his own chest. "I know my rights and I know I'm entitled to a goddamn lawyer."

Shanahan said nothing, instead dropping the brown file folder he'd been carrying on the table. The prisoner jumped at the crack the folder made. The echo reverberating inside the small room was almost disorienting to him. Shanahan made a show of licking his finger before he opened the stiff cardboard cover of the folder. Inside were about a dozen sheets of paper with a top sheet that read: Property Dossier, Federal Bureau of Investigation, U.S. Government. Eyes Only.

Shanahan flipped to the first sheet beneath it and began to summarize. "Your name is Manan Hadariik. According to our records, you were born in this country to one George and Mary Hadariik, both deceased. You attended high school in San Jose, California, followed by a maritime structural engineering school in Austin, Texas. You have only one surviving sibling, a married sister with two children and a husband who works in the banking industry. You don't talk to her, you don't see her and you don't appear to have any sort of legitimate income since you lost your job two years ago with a maritime company that went under after the economic recession. Yet you seemed to be doing pretty well for yourself, Mr. Hadariik. Would you like to explain that?"

"I do not have to tell you anything. Like you said, I was born and raised in this country and I know my rights. And I also know that if I request an attorney, you can no longer talk to me or ask any questions until he arrives."

Shanahan pulled the chair back and dropped into it. He put his hands behind his head and swung his feet under the table. "Well, that's where you're wrong, sir. Actually, under the U.S. Patriot Act I have the authority to hold you up to twenty-four hours incommunicado if I have reason to believe that allowing you access to anyone else outside of the law-enforcement community could threaten national security."

"You don't have any such proof," Hadariik replied with a sneer.

"On the contrary," Shanahan snapped. "Let me explain something to you about this country since September 11, 2001. We don't like terrorists, Mr. Hadariik, and we especially don't like Americans who would betray their own country for a few bucks. No, you have no job, you have reported no income on your taxes for the last five years and yet you live in a nice house in the suburbs and you don't look malnourished. In addition to the fact you were caught by special agents of another law-enforcement agency breaking into a business in the middle of the night with the intent of killing the two proprietors therein. Fortunately, those men prevented you from finishing your little mission."

"So you have proof that I tried to kill somebody," Hadariik had said. "So what? People are getting killed all the time in this country. The fact that I was trying to kill these two men is not proof I'm a terrorist."

Shanahan smiled—now he had him. "No, you're right, it's not proof that you're a terrorist. But the fact that the three men who were with you tonight are all in the country illegally and they have Middle Eastern backgrounds is. And the fact the weapons you were carrying were imported from a country known to support terrorist activities pretty much clinches my case. Now I have a choice. I can put you into protective custody if you tell me everything you know about the terrorist activities here in Charleston, or I can turn you over to the CIA or NSA or some other agency that will make you disappear. What's it going to be?"

Hadariik didn't say anything, and Shanahan decided to let him stew on it for a time. Without question, the guy had information on terrorist activities and was most likely a member of a terrorist organization. Maybe it was al Qaeda, maybe another fundamentalist Islamic group. Shanahan didn't really care which one; all he cared about was diverting a potential disaster and preventing another attack like the one that resulted in the loss of more lives than the Japanese attack on Pearl Harbor in 1941.

"You know what, you can play hardass all you want," Shanahan said. "But you won't be very tough when they drop you into a military prison at Fort Leavenworth or some other godforsaken place. Maybe if you talk to me, I can make things go a little easier. Maybe you could spend your time in a nice, cozy federal penitentiary rather hard-labor camp or a place like Joliet state prison, where when they find out inside that you're a terrorist, and I guarantee you'll never be able to keep that secret, you'll be sodomized to death inside of an hour. How does that sound?"

Shanahan didn't say anything else, letting his prisoner squirm a little bit longer. Of course, he knew that if Hadariik held out for twenty-four hours he would be entitled to an attorney at that point, and any chance Shanahan had of finding out what he knew would be most likely gone forever. The other thing Shanahan wanted to know was what Hadariik knew about the three men who had stopped him. Maybe he didn't know anything and then maybe he knew a whole hell of a lot. Whatever the case, Shanahan would get him to talk one way or the other.

"You're running out of time. What's it going to be?"

Hadariik continued to say nothing and simply stared at Shanahan, his eyes burning with hatred for him. Shanahan thought he could almost see smoke pour from the guy's nostrils as if he were some sort of angry dragon. Shanahan decided not to press the guy at this point.

He got out of the chair and put his hands on his hips. "Tell you what. I'm going to give you a little more time to think about your options here. I'll be back in a little while, at which point you can tell me what your decision is."

"I've already told you my decision."

Shanahan said, "Nah, I'm not ready to accept that. You need to think about this for a while, not make any snap decisions just yet. You need to think about how you protect yourself from what happens to guys like you in prison. If you want to die a horrible and gruesome death, Hadariik, that's your business. But my business is trying to save your life, and I think it's important to give you every opportunity to reconsider if for no other reason than I'll sleep better at night knowing I tried. So you think about that, pal. You think about that long and hard."

Shanahan stepped out into the comparative coolness of the hospital hallway. He walked down to the nurses' station, informed them that they could return the prisoner to his room, and then phoned in to headquarters to make his report to the SAIC. Once he completed that, he went downstairs, out the door and climbed into the sedan where his partner waited in the passenger seat.

Buddy Davis was an extremely large black man, bald, with biceps probably as thick around as Shanahan's thighs. At the moment he looked peaceful, almost demure with his hands clasped across his chest. That muscular chest rose and fell with eerie regularity, and yet even with his mouth open and his head back against the seat he didn't make a sound. Most men would've thought a guy that size would snore like a chain saw. Not Buddy Davis. No, Davis was a picture of silence, a giant of a man who was actually soft-spoken with just a hint of a Southern drawl, the remnants of a life he'd known raised in the backwoods of Mississippi.

Shanahan closed the door quietly, not wanting to disturb his partner's sleep. They had been on the night shift but since catching this case they were now basically on an around-the-clock vigil until the matter was concluded. Or until Hadariik decided to roll over on his terrorist friends. In spite of his attempts to be quiet, the sound of the door clicking against the latch broke Davis from his nap.

He sat up in the seat, the top of his head coming within inches of the roof of the car, and yawned. He smacked his lips a few times trying to get moisture back. "What time is it?"

"Almost ten o'clock," Shanahan said. He didn't have to look at his watch as he'd noticed the time on the massive wall clock on his way out of the hospital. "You hungry?"

"I'm famished."

"Any particular request?"

"Nothing comes immediately to mind. I'm open to just about anything as long as it involves lots of coffee."

Shanahan nodded as he started the car. "There's a diner I know, just down the road, that serves an awesome breakfast. What say we go there so we can sit down and have a bite to eat in peace?"

"Sounds good to me."

As they rode to the breakfast spot, Davis asked Shanahan about his interview of Hadariik. Shanahan gave the lowdown and the two men discussed what some other options might be. Frankly, neither one of them figured that much would come of it. As long as Hadariik wasn't willing to cooperate, there wasn't a whole lot they could do. And if the guy did in fact decide to lawyer up, there would be even less chance that they could discover whoever was behind the murder of one of the proprietors of the maritime shop and attempted murder of the other.

Once they were seated and placed their order—the waitress brought their coffee right away—the discussion turned to the three mysterious men who had disappeared shortly after sunrise. Shanahan hadn't been exactly happy about that fact since he had some questions that he thought only they could answer, but the fact remained that he didn't have any authority over them. The SAIC had told them not to interfere with the three men in any way.

"What the hell does that mean?" Davis asked.

Shanahan shrugged. "Your guess is as good as mine, D."

Ever since Shanahan had known him, Davis went by the nickname "D." They hadn't started off as partners; that came much later, after they began working together when one of the men on the squad retired. Shanahan and Davis were part of the Violent Criminal Apprehension Program, or VICAP. Most of their cases involved going after individuals who were well-established criminals, known throughout the country and typically sitting somewhere in the top twenty of the Bureau's most-wanted list. Hadariik presented a special case for them, not only in the fact that he had no previous criminal record of any kind but also that he fit the profile of an Islamic extremist and terrorist.

Midlevel education; young man in his late twenties, early thirties; Middle Eastern descent but a natural-born U.S. citizen with either naturalized parents or parents who were U.S. citizens. Poor relations between some of the Middle Eastern countries and the United States and her allies hadn't always existed. There had been a time when many of the Arabs got along nicely with the West. Certainly there had been an alliance of sorts, shaky maybe but an alliance all the same, during the country's efforts in the early 1980s over the Afghan-Soviet War. That's when the United States lent weapons and CIA intelligence support to the mujahideen rebels.

That had been a different time, a time when the greatest threat to American freedom had been communism and Soviet tyranny. Now it was terrorists and Islam, or at least a very radical form of it, and a group of subversives who felt that their views of Western traditions and the freedom of the masses to worship and conduct their lives any way they chose were too dangerous to be permissible.

Davis used one of the thick, cheap paper napkins to wipe at a bit of sweat that snaked its way along his neck. "Well, if you ask me, it sounds like a whole bunch of Wonderland bullshit. If those three cats were so important to the situation, then why didn't they have at least enough professional courtesy to stick around and maybe help us out with this?"

"You got it exactly the way I got it from the SAIC. He told us in no uncertain terms that we were to leave them alone, and I took it to mean just that. Apparently we didn't have enough juice to detain them or question them. It sounded as if basically they were allowed to operate with complete autonomy and we weren't in any way to touch them."

"Well, pretty unlikely that they were spooks since it's allegedly illegal for the CIA to operate within the United States. The new director has been pretty good about keeping them at bay, I hear told."

Shanahan had to agree with that. Since the new President came into office, quite a number of things had changed. For one, the CIA had gotten its hands slapped for all of the various indiscretions they had committed since the onset of the Iraq war. The debacles in treatment of prisoners and allegations of summary executions taking place in areas of Afghanistan and Iraq were largely a propaganda tool. Nonetheless, they had done the kind of damage that was needed to return control to the FBI. As the top law-enforcement agency in the country, the Bureau was under constant scrutiny and not able to get away with many of those things.

Not that Shanahan wanted to. Tom Shanahan had always played things by the book, at least as often as he could, and while that had bought him a certain amount of credibility it had also bought him a lot of trouble. Agents who revealed too much about themselves and held too strongly to a specific set of moral and ethical codes, codes that weren't necessarily always in line with the Bureau's party line, tended to get passed by for promotions. More often than not. Nobody in the upper echelon would have admitted that, but pretty much everybody knew it was true. And Shanahan happened to be one of them, because he'd been the victim of that culture for many years.

Well, maybe not a victim but certainly an unwitting party.

"I'm with you, D. I don't think they're anybody special and I sure as hell don't believe they should have been allowed to walk away without giving us any information. But as I said, it was the SAIC's decision and not mine."

Davis nodded. "Well, at least we were able to take custody of Hadariik. That should count for something."

"It should, but I don't know whether to view that as positive or a negative yet."

The men clammed up when the waitress brought their food, and neither of them spoke until they were certain she had passed out of listening range. Shanahan even lowered his voice, cognizant that there were a few more customers than there had been when they first arrived at the diner.

"I think for now it's in our best interest not to worry about them. We should concentrate on getting whatever information we can out of Hadariik before he lawyers up. By whatever means necessary, if you catch my drift."

"I do," Davis replied. "And I agree. It's just that I get the sneaking suspicion we haven't seen the last of those three guys."

"Yeah. Me, too."

CHAPTER FIFTEEN

Across the city in the waterfront district, unbeknownst to the two FBI agents, Carl Lyons was thinking much the same thing about them.

The Able Team leader still couldn't understand why Hal Brognola had told them to leave this mission, or at least the terrorist, in the hands of the FBI. After all, Stony Man knew as well as Able Team did that the man named Hadariik was their only lead. It almost seemed as if Brognola didn't want Able Team to find the terrorists, although Lyons knew better than that. He'd been working for the outfit too long to think they would allow their hands to be tied by bureaucratic red tape. No, there was something else behind Brognola's move here.

And if the Stony Man chief had an alternate plan, Lyons knew it wasn't up to him to argue it.

"There it is," Blancanales said, pointing at the terrorist van through the windshield.

In spite of the fact the Able Team commandos knew there weren't any terrorists manning it—and if there had been they would've been long gone by now—they still approached with extreme caution. They kept their pistols held at the ready position, taking it one step at a time and moving in leapfrog fashion so two could cover a third.

Lyons approached the van and gingerly tried the passenger door, which gave easily and popped from the latch with a soft click. The van was a recent model with a totally customized interior. While Lyons rifled through the glove box, Schwarz and Blancanales went through the back with a fine-tooth comb. They found maps of the region covered in heavy plastic with some areas marked in grease pencil, but none of them were near the shore.

"You don't suppose the base could be more inland, do you?" Blancanales asked.

Schwarz shook his head. "I don't think so...at least, I don't see how such a thing could be practical. There would be more than just a metalworking shop to complete the submarines, and they would need access to a dry dock."

"What about a natural inlet?" Lyons said.

Schwarz expressed curiosity. "What do you mean?"

"Well, there's always a possibility they're not on the shore at all. Maybe they found some sort of a natural river that takes them far enough inland it would be the last place in the world anybody would think to look."

"I thought about that myself," Blancanales interjected. "But I thought about that more along the lines of something along one of the waterways. Those subs could easily maneuver through the natural waterway system here in Charleston without drawing any attention."

"Oh, I think they would draw attention," Schwarz said. "I find it very difficult to believe they'd be able to go deep enough that somebody wouldn't detect them. The waterways are too shallow here. Maybe some place like San Francisco or New Orleans or even up north in the Washington State area. But here? I highly doubt it."

Blancanales had been only half listening to his friends, instead scrutinizing each and every map they had discovered. Over the next minute or two, a pattern began to form and eventually it dawned on him.

"You know," he said to his comrades, "I think this may be of value after all."

Carl Lyons took his attention from searching the front of the van and looked at the maps spread out on the rear floor with a bit more interest now. "How so?"

Blancanales pointed to the various circled areas. "Most of these are actually residential districts. At first I thought that maybe they were other commercial buildings in which the IUA conducted business. You know, like they did here. In order to build the subs they would need to obtain their materials from somewhere."

Schwarz shook his head. "Agreed, but I'm not sure what you're driving at. Didn't you just say all of these were marked as residential areas?"

"I did," Blancanales said. "What I'm driving at is that these may not be where they got their resources from, but there's a better than half chance this is where we can find additional personnel."

"What makes you think so?" Lyons asked.

"Think about it a minute. The IUA is going to need materials to build these prototypes. I think we can all agree about that. But they're also going to need people who specialize in shipbuilding, like engineers and welders, metalworkers and electricians. There's no way it would be easy for them to smuggle people with that kind of experience into the country. We already know that Hadariik is a U.S. citizen, and that he has a background in maritime engineering."

A smile played on Schwarz's lips. "Hey, I get where

you're going with this now. You think these may mark the
locations of key personnel at the IUA who were recruited."

"Wouldn't it make sense?" Blancanales said. "Look,
this house here is marked as being on Portage Avenue.
Doesn't that ring a bell with either of you guys?"

It took Lyons only a moment to remember where
he'd heard that address. "It's the street that Hadariik
lives on."

And those two that we took down in Washington,
they lived in Charleston, as well. I believe it was down
on 125th Street, if memory serves correct. They lived
together in an apartment complex of some kind. I don't
recall the exact street address. But there is a fairly large
location listed here with a circle around it. And it's just
the right size to be an apartment complex or condos or
town houses. I don't think there's any question about
what we have in our possession here."

"Well, we don't have much else to do," Lyons said.
"Sounds to me like it's well worth checking out."

"Where do you want to start?" Schwarz asked.

Lyons nodded in Blancanales's direction. "It was Pol
here who first saw the pattern. I say we let him choose."

Blancanales appeared to give it careful consideration.
Although they were waiting for the victim to come out
of surgery and regain his senses long enough to talk to
them, they didn't have an unlimited amount of time and
resources. Blancanales knew they couldn't spend the
entirety of their day hopping from one place to the next,
checking out each and every area. For a moment he
supposed that they could skip the residence down on
125th Street, as well as Hadariik's place. After all, it was
entirely likely the FBI would conduct a thorough search
of the latter. That left about three other places that they
could check, and based upon their locations, coupled

with the likelihood traffic wouldn't be too bad this time of morning, Blancanales thought they could cover every area by late afternoon.

"You know, there's nothing saying we couldn't call Shanahan and ask him to help us cover the area," Schwarz suggested.

Lyons produced a scoffing laugh. "Not sure I want that guy involved in any of this. He's got his hands full already with Hadariik, and it's probably not wise to take him off that to go on what could turn out to be little more than a wild-goose chase."

Blancanales shrugged. "I admit that this entire thing is sketchy and that it would not be a way to win friends or influence people at the FBI if we wasted Shanahan's time. But I almost want to agree with Gadgets on this one, Ironman. We could definitely use their help right now, and it might show our willingness to cooperate. Maybe if we agreed to scrub his back, he'd return the favor when we need it most."

Lyons didn't like the idea but he had to admit that his friends were right. They were going to need the FBI's cooperation as long as Stony Man was putting up a front to protect Able Team's cover. It seemed that with all the recent activity, it had become more important not to make waves with a local agencies than to find the IUA terrorists. Lyons knew that wasn't a very likely scenario, but it still rankled him every time he thought of it.

"Come on, Ironman," Schwarz said. "You know we have to play the game here if we expect to resolve the situation quickly."

"I know, I know." Lyons waved them away. "It's just I hate pussyfooting around with these guys. Shanahan strikes me as a little too cocky for his own good."

"Now, now, don't be grumpy," Blancanales said.

"Remember what you told me back there about cutting the doctor a break?"

"Using a little of my own psychology on me, are you?"

Blancanales smiled. "That depends."

"On what?"

"On whether or not it worked."

Carl Lyons sighed. "Okay, you win. Let's grab up all the information we can and then do one last sweep inside that shop. It won't be long before the federal boys arrive, and we don't want to be within half a block of this place when they do."

Schwarz looked around the interior of the van. "I wonder if we shouldn't take this puppy out of here. We may find some additional evidence. Or maybe even destroy it."

"We'll leave it for the FBI's criminal forensics team," Lyons said, shaking his head. "We don't leave it here and give them something to discover—" Lyons held up his fingers and gestured with the quote signs "—they'll get suspicious."

Schwarz nodded his understanding and the three collected what evidence they had found and headed back toward their SUV. Once they were on the road, they agreed they would call Stony Man and relay the information. While Aaron Kurtzman probably had enough work on his plate, they would need his assistance in tracking down any other potential significance to these locations since they no longer had the computer equipment that had been aboard their van.

The very fact they had lost such a valuable tool so early in this mission was still a sore spot with Schwarz. Both of his teammates knew it, so neither one of them made any mention. Under other circumstances they would have rubbed his nose mercilessly in it, but right at the moment they knew such a ribbing wouldn't have been well received. There would be time enough later to make him miserable.

At the moment, Able Team had terrorists to find.

And the hunt was on.

TOM SHANAHAN COULD HARDLY believe his ears when a call came in from the guy who called himself Agent Irons. Less than an hour earlier he and Buddy Davis had finished their breakfast and then returned to their headquarters to begin the long and arduous task of paperwork. On the way, Shanahan had taken the opportunity to stop at his home, grab a quick shower and change clothes. He'd been seated at his desk, tapping away at his computer and filling in fields of the secondary report when the phone rang at the desk of an agent near him. The agent picked up, grunted some sort of response and then stabbed the hold button.

"Hey, Tom," he called. "Some guy on the phone calling himself Irons. Says he needs to talk to you right away."

The name didn't immediately ring a bell, and then Shanahan realized it was the big blond guy with the cold blue eyes who was part of the trio that duked it out with Hadariik and his friends. Shanahan took a moment or two to gather his thoughts and then nodded for the agent to put the call through. When he picked it up, Irons began speaking immediately.

"Shanahan, this is Irons. We met this morning. You got a minute to talk?"

For just a moment Shanahan experienced something that bordered on irritation. He didn't really see any reason why he should be cooperating with these guys, especially since they had left so abruptly and provided very little information themselves. Now this Irons guy was calling and actually had the audacity to want to talk. Something about that just didn't seem right, or fair; then again, nobody had promised him a fair shake in the Bureau.

"Listen, Shanahan," Irons said without bothering to wait for a reply. "I know you got the raw end of the stick on this. And I know that you feel like you're being kept in the dark. And maybe on some of the stuff you are. But we got our marching orders, just like you've got yours when it comes to Hadariik, and that's just the game us pawns must play. Fortunately, I'm a reasonable guy, and I happen to think you are, too…at least that's what my partners think. So in the interest of good relations between us, I'm willing to offer a broken arrow up front."

The little speech took Shanahan completely off guard at first. He'd expected Irons to begin spouting off a list of demands or ordering him around. He thought a moment, listening to the tone and inflection in the guy's voice, looking for any deceit. He didn't get that impression, though. It seemed as if this guy was on the level and Shanahan would've been nothing less than a jerk if he wasn't willing to at least give Irons a chance. After all, they *were* on the same team and they probably wanted the same things. How did Shanahan know what kind of bureaucracy Irons had to put up with? If his job was anything like Shanahan's, he probably had his own fair share of red tape.

"I'm listening," Shanahan said.

"We have some information here. It pertains to what we think might be the residences of some of the other terrorists, or at least people who are affiliated with the same group Hadariik is."

"You know for a fact that Hadariik is attached to a

terrorist organization?"

Irons let out a disbelieving chuckle. "Of course we do. You telling me that you didn't?"

"I wouldn't have known anything, unless it came directly either from you or Hadariik."

"What are you talking about, Shanahan? The whole slew of information on this—it was my understanding that all of it had been passed on to you. At least that's what we've been told, which is why we didn't bother to stick around this morning to chitchat."

"Well, then, we got a real communication gap somewhere, pal, because nobody has told me a goddamn thing. All I know is that you three shot it out in the middle of the night on the wharves of Charleston with a bunch of guys who are, in turn, shooting allegedly law-abiding citizens and assassinating legitimate business owners. The fact that Hadariik is even attached to terrorists is a conclusion I came to on my own."

"And how's that?" Irons asked.

"You're kidding me. Right?"

"I don't kid, and you can skip the wit. For now, just assume that I am completely ignorant and as much in the dark as you are. So I'll ask again. How did you connect Hadariik to terrorism?"

Shanahan took a deep breath, sighed and leaned back in his chair. It was an older chair, one of those gray metal ones that rotated and reclined. Shanahan had pulled it from a dusty basement, one of many in a graveyard of similar chairs and gunmetal-gray desks from bygone days. He preferred these older chairs to the newer, more stylish ones the government purchased in bulk at ridiculous prices. There was something G-man about these older furniture pieces that made him feel like part of the FBI he had once known.

"Well, first of all, everything about this guy fits the profile of a domestic with ties to al Qaeda. Second, his three deceased friends all happen to be from the same region in Iraq. Refugees that we had allowed into the country during the latter days of the war. Somehow those guys fell off our radar, and as a result of the entire mismanagement of the program we now have four dead people and two severely wounded to deal with."

"What would you say if I told you I could see to it that those cases get wrapped up pretty well? In fact, I might be able to arrange to have them wrapped up in a package so nice and tidy that you'd be looking at the front end of a promotion when we're through."

Shanahan couldn't help but laugh at the absurdity of the remark. "Oh, I'd probably tell you that you were full of shit."

"And if I were affiliated with just any other law-enforcement organization in the federal government you'd be correct," Irons said. "But I'm here to tell you this time that I don't make promises I can't keep from this point forward. Understand something here and now, Shanahan. If I tell you that I can do something, I can do it. All you have to do is be willing to trust me."

"I don't know you, mister."

"And I can understand your misgivings," Lyons said. "But that doesn't mean that we can't put those aside and work together. You just got done saying yourself that you couldn't do some of this stuff unless we told you or Hadariik told you. We sure as hell know that Hadariik giving you any sort of useful information isn't likely. That means if you want to get in on the ground floor of this thing, you have to listen to us. And if you want to participate in what I'm about to tell you, then there are going to be some ground rules."

"I'm not sure I can do that without authorization," Shanahan said. "And I'm not willing to do anything without taking my partner along. This is his case, too, and I don't know how you do things where you're from, but in the Bureau we work as a team."

"Believe me, you aren't going to have to worry about authorization," Irons replied. "I can get the cooperation of your entire section with one phone call. If we want to attach you to work with us on this particular case, you can be sure it'll happen in such a way as to leave no room for doubt or argument by your superiors."

"What, you got some sort of direct line to the Oval Office?"

"No, but I have the next best thing on speed dial."

Shanahan stopped to consider that. After what the SAIC had told him, he had little reason not to suspect that Irons probably wasn't talking out of turn. Shanahan had suspected right from the start that these guys were much more than they appeared, and the very fact they were now calling and asking—if not in a very round-about way—for his help led Shanahan to believe that they could probably be trusted. Irons had struck him as one of those guys who didn't have a whole lot of time for nonsense and wasn't overly willing to play the politics.

"Okay, Irons, you have yourself a deal," Shanahan said as he picked up a pencil from his desk and slid a pad close to him. "Where do you want to meet?"

CHAPTER SIXTEEN

Barbara Price poured a cup of coffee and then sat in front of the computer terminal in her office.

Her contacts at the National Security Agency had forwarded additional information from the satellite pictures they had taken of the mining facilities in Namibia. She had reviewed them briefly and then sent them on to Kurtzman for further analysis. He hadn't come back with a final report yet, nor had he indicated they were any closer to actually locating mines. Still, she believed he'd have something before long.

Price took a sip of her coffee and began to review other information gleaned from Able Team's prisoners. She had just finished reading the updated information Schwarz had sent via his PDA regarding the maps they had discovered in the terrorists' vehicle. Price wasn't exactly sure she was comfortable with their choice to involve agents of the local FBI station in Charleston, but at the same time she couldn't really blame Able Team. Stony Man hadn't been able to give either of the teams much support on this mission. The intelligence they had on the IUA had been thin to start with. Whoever was in charge of the group had managed to keep himself under the radar. Up until this point, working without intelligence had made it extremely difficult for the field teams to operate efficiently.

In a lot of respects, much of what the IUA had done didn't make any sense to Price. Their tactics didn't seem to fall into line with those of previous terrorist operations. They'd taken risks that they hadn't taken before, and Price couldn't help but wonder if they were responding to pressure being placed on them now that Stony Man was involved. Up until this point, after all, they had been able to operate with significant autonomy. Now they were being hammered at every angle, and they were pulling out all the stops—at least it seemed to Price and the rest of the Stony Man team—in a last-ditch effort to complete whatever it was they had in mind.

So how did a terrorist organization like the Revenge of Allah penetrate the United States undetected, subvert computer security to the point that they were able to obtain top-secret plans to a submarine prototype and put together an entire team of maritime engineers and construction specialists without drawing any attention to themselves? Price supposed that they had done it in much the same way as the terrorists who had flown planes into the World Trade Center and Pentagon. At that time, their plans hadn't really taken too much thought, either. It was the complacency of American intelligence communities that allowed the terrorists to get away with such a simple plan. In fact, their entire plan had been based on lackadaisical security and inefficient screening equipment. The terrorists had taken entire planes of hostages with nothing more than a couple of box cutters and the threats of explosives.

In this case, their plans had been much more complex

and detailed. Here they had gone to the lengths of murdering a computer scientist, paying off government officials and even acquiring local talent. That last part, especially, could have exposed them to significant risk. But somewhere along the way they had gotten lucky. Well, if Price knew anything about the eight men in the field right now, it was that the IUA was about to be driven to its knees. Perhaps their efforts would even result in the complete eradication of the group.

A soft, steady beep demanded her attention. Price turned toward her computer monitor and pressed a button that activated the Web cam. There was a flicker as the communications software made a connection to the Annex, and then the face of Aaron "the Bear" Kurtzman filled the screen. Price immediately smiled at her friend.

"Good morning," Kurtzman greeted her in his booming voice.

"Morning," she said. "I didn't even think you were up yet."

Kurtzman expressed curiosity. "Why wouldn't I be?"

"Well, I saw Hal first thing this morning as he was leaving for the Oval Office and he told me that you'd been up most of the night looking over that geographical data."

"Yeah, I guess I was up until about 0400 hours or thereabouts. These days, I only need a few hours of sleep, certainly not like I used to."

"I'm not sure if that's a sign that you're getting younger or older," Price said with a chuckle.

Kurtzman smiled. "I think we're all getting younger, honey. It's the job that does it to you, or at least that's what Schwarz is always telling me. We age backward in this business."

Price couldn't immediately say why she found that so funny, but she burst into laughter. It wasn't often that she let herself relax like that but it felt good all the same. They had been undergoing a lot of stress in the past twenty-four hours so a little release was nice. Leave it to Kurtzman to know just the right thing to say at the right time.

"Someone a little giddy this morning?" Kurtzman asked.

"A little overtired maybe."

"Well, I guess I can add some fuel to your joyful mood."

"You found the location of the yellow-cake mine?"

Kurtzman nodded with a big grin. "I sure as shootin' did, and I'm sure once we get the information to Phoenix Force it's going to make McCarter all that much happier."

"How so?"

"Well, I can't be completely positive, but if we're correct about its location, accessing it should be easy. And it won't take much for them to neutralize the area. The yellow-cake is on a layer just below the outside strata. Looks like it's a fairly rich deposit, but not very large, and it also appears that the terrorists may have been using a lot of manual tools to mine it out. There wasn't much heavy equipment involved, which is why it took us so long to find the mine. I have to admit they did a pretty good job of keeping it hidden."

"That's excellent work, Aaron," Price said. "Really excellent work."

"It's you and the friendly contacts you've maintained inside the NSA we have to thank for it. I just evaluated the information. If it weren't for those satellite pictures we could have had Phoenix Force wandering around the Namib Desert forever trying to find the mine."

While Price wouldn't have wanted to admit it, Kurtzman's statement—like most of them—was one of undisputed fact. While Stony Man's resources reached far and wide, the reality was they didn't have an unlimited budget. Over the years, Senate finance committees and other political groups had tried to bring transparency to the spending allotted toward intelligence activities. Fortunately, laws existed to protect the President and the government from having to reveal the actual amounts and budgets of intelligence agencies like the NSA, DIA and certain sections of the CIA. In fact, the NSA's budget and the number of its personnel remained classified information. While Stony Man did maintain a dedicated communications satellite, the reality was it didn't have the money necessary to deploy and oversee satellites dedicated strictly to its operations. This meant that quite often the Farm had to piggyback off of satellites maintained by the CIA, DARPA and NORAD. It even had a feed into the two main orbiters maintained by NASA.

"Well, I just got some intelligence from Able Team and I'm disseminating that now. Since Hal is out, why don't you contact David directly and let them know what we've found? Also tell him they have authorization from Hal and me to proceed to destroy that mine by whatever means he deems fit. And make sure he knows that we can't risk anyone at the mine to escape. That could put the responsibility for a massive radiation exposure in our laps, and that can't happen for obvious reasons."

"I can do that," Kurtzman said. "But are you sure you wouldn't like me to look at Able Team's information?"

Price shook her head. "Not right at the moment. I have something else for you to do once you've contacted Phoenix Force."

"I'm all ears. Shoot."

"Get in touch with Kissinger," Price said, referring to Stony Man's resident weaponsmith and armorer. "Work with him to come up with some tactical equipment requirements for weapons we can send on to Able Team. We have to have a contingency plan in place in the event that the IUA manages to get any of these submarines into the water."

"Understood and noted."

"And, Aaron."

"Yes?"

Price smiled. "Again, *really* nice job."

"Anytime."

TOM SHANAHAN AND Buddy Davis were to meet Irons and his partners at an abandoned warehouse on the fringe of the waterfront district. Shanahan had suggested the place, knowing that it was used by the FBI for outlying storage and the occasional sting operation. Being a port city, Charleston had its share of smuggling—criminals brought everything from drugs to weapons to human slaves through the city—which had led to the seizure of the warehouse some years back on a case broken by the FBI. It was on this case that Shanahan and Davis first started working together, and shortly after that they became partners.

"Seems almost apropos we meet them here," Davis said with a grin.

Shanahan agreed with a nod, but his mind was on the meet ahead of them. He still wasn't absolutely sure he trusted Irons, but after talking it over with his partner, he'd felt a little bit better about the situation. At least he wasn't going into this by himself. He really did want to make it work between him and Irons, but he just wasn't sure he could trust him. It was going to take some serious convincing by these three men to secure Shanahan's cooperation. After all, he'd been told he could not interfere with them. Nobody had informed him, including the SAIC, that he was to cooperate with anything they were doing or to share information he acquired in his investigation. In fact, Shanahan hadn't even expected to see them again, which was another reason the telephone call had been a surprise.

Davis brought the vehicle to halt and for a moment or two, the pair thought that they had beaten the mysterious trio to the rendezvous. Then the men appeared seemingly out of nowhere and approached the vehicle. Their steps were slow and purposeful, almost as if they were being cautious in making sure they weren't stepping into some sort of ambush. Shanahan thought that was weird, and he wasn't sure if Davis noticed so he decided not to make any mention of the observation. At least not right now.

"Well, there they are. Let's go do this."

SHANAHAN'S REACTION to his call surprised Carl Lyons.

The Able Team leader couldn't understand why anyone, least of all Stony Man, would have kept the FBI in the dark. Something here just didn't sound right at all. Lyons could understand that his people were operating off limited information, that they were going to be extremely discreet about who got told what. At the same time, however, Brognola had literally tied their hands with some of this stuff and he couldn't understand why. He was used to operating with pretty much carte blanche in these situations.

As soon as Able Team spotted the sedan pulling into the parking lot of the abandoned warehouse, the three men left the shadows and approached the vehicle. Lyons had suggested they do so with caution and keep themselves spread at a distance that wouldn't allow them to be taken at one time. The last time they had approached what was supposed to be a friendly meet, they had nearly gotten their heads blown off. Carl Lyons didn't intend to make that mistake twice.

As he had told Blancanales and Schwarz, "I'm kind of addicted to breathing."

When they reached the FBI sedan, Lyons reached out his hand first and Shanahan took it. He was about Lyons's height, maybe an inch or two taller, with short brown hair peppered with gray. He looked to be in pretty good shape, his legs long—proportioned almost like those of a guy who did a lot of running—and his light tan suit hung well on his frame. Lyons could tell immediately the suit had been tailored specifically to be friendly to the kind of work Shanahan did by concealing the bulge of his pistol.

Able Team had reviewed the federal cop's dossier, and Lyons had to admit the guy had a pretty impressive record. Shanahan certainly wasn't a bureaucrat or asskisser; the number of times he'd been passed over for promotion confirmed that much. Especially in light of the fact that he had a superb rate of arrests and convictions since coming on board with VICAP six years earlier. After shaking hands all around, and a formal introduction to Buddy Davis—a hulking black guy about as big as a California redwood—Shanahan suggested they move inside the warehouse.

They entered through a side door with a double bolt locking system, for which Shanahan had a key, and walked down the narrow hallway that opened onto a set of small offices. In what had once doubled as a conference area and kitchenette, the men sat in chairs arranged around a table with a thick plastic cover. They were careful not to touch it, as there was a thick layer of dust coating the plastic.

Schwarz made a show of looking around before he said, "Use the place much, do you?"

"Yeah." Shanahan produced only a half smile. He then turned his attention to Lyons. "Okay, Irons, so we know your names and you know ours. But you still haven't told me who you're working for."

Lyons shook his head, trying not to seem irritated. "Look, Shanahan, you and I both know I can't tell you that. I indicated at the hospital that who we work for is unimportant but that we are both on the same side. And I basically told you the same thing on the phone. If you can't accept that and take it on faith that our intentions to meet with you are honorable, I'm afraid you wasted your trip out here."

Shanahan looked as if he wanted to reach out and throttle Lyons, and perhaps he did, but he didn't say anything.

Blancanales inserted himself at that point in the hopes of salvaging what little credibility they had. "I think what my partner's trying to say, Shanahan, is that we appreciate you meeting us like this. I know integrity means a lot to a guy like you and we can all certainly appreciate that here. But as we've already told you, we have rules to follow and you have rules to follow. We'd like the opportunity to work with you, and we called this meeting for the express purpose of giving you some information."

"You know he's right," Schwarz said. "We didn't have to call you and we didn't have to agree to meet you, but we did. So please give us the benefit of the doubt and listen to what we have to say. You don't like what you hear, you can walk away and do your own thing. Fair enough?"

Shanahan nodded. "I'll give you ten minutes to explain this to me."

"All right, now that we got that out of the way," Lyons said, "let's talk business. Your assessment is absolutely correct that Hadariik belongs to a terrorist organization, but it's not al Qaeda. This is a new group, one we've not seen before, and I can assure you we have significant experience with most of them. We estimate this new cell to be somewhere in the area of one to two hundred active members. There's probably a lot more supporting them, but right now we don't have much more we can tell you about them."

Blancanales added, "What we do know is that their leader is one clever son of a bitch. The group calls themselves Intiqam-ut-Allah, or the Revenge of Allah. You'll usually just hear us refer to them as the IUA. They broke off from al Qaeda some time ago, but nobody is really sure why other than the numbers got large enough that apparently they decided to go their own way."

"What do they want?" Davis asked.

"That's what makes them so difficult," Lyons said. "They're not politically motivated and they're not religious fanatics. The IUA thrives on the destruction of Westerners. Period. They don't care about American foreign policy and they don't care about religious freedom. This group simply hates America and everything she stands for, and any way they can interfere with us or wreak mayhem in the country, they will. That's what they consider to be most important to their cause."

"Jesus," Davis muttered.

"Exactly right," Schwarz said. "And this probably would be a good time for prayer."

"How did this all start?" Shanahan asked.

Lyons cleared his throat and began, "Yesterday morning, our team was dispatched to investigate the attack of the federal convoy of U.S. marshals. This group was on special assignment to escort a naval warfare scientist to a briefing at the Pentagon. Now, we're not at liberty to discuss exactly what the nature of this meeting was."

Shanahan started to get to his feet. "Well, give me a call when you are at liberty to discuss it."

Now it was Blancanales who had begun to lose his patience. "Sit down, Shanahan. This is no time to be obtuse."

For a very long moment, nobody said a word. Even Lyons had to admit that his friend's sudden outburst came as a surprise. Blancanales hadn't really raised his voice, and his tone hadn't been one of ridicule. No, this had been more of a soft but strong command, one of those occasionally spoken by the man they knew as Mack Bolan, the Executioner. Like that consummate soldier and warrior, every man in Able Team and Phoenix Force had been hand selected partly for his ability to take command of the situation and maintain an air of authority. Blancanales was exercising that talent now, and nobody in the room decided to argue the point.

Shanahan's eyes narrowed a bit, but he relaxed and took his seat.

Blancanales nodded. "Thank you. Now, it didn't take us very long to figure out that it was the IUA who had attacked the convoy. They murdered every individual there, including a scientist and four United States marshals. You can imagine we weren't too happy about that."

"So why are you telling us about this?" Shanahan said.

"Because the stakes have just gotten much higher," Lyons replied. "Within the next twenty-four to forty-eight hours, we suspect the IUA will launch anywhere from one to six tactical submarine prototypes equipped with nuclear-tipped missiles. We think that they're going to fire those at select targets here in the United States. We just don't know what targets and we don't know where the subs will be launched from."

"We did come into some intelligence," Schwarz said. "We think that this information might lead us to other members of the IUA, and that one of them may very well possess the location where the terrorists are hiding and building these weapons."

"This is your city," Blancanales said. "You would know much better than we do where to start our search based on this intelligence. Will you help us?"

Shanahan managed a smile. "Are you kidding? Wild horses couldn't stop me now."

CHAPTER SEVENTEEN

As the military chopper left the pad behind the White House and headed back to Stony Man Farm, Harold Brognola looked out upon Washington, D.C.

Lights begin to twinkle starlike in the nation's capitol as sunset quickly approached. Brognola wished his news had been better but the situation was what it was. This was the first time in some years that Brognola could remember sending Able Team and Phoenix Force against the group as elusive and violent as the IUA. To be sure, the field teams had seen their share of tough missions, and on that count this one couldn't really be viewed much differently. But the group calling itself the Revenge of Allah had proved tough and resourceful, clearly organized, and with significant intelligence and material resources in the country.

Far below him now, the nation went about its daily tasks. The vast majority of Americans took their days in stride and their evenings with peaceful mediocrity. But that kind of freedom came with a price, and it was a price the men of Able Team and Phoenix Force had learned to pay many times over.

These were the men and women alongside whom Harold Brognola prided himself as having the privilege and honor to serve, and he knew no matter how this day ended that when the new day dawned the teams would have secured absolute victory. He didn't doubt it for a moment. Something in his heart and mind told him that it was true.

The transit from Washington to Stony Man Farm—nestled within the Blue Ridge Mountains—took just under forty minutes. As soon as the chopper touched down, Brognola stepped onto the pad and moved purposefully, squinting his eyes and ducking to remain below the rotor wash, in the direction of the entrance to the underground Annex. This part of Stony Man Farm had been constructed well after the farmhouse itself, which had initially served as quarters, armory and all-purpose facility to Stony Man operations for many years.

The addition of the Annex had been the brainchild of Aaron Kurtzman, with contributions to its construction from every member of the sensitive operations group. Built between a wood chip mill—a flat-roofed concrete-block building with a two-story silo—the Annex sported a power supply provided by soundproofed generators positioned in the subterranean complex with fuel tanks attached. It included a computer room complex, communications center and a security operations room. The computer room was primary home to Aaron Kurtzman, and featured a massive array of quantum-capable computer systems, massive LCD screens and a monitoring and control system that would have made even officials at NASA green with envy.

The communications center was connected to a secure internal telephone system. The communications center also warehoused all of the equipment used to piggyback the satellite systems of various agencies. The operations area accommodated workstations not only for Price and Brognola, but also members of the black-suits who provided perimeter security to the entire complex and surrounding farm, as well as the workers who were actually highly trained members of that detail.

It was some wonder nobody had discovered that the operations of Stony Man Farm were more than they appeared. That was likely due in large part to the continuous show that had been put on by Stony Man's security force. While the Farm existed in a remote area, it did not operate in a vacuum. There was a major highway that ran near the Farm, the only main thoroughfare between the Shenandoah National Park and the federal forest preserves. In fact, these areas experienced a fair amount of traffic during the tourist season; maybe that in part was what made the location seem unlikely as a secret government facility.

As soon as Brognola reached the operations center, he had Price and Kurtzman darkening the door. Brognola sighed. The job of the Stony Man chief was never done, but he knew that he'd taken quite a bit of time to brief the President on their current situation and he could only hope that the news they were there to deliver would be better than what he'd gotten so far.

"I hope you're here to make my day," he told Price.

"I don't know if the information I have will, but I'm certain that you'll be delighted to hear Aaron's news." She looked to Kurtzman, who sat straight and tall and resolute in his wheelchair. "Go ahead, Aaron, I'll let you do the honors."

Kurtzman wheeled himself over to a nearby terminal. He tapped a key to dim the lights, and then another key to project a map onto the massive LCD panel at one end of the room. The glass enclosure of the operations center had a large briefing table and Brognola had seated himself at one end of it. Often times, they held briefings of the field teams in the War Room at the farmhouse. There was something nostalgic about that place, something that seemed to put the teams at ease. Brognola wasn't exactly sure himself what it was, but he knew he felt the same way they did about it. Sure, this briefing room supported all of the latest in high-tech gadgetry and when the field teams were away, it made for a convenient spot from which to plan.

"This is a picture of the map that we overlaid based on the satellite terrain photographs received from Barb's NSA contacts." Kurtzman tapped another key, and a central area on the map lit up while the rest of it went gray. This area then magnified and little lines marking a couple graphical areas glowed yellow. "What you're seeing here are the strings of yellow-cake, or U-92 raw ore. It took us a while to find the site because, as I explained to Barb, the terrorists weren't using much in the way of heavy equipment. They certainly weren't using any personal protective equipment, which is why they were exposed to the radiation."

"Outstanding work. Have you gotten this information to Phoenix Force yet?" Brognola asked.

"I told Aaron to notify them as soon as we got the information," Price answered.

"Good. Now all we have to do is hope that they can shut down the operation before they get the yellow-cake out of the country."

"Unfortunately, we may be too late for that," Price said.

Brognola shook his head. "I suppose this is the bad-news part of the briefing."

"Believe me when I say I'm the first to wish that it

wasn't, but we have to put all our cards on the table at this point." Price brought him quickly up to speed on Able Team's plan to ally themselves with the members of the FBI in Charleston. "Lyons is convinced that this is their first and best chance of locating the construction facility. That's assuming, of course, that the two men they captured here in Washington were telling us the truth."

"Well, I've spoken with the President, who in turn talked with the director of the CIA. Apparently we've known for some time that there was a possible operation by an al Qaeda terrorist group inside the U.S. We just didn't have any leads and so we had no way of getting in front of this thing."

"Well, now we have some additional information that might well give us the upper hand and afford us an opportunity to shut this thing down once and for all."

"So tell me about these locations that Able Team discovered."

"It was actually Blancanales who figured it out. Smart cookie." Price handed Brognola a sheet of paper with a brief she had prepared analyzing the team's intelligence. "The terrorist they took alive in Charleston is Manan Hadariik. He's a U.S. citizen who up until this time had no known ties with any terrorist organizations. Apparently our information on Hadariik wasn't as reliable as we thought. Among the several locations that Able Team found were Hadariik's residence, as well as those of the other three, who were in the country illegally. Able Team is convinced that the remaining locations may also be inhabited by terrorists. They think these terrorists will be able to lead them to the construction facility."

"Sounds like a pretty reasonable theory to me. I assume you told them to proceed."

"I did," Price said with a nod.

Brognola couldn't help but feel satisfaction. At last they had come upon something tangible, something they could use. The intelligence was solid and if there was something to be found, Able Team would find it. And now that they knew the location of the mine in Namibia, Phoenix Force might be able to provide some additional time to close the book on this thing. Brognola felt a little guilty that he hadn't been able to express the reason for his reservations in keeping this as quiet as possible. The President's mind had been focused elsewhere, on things that were much more important at the moment. The economic depression and the precarious state of foreign relations with nuclear-capable countries had the entirety of America on edge. Yes, the country hadn't been running any popularity contests with the rest of the world, even with some of its allies, and this distraction would only escalate those matters if it got out.

"The Man has told me in no uncertain terms we need to wrap this up, and we need to do it quickly," Brognola said. "There's a lot at stake here. I told him that he has done some things recently that have tied our hands politically, and that we do not have the ability to operate without some leeway."

Kurtzman frowned. "How did he take that?"

"I'm not sure," Brognola replied with a shrug. "But I can tell you that he is a man who appreciates candor, and I think he's more or less decided to loosen the leash for the time being. So I bought us a little bit of latitude… I just don't know how much or for how long."

"Able Team and Phoenix Force have never let us

down, no matter how tough it gets," Price said. "They know the kind of pressure you're under. They'll come through, Hal."

Brognola looked tired as he locked eyes with Price. "I know. And when they do, there isn't a force in the world the IUA could throw at us that would stop them."

Kurtzman chuckled. "Amen to that, brother."

TOM SHANAHAN PROVED true to his word.

After looking over the information obtained by Able Team, Shanahan settled on an area deep in the heart of Charleston's historical district. The area in question featured architecture dating all the way back to the post–Civil War era. The homes were large and spacious, the grounds tended by professional landscaping companies, but it was an expensive place to live. Lyons had to wonder for a moment about his selection but he decided to keep his opinions to himself. They had brought Shanahan and Davis on board because of their knowledge of the area, and to question it now wouldn't have been right.

The two FBI agents showed up at the rendezvous in standard garb, trading their suits for black cargo pants, T-shirts, Kevlar vests emblazoned with FBI in yellow letters and combat boots. Both of them toted an M-16 A-3 carbine and bandoliers with two spare magazines each of 5.56 mm ammunition.

For Able Team's mission in Charleston, John Kissinger had packed top-of-the-line armament. There was a brand-new SG-551—a carbine version of the Swiss-made SG-550—which boasted a 30-round detachable box magazine clipped to a second magazine just like it. With a cyclic rate of 700 rounds per minute, the weapon would prove formidable in capable hands. Hermann

Schwarz snagged the weapon from the back of their SUV and checked the action before popping a magazine into it and putting the weapon into battery.

Blancanales retrieved an Italian-made RS-202 M-4 combat shotgun designed by Benelli Armi and handed it to Lyons. The RS-202 chambered two-and-three-quarter-inch 12-gauge shells in under-barrel, tube-fed magazines. Lyons popped open the breech and quickly spied the first shell, smiling with satisfaction when he noted the special markings. The shotgun had been loaded with Lyons's favorite shells, a mix of No. 2 and double-0 buckshot.

Finally, Blancanales procured an H&K MP-5 40 for himself. The weapon was identical to the 9 mm MP-5 A-3, with the exception this one was chambered for the .40 S&W cartridge fed by a sloping magazine. Additionally, these weapons had been modified for single shot, two shot and full-auto.

The weapons sported by Able Team didn't escape the notice of either Shanahan or Davis. The FBI agents looked at their own weapons for a moment and then back at the very unconventional RS-202 shotgun displayed almost peacock proud by Carl Lyons.

"Those are some pretty fancy toys," Shanahan said.

Lyons flashed him a wicked grin. "Are you jealous?"

"It's not any sort of subconscious penis envy, if that's what you're asking."

The crass humor took all three of the Able Team warriors by surprise. At first they had taken Shanahan for being just another stuffed-shirt federal agent with too much starch in his collar and not enough fabric softener in his underwear. But the more they were exposed to the guy, the more they were beginning to like him. In some respects, Shanahan reminded Lyons a little bit of himself in his younger days with the LAPD.

Schwarz and Blancanales had agreed upon a similar sentiment between themselves but in the interests of maintaining peace, they had decided not tell that to their friend.

"Well, just remember," Schwarz said. "It's not the length of the pipe, it's how you lay it."

"Too much information, man," Blancanales said.

Lyons got down to business and inclined his head in the direction of the house. "All right, this is your show, Shanahan. What's the plan?"

"Well, I had to call in a couple of favors but I did manage to get a warrant. We should be able to enter the property under the assumption that the occupants are armed and dangerous. But I have to tell you, I didn't feel right getting this warrant without seeking the approval of my SAIC first."

"I understand you want to cover your asses, Shanahan," Lyon said. "But I can guarantee you're not going to get in trouble for this. Anything you do from here on out you'll be doing under my authority. Just don't go all vigilante on me. First and foremost, we protect any innocent bystanders and we won't draw down any heat from on high, if you catch my meaning."

Shanahan nodded. "I read you, Irons."

Lyons looked at Davis, who also acknowledged him with a curt nod.

"I don't know if Shanahan here has any sort of a plan," Blancanales said. "But I would strongly suggest we take a soft-probe approach first. It may not go well for us if we choose to come in with guns blazing. If there are terrorists inside there, it's probable they're going to be waiting for us. We'd do well to keep that in mind. Try to use surprise to our advantage."

Lyons looked at Schwarz. "Any objections?"

"I'm down with that," Schwarz replied.

"You two?"

Shanahan and Davis shook their heads.

"Okay, then, it's unanimous," Lyons said. "Let's get her done."

The afternoon sun was quickly dipping behind the horizon, and the shadows along the quiet street covered their approach. Lyons had considered the possibility that terrorists had some type of electronic security set up on the perimeter, but Schwarz had quickly dismissed the idea. Such an extravagance, even in a neighborhood like this, would have drawn quite a bit of attention, just the kind of attention the IUA didn't want. In fact, if they had done such things, they probably would have been discovered by now.

Fortunately, Able Team didn't have to break in either Shanahan or Davis. The two FBI agents had plenty of training, and the tactics they used really weren't any different from those in which Able Team trained. The main difference was that Able Team trained on those tactics on a nearly daily basis, whereas the FBI did not perform training of that nature on nearly such a regular schedule. Still, Shanahan and Davis had been in the business long enough that it was obvious even as they made their approach the two knew what they were doing. Lyons had every confidence they could hold their own. He would've never permitted them to participate otherwise.

The ball in motion, the Able Team warriors and their FBI allies converged on the terrorist hideaway.

CHAPTER EIGHTEEN

Phoenix Force wasted no time using the information provided by Stony Man to plan their assault.

Sheinberg and his staff had been able to procure a sufficient amount of equipment that would protect them from any exposure to radiation. He also gave every member of the team a lesson in the signs of radiation exposure and how to read the badges that were attached to the suits. Night had fallen on the Namib Desert, and the only saving grace the Phoenix Force warriors had was the fact the suits would at least insulate them from the cold, biting winds.

David McCarter could think of no less hospitable place to conduct an assault against terrorists. The terrain they would be going into was cold, rocky and treacherous to cross at night. The winds were also brutal and could exceed seventy-five miles per hour. They would be without any support, save for an evacuation team provided by the Namibian militia. While the Namibian government had agreed to cooperate by promising the Oval Office to turn its head—effectively the Namibian authorities would look the other way while a foreign power conducted clandestine operations against the IUA terrorist force—such a promise implied they would require complete deniability if things went wrong.

McCarter could understand it, although he didn't always agree with it. Politics was the single greatest soldier-killer of all time. The Briton had fought with honor, first as a member of the Special Air Service and then as a covert-operations specialists with Stony Man. McCarter did it because of duty, sure, but he also did it because he didn't bloody well know how to do anything else. This was what he knew, this was the life he preferred because he was good at it and he would've been the first to admit that he loved the action, every bit of it. He could have done without the sacrifice, the deaths of men like Justus Matombo, but there was something in his blood that predisposed him to this type of work.

"So our approach isn't going to be easy," McCarter said as their SUV bounced across the rugged terrain. "We'll have to stop at least five hundred feet short of the perimeter and take the rest on foot. It's going to be dark and we can't risk using any illumination whatsoever. I've also been told that there's a sandstorm predicted to pass through this region tonight, so we could be in for a long wait if we experience any sort of delay. Does anybody have any questions?"

From the backseat, Hawkins held up a hand. "Yeah, I was kind of wondering when they were going to ask us to move heaven and earth while we're at it?"

"I know it's a tall order, mates," McCarter said. "But we owe this to the Namibians and we owe it to Matombo."

None of the men said another word, each lost in his own thoughts. For the sake of expediency they had decided to don the protective wear before leaving. The suits were hot and uncomfortable, and they made each of the men itch in places where they couldn't even scratch, but it was much better than stepping into a combat situation where they could succumb to radiation poisoning. Something about vomiting, hair falling out and skin cancer seemed much less appealing than a few hours of discomfort. And they tried to look on the bright side, as the suits would offer extra protection in the event they were caught in the forecasted sandstorm.

"There's one other thing," McCarter said. "This isn't going to be a normal assault."

"In what way?" Gary Manning asked.

"In the way that we won't be taking any prisoners. I can't be any clearer than that. Every one of the individuals there has been exposed to significant amounts of radiation, amounts that Sheinberg tells me can only result in fatal effects. Maybe those effects won't manifest themselves for two months or three months or even six months, but he has indicated that based on the subjects they were able to assess, there is no doubt every one of them has already signed their death warrant by working in this mine without protection."

"So what are you saying, David?" James asked.

McCarter looked at each of them in the backseat, and even elicited a look from Encizo behind the wheel, before he said, "I'm saying that the Namibians can't afford to have any of their citizens exposed to that kind of poisoning. I'm telling you this is a scorched-earth policy. We're shutting this operation down and we're shutting it down for good, and nobody on the other side is to walk away from it."

The interior of the SUV became deathly quiet. In all the time that they had worked for Stony Man, not one of them could ever remember an order of genocide coming out of the mouth of the team leader. But in this case, McCarter hadn't left any room for doubt. They were not to take prisoners and they were not to show mercy. This was one of those situations where the only mercy they could show was a bullet in the head. The rules had changed, no doubt about that, and each one of the men knew he would have to look inside himself and dig up what was needed to execute this operation.

The bottom line was this: they were faced with a situation where the lives of many outweighed the lives of the few. So the terrorists were human beings. The innocent citizens of Namibia and those of the United States were human beings, too. And they had not made the choice to go digging around for the raw ore needed to inflict widespread terror upon others. This was a case where the ends would have to justify the means, and every one of them would have to live with that.

But it was something that every member of Phoenix Force understood. Ultimate war. Scorched-earth and take no prisoners was the order of the day. And no matter how difficult it was, they would follow those orders.

Anything less would mean the death of millions of innocent people.

THE WINDS WERE GUSTING at least thirty miles per hour by the time Phoenix Force reached their target. A wall of sand and grit and dust obscured their view of the layout. Positioned behind a V-shaped notch in a slight rise overlooking the mine, McCarter stared through a pair of night-vision binoculars at the terrain below. The winds were making it very difficult to see the positions of sentries, but McCarter didn't feel comfortable going in utterly cold. They needed to have some idea of what they were up against before they just charged down the hill with their weapons on full-auto burn.

They were now fully attired in their suits, the masks in place. McCarter felt like an astronaut on some inhospitable planet. The scene around him seemed almost surreal, being protected inside the suit while the winds buffeted the team, whistling and howling their way through the cavernous pocket of the yellow-cake mining operation. At one point, the dust cleared long enough for McCarter to spot what looked like a large bulldozer.

McCarter lowered the binoculars and then keyed up his mic as he passed them over to Encizo, who lay next to him. "You see that dozer?"

Encizo lifted the binoculars to the faceplate of his suit as McCarter pointed in the general direction. It took the Cuban about a minute to get settled on the regular shape, but eventually he caught sight of it. "I see it."

"You think if we can get you down to it, you can work that thing?"

Encizo knew why McCarter was asking him. During his time as an insurance investigator and construction supervisor, Rafael Encizo had gained some experience and training with the operation of heavy equipment. This had been required because there were times when he had to investigate accidents at construction sites. Such investigations would go a lot smoother if the investigator had some familiarity with the equipment involved, knowing its capabilities and its limitations, and what could or could not be done with it. Quite often there was a lot of money involved as heavy equipment operators would try to ride workers' comp claims by claiming their equipment was faulty. Encizo would then have to disprove that theory by demonstrating that a worker operated the piece of equipment in an improper fashion or violated some safety procedure.

"Probably. What did you have in mind?"

"I was thinking that if you could get that puppy up and moving, we could use it as a shield on our approach. Make it more difficult for the enemy to see us until we were on top of them."

Encizo nodded, although he wasn't sure McCarter could see the gesture. "Sounds like it might work. I'm certainly willing to give it my best shot."

"Okay, then, let's get back with the rest of the group and tell them what we've got planned."

The pair scrambled down the back side of the hill, both of them cognizant of their footing as they traversed the uneven and precarious terrain. They found the other three in the huddle where they had left them, their weapons held at the ready and each of them keeping vigil on a different part of the perimeter. McCarter instructed them to form on him so they could discuss the tactics.

"Okay, listen up," the McCarter said. "I don't see a whole lot of movement down there. I think I counted two sentries. They probably don't have a lot of personnel working guard right now just because they wouldn't consider this the most opportune time for someone to try to breach their security. We're going to use that to our advantage. I spotted a bulldozer down there, so we'll use that to provide some cover, as well as a distraction.

"Gary, you and Rafe are going to execute the forward action. It looks like the security detail has formed up near the entrance to the mine. I want you to make your approach on the leeward side. The rest of us are going to fan out and make our way slowly down the pocket until we reach ground zero. As soon as we see the dozer start moving, Hawkins will start up with the machine gun. Each of you keep your fire zones narrow and watch for your teammates. The visibility is going to be bloody next to nothing down there, and I don't want us shooting each other's asses off. Keep the body count to the terrorists. Questions?"

Each man nodded his understanding and without another word they broke the huddle. Hawkins ascended the hill right there with the M-60 E-4 cradled in his arms. Manning and Encizo moved off to the right before making their own ascent, while McCarter and James headed to the left. Before long, Hawkins couldn't see any of his teammates. As a member of Delta Force before joining Stony Man, Hawkins had been drilled on all the CQB tactics in the U.S. Army's arsenal. That had been a great preparation for his induction into Phoenix Force, but this situation was somewhat different. He remembered the instructions they had received from McCarter during transit. There were to be no prisoners, no survivors. That meant if it moved, shoot it, but in a sandstorm he would have to make absolutely sure of his target before he let fly. Yeah, this was going to be one hell of a tall order.

Hawkins picked his way down the rocky, slippery slope and into the pocket of the yellow-cake mine. As he got closer, he was able to make out the entrance to the mine directly ahead of him. Hawkins went to his belly and extended the legs of the bipod. He wedged them against a large rock and flipped up the sight, then pressed the stock tightly against his shoulder and leaned his face as close to obtain a good sight picture. The damn mask he wore was making it practically impossible to do that.

Aw, stop your grumbling, T.J., he told himself.

Confident of his position and his fire zone, Hawkins settled in and waited for the signal.

IT TOOK THEM a lot longer to get to the dozer than Encizo had thought it would, but they reached it unchallenged.

Gary Manning covered Encizo with his MP-5 as the Cuban climbed into the cage of the dozer. Encizo took only a moment to familiarize himself with the controls. All of the writing was in a language he didn't recognize, but that didn't really matter. The controls were standard for a dozer like this one and Encizo didn't need to be able to read the instruction plates. Within a minute he had deciphered where everything was and what it did.

Encizo reached toward the key, which was still positioned in the ignition lock, and then set the choke to full open. He double-checked that the brake was in the upright and locked position and then turned the key to start the engine. The dozer engine roared to life, although its sound was muted by the sealed mask. Encizo gunned it a couple of times, feeling the power of the machine as it vibrated through the seat and shook his entire body to the bone. Encizo released the brake and stepped on the accelerator, flipping the lever to unlock the blade and raised it up high enough to cover him in the cab, but not so high as to obscure his view of the area ahead.

At one point Encizo looked behind him to see Manning following with ease. He couldn't see the Canadian's face but he took a very clear understanding from the okay sign his friend threw him. Encizo returned his attention to the area ahead of him, watching as somewhere near the entrance to the mine flashes of light ensued, a signal the battle had begun.

IT HAPPENED SO FAST Calvin James barely had time to react.

He'd somehow managed to pick his way to the bottom of the pocket without breaking his neck, and with barely enough time to catch his breath when he saw the dozer lurch into motion. A heartbeat later, he heard or rather felt the steady thumping of the M-60 E-4 as Hawkins opened up on the enemy. James scrambled to his feet and rushed the enemy's position. As he drew nearer, his face mask began to fog some but James didn't let that bother him because Sheinberg had told them the mask would fog initially and then clear up.

Still, it was almost like fighting while encased inside a turtle shell. James thought back on the many missions he'd conducted, and he couldn't recall one that had been quite so mentally *and* physically demanding as this one. They were going against a force that may or may not have been numerically superior, but at the same time they were up against radiation-poisoned zombies who were basically nothing but shells of human beings. The terrorists were already dead, whether they knew it or not, and therefore had very little to lose.

James tried not to let the grisly aspects of this mission affect him as the initial fog cleared from his face mask. For some reason, the winds had not reached this part of the mine and there was almost an eerie calm about the area. It was a good thing, too, because James might not have spotted a terrorist sighting on his position with an assault rifle. James dropped to one knee, brought the MP-5 into position and verified his fire zone before opening up. James had triggered his weapon at the exact same moment as the terrorist fired on him, and a few of the rounds came uncomfortably close before the 9 mm Parabellums did their job. The rounds struck the terrorist in the chest and knocked him off his feet. He dropped out of sight behind the massive natural rock wall he'd been using for cover.

James jumped to his feet and continued for the rear of the dozer. He was within ten yards when he saw movement to his left and turned to see McCarter on a similar course. Throughout their approach Hawkins had not let up with the machine gun. They had traded out all of their standard rounds for tracers, and these were obviously helping the Phoenix Force warrior as Hawkins took out two of the sentries at the mine entrance before the remaining members of his team even got close.

James and McCarter ended up reaching Gary Manning's flank about the same time. The Canadian whirled when his combat sense alerted him of the approach, but he quickly verified they were allies and turned his attention back to the task at hand. A boulder to the left concealed a terrorist who popped up with an assault rifle held high and at the ready. A scarf covered his nose and mouth, and he wore goggles over his eyes. Unfortunately for him, he was one man against four. The terrorist squeezed off a short burst before the autofire from a quartet of MP-5s cut him to shreds. Even Rafael Encizo had spotted him in time to bring his weapon to bear. The terrorist danced under the assault of rounds and pitched forward into the dust.

When they reached the mine entrance, three more terrorists emerged from the enclosure and fired indiscriminately at the dozer. Most of the rounds glanced harmlessly off the blade, and the terrorists were so preoccupied with shooting at the dozer they took scant notice of the trio on the ground.

McCarter got the first terrorist with a rising corkscrew burst that cut across the terrorist's abdomen and chest. The last two rounds blew his skull apart and he collapsed to the ground. James got the next one with three rounds to the stomach, shredding the tender flesh of his abdomen and spilling the terrorist's guts. Manning held the MP-5 tight against his hip, remaining cognizant of the order to maintain a narrow fire zone. He triggered the weapon and stitched his target from crotch to sternum with at least a half dozen 9 mm slugs. The impact was close enough to knock the terrorist off his feet and dump him onto his back.

No further terrorists came out of the mine entrance and a quick check-in from Hawkins confirmed there were no further sentries spotted at the ground level.

"Any chance that there's another way out of that mine?" McCarter asked the team.

"We weren't able to get that kind of data from Bear," James replied. "But it's highly unlikely, unless there's some natural egress."

"Rafe," McCarter said, "I want you to put that dozer at the mouth of the mine entrance."

"I assume you want the blade to cover it," Encizo said.

"You got it, mate."

Encizo did as instructed and then quickly disembarked as McCarter sent Manning a prearranged signal by opening and closing his fist several times. Gary Manning, the team's explosives expert, knew exactly what to do. Within a few minutes he had set charges at specific points around the perimeter of the mine entrance. The members of Phoenix Force swept the area to ensure they had cleared it of any terrorists who might be hiding, waiting for them to leave, and then retreated to a safe distance.

As soon as they were over the rise in the pocket and

beginning to descend to the other side, Manning reached into his utility belt and withdrew a small black box. The winds were beginning to pick up again, and the Phoenix Force team knew before too much longer that the mother of all sandstorms would hit the Namib Desert. The explosion that followed when Manning triggered the remote detonator seemed woefully weak in comparison to the havoc that Mother Nature was about to wreak on the entire region.

The echo of the blast had barely died out when Hawkins gestured to a point just to the right. Through the blowing dust and sand they spotted what appeared to be headlights that swept out of view a moment later.

"Blast it!" McCarter let out a series of curses. "They had a remote observation post."

"We can't let them get away," James said.

"Let's get to our wheels," McCarter urged.

With that, the five warriors broke into a mad sprint for their vehicle.

CHAPTER NINETEEN

When Latif al-Din heard Hezrai's report, it took quite a bit of self-control to not reach out and strangle the man to death.

Unfortunately, al-Din needed Hezrai right now, although he would make sure that when their mission was completed he would have this incompetent beheaded. Hezrai had not trained the men appropriately; it was just that simple. And al-Din could not afford to have someone in Hezrai's position fail him again and again. Not to mention the fact that these latest incidents—the bungled attempts on the lives of the two Americans who had sold them the diesel engines and their success deceiving al-Din into thinking their assassination of the two men who had been captured in Washington had succeeded—was costing him valuable time and diverting him from their mission.

Now the three Americans who had slaughtered his entire field team in Washington had somehow found their way to Charleston. They had come close, uncomfortably close, to the operations and al-Din knew that it was only a matter of time before they succeeded in

locating the construction facility. This would not only
force him to move up his timeline but it would also
require him to take additional personnel and divert them
to ensuring the security of their operations.

Hezrai didn't apparently agree with al-Din's assessment when he verbalized this to him: "You will forgive
me for being so bold, but I do not think it is wise to
commit any more men on this particular situation."

Al-Din smoldered inside but kept his voice quiet and
level. "Oh, you don't. And why is that?"

Hezrai cleared his throat. "Every detachment that
we have sent to try to throw the Americans off our trail
has only ended in disaster. I understand that you are
trying to be proactive about this, but I believe that the
fear of discovery may be clouding your judgment."

"I have to wonder what would compel you to say
these things to me, Hezrai. Particularly when you know
that I'll kill you for your insolence."

"If my death will satisfy you, will satiate your anger
so that you may refocus your efforts on destroying the
great Satan, then I will gladly give it up."

Al-Din was completely taken aback by his statement.
He had always faulted Hezrai for not being a stronger
leader, had always worried about the man's lackluster
performance as a trainer and disciplinarian of the men.
But now here he was, that same man who had repeat-
edly demonstrated a lack of ability in those areas, pro-
fessing self-sacrifice for the betterment of their mission
against America. Al-Din looked for some bit of deceit,
some contempt in his words, but he saw nothing to
indicate Hezrai was mocking him.

"You are sincere in this," al-Din said, doing nothing
to hide the surprise in his voice.

"I am quite aware that over the past years you have

not been completely satisfied with my performance. And I'm also aware that there are others among our ranks who would probably do a much better job in my capacity than I have done. But I have always loved what we stood for, and I've always admired your passion for our people, and I would never purposefully do anything that I thought would be a disservice to you."

"You are an enigma, Hezrai, a great enigma that I may never understand. And while my position about your aptitude and abilities has not changed, my personal opinion of you most certainly has. And it is in this that you have done well, because today you have saved your own life by your willingness to give it up."

"I am here to serve you, Latif. And I will continue to do so as long as you let me."

"I would agree that sending any additional resources to combat the Americans might be unwise in other circumstances," al-Din said. "But in this case, I think you are mistaken. I think that we must ensure that they do not locate us. In order to do that we must silence all potential liabilities, and we must take the fight directly to these Americans."

"I do not believe we have any liabilities remaining."

"What about the two prisoners they have taken, our men that are being held in Washington?"

"Neither of those men knew the location of this facility," Hezrai pointed out. "I should also point out that if they had known our location, the Americans would surely have attempted to strike here by now."

"And what about Hadariik?" al-Din asked. "Indeed, he knows a considerable amount relative to our operations, not to mention the location of this facility. Additionally, he possesses engineering knowledge that I do not think any of the other resources we currently have here possess. Would you actually have me believe that he's not a liability?"

"Hadariik is an exception," Hezrai admitted. "But he is the only exception and he is easily dealt with. He is not under significant guard at the hospital where they currently have him, and I believe we should be able to send in just one man to silence him once and for all. As to the information that he has regarding engineering, he has already drawn the plans for us and all of those things that are in his area of expertise have been completed."

Al-Din gave that statement serious consideration. There was no point arguing with Hezrai; he knew the man was right. Hadariik had become a liability, and al-Din had to wonder if perhaps Hezrai hadn't purposely sent him on the mission to assassinate the two engine-builders with the thought they might actually fail. Al-Din had never known Hezrai to be a man of cunning, but it was usually the most cunning men of all who were able to make all of those around them think just the opposite. Al-Din was beginning to see Hezrai in a whole new light, and he wasn't sure if that pleased him or worried him. As they progressed, al-Din knew that he would have to keep his eyes on Hezrai at all times.

Hezrai may very well have been like a serpent, slithering through the night until it crawled into bed with its own prey and struck with a venomous bite.

"And what of the construction?" al-Din asked, assuming they had now closed the subject on Hadariik's fate. "I understand that the first shipment of U-238 has arrived."

"It has, although it was not as large as we had hoped. A significant amount of the raw ore is required in order to produce even a semi-effective portion of the pluto-nium required to make the warhead effective. They were only able to produce enough to equip two pairs of war-heads."

Al-Din considered this new wrinkle. It had been his desire to launch all six of the submarines at one time, but now he knew he would probably have to amend his plans. Between the Americans putting the pressure on his people here in this decadent city and the recent events in Namibia, al-Din knew they might not get their chance if they didn't speed up the timetable.

"Even the launching of four warheads would be a sig-nificant blow. It might even buy us enough time to find another source of ore while the Americans are recover-ing from a first strike. Four warheads mean that we could at least dispatch two of the prototypes. I will in-form the work-master to choose the two submarines that are nearest completion and have them double their efforts on those. We should be able to get those craft launched within the next sixteen hours."

"I would completely agree that such a task is not im-possible," Hezrai replied.

"See to it that the missiles are loaded and configured as soon as possible. I don't want any more delays, and I don't want excuses. I'm relying on you to make sure that this gets done, Hezrai. Don't fail me again or there is no amount of words or deeds that will prevent me from personally separating your head from the rest of your body."

"You may consider it done, Latif."

With that, Hezrai turned on his heel and left his master's office.

For a long time, al-Din didn't move from his spot. Surprisingly, he didn't feel like taking his usual walk so that he could think; he didn't even feel like having a drink or participating in the company of a woman. No, he had entirely too much on his mind. Things had begun to spiral out of control in the past few days. Maybe his decision to murder the American scientist had been a mistake. Yes, perhaps he had played his hand a little too soon and shown the enemy his intent before the time was right.

Whatever happened now, al-Din knew that he could not second-guess himself. If he showed the men around him any weakness, any hesitation whatsoever, they would see it in him and he would lose their allegiance. Those inside the Revenge of Allah were not like those who chose to follow other groups. The men that he led were cutthroats, murderers, rapists and criminals who had decided that they enjoyed the way of life he afforded them. But it didn't mean that they couldn't spot weakness and nobody was above reproach.

Al-Din then decided things had reached a point where he would have to put an alternate plan into action in the event the Americans found him before they could launch the submarines. Al-Din leaned forward and plucked the cell phone from his desk. He dialed the special number he'd memorized and a gruff voice answered midway through the second ring.

"Yes?"

"I think the time may be coming," al-Din said. "I believe it is time to put our alternate plans into motion."

"Have you been compromised?"

"I believe so," al-Din said, trying not to sound uncertain in his response. "There are those within my own ranks whom I don't trust any longer. In fact, I'm not sure that I ever did."

"Very well," the man replied. "We shall be prepared for your arrival."

The line went dead.

Al-Din set the now worthless phone on his desk. With that final call, he knew in five minutes a special program would fry the interior of the phone, melting the chip and SIM card into slag. A fail-safe so that nobody would be able to track him. Unlike Hezrai, the man he'd talk to would also ensure that the three Americans did not survive the night. They were as much a threat now to him as his own, the way al-Din saw it. He could not afford that kind of liability. Yes, he had truly lost control.

And it was time for Latif al-Din to cut his losses.

DESPITE THE HEAD START the vehicle had on Phoenix Force, they somehow managed to catch up to their quarry.

At first, they thought to overtake them, but McCarter decided to rethink that scenario. It was possible the vehicle would lead them directly where they needed to go, so Encizo followed from a distance in total blackout mode. A few times, the Cuban nearly put the vehicle in the ditch but somehow he managed to recover and steer back onto the makeshift road. They couldn't be entirely sure, but Gary Manning convinced them that the road they were taking led to Walvis Bay.

After one particularly nasty bump that nearly bottomed out the SUV, James asked, "Are you sure that using the taillights of the vehicle in front of us as our only guide is such a good idea?"

"I think I might agree with him," T. J. Hawkins added. "My ass is beginning to feel like somebody's used it for a washboard."

"What do you think this is?" McCarter asked. "Some kind of a limo service?"

"I just hope it's well worth it," Manning said.

"It would be a damn shame if this turned out to be nothing more than a wild-goose chase," James said.

"Kids," Encizo said. "Can't take them anywhere anymore."

They hit another bump and Hawkins said, "You know, this is why we can't have nice things."

For a time they fell silent, the bantering falling to the wayside as the exhaustion from the past twenty-four hours began to set in. McCarter couldn't say that he blamed his team for being a little punchy. He was feeling pretty drained himself at this point, and he was betting that wherever this vehicle led them it would only spell more trouble. Still, while they had rescued the medical team and sealed off the mine, they still hadn't managed to prove or disprove the theory the terrorists were trying to smuggle the raw ore out of Namibia.

One thing he counted as good fortune was the fact that they seem to be pulling away from the storm. Trying to follow the mysterious vehicle would have been next to impossible in a desert sandstorm, not to mention they would have probably been unable to contact Stony Man or the Namibian militia personnel who were presently on standby. Still, if this paid off and they were in fact headed to Walvis Bay, it would put them one step closer to returning home. And they would also see a familiar face, that of Stony Man pilot Jack Grimaldi.

The satellite communications phone on McCarter's belt rang for attention. The vehicle they had been following had now veered onto a hardball road, and there were vehicles both in front and behind them. As McCarter unclipped the phone from his belt, he indicated it was probably safe for Encizo to turn on the headlights. The Cuban didn't have to be told twice and immediately complied as McCarter answered the phone.

"Talk to me," McCarter said, knowing it could only be one of three people on the other line.

The voice of Barbara Price rang sweetly in his ears. "Hanging in there?"

"I'm doing okay, love," McCarter said. "Although the natives are getting a bit restless."

"Well, then you can pass on a little bit of good news from me," Price replied.

"I'm sure it will be well received right now."

"I thought you could use it. Okay, I have a couple of updates for you. First, we looked into the men you encountered on the road back to Lüderitz. It looks like Gary was right on the money. All three of the men were known mercenaries for hire, and one of them out of Italy had quite a bit of experience. We weren't able to find a tie between any of them and the IUA, but we did discover that they were staying at a hotel in Walvis Bay. Aaron's working on a way to run down the phone system there, get inside to see if he can find out if there were any communications. But that's going to take some time and we can't even be sure it'll tell us anything we don't already know."

"Or at least suspect," McCarter said. "What else?"

"Able Team thinks they may finally have a lead on the terrorist facility in Charleston," Price continued. "They're working with a liaison in the FBI to find some other specialists who might have been involved in the construction of the prototypes. If they can find one of those individuals, they think they might be able to pin down the location once and for all."

"Well, we have finished neutralizing the mine and you can tell Hal there won't be any more problems. We sealed the mine with explosives, so at least they can send cleanup teams and be confident they're in the right place."

"The Namibian government will definitely be glad to hear that. Also, we started digging around about your theory relative to the conversion of the raw uranium ore into weapons-grade plutonium. None of us here is an expert so we had to reach out to one of the staff members at the Nuclear Regulatory Commission. He indicated that it was more than possible to set up a nuclear reaction aboard a reactor-based ship of any significant size. All that's required to extract weapons-grade plutonium from U-238 is to bombard it with a single neutron."

"So you're saying that it only takes a nuclear reactor to produce the plutonium?"

"More or less, is the least complex answer. Producing weapons-grade plutonium doesn't necessarily require an advanced military reactor. In fact, there are many cases where reactor-grade plutonium was sufficient for the production of a nuclear weapon. The only difference here would be the yield, which, depending upon the amount used, is typically less than twenty kilotons. It's highly doubtful the IUA would ever have the resources available to get their hands on a military-grade reactor, but it is possible they could use the standard nuclear reactor aboard a ship to produce weapons capable of inflicting significant destruction."

"Are there any commercial vessels out there that have nuclear reactors?"

"Absolutely," Price said. "Although those ships are very well protected and strongly regulated. It doesn't seem likely that terrorists would be able to get access to them quite so easily."

McCarter told her about the mysterious vehicle they were following. "We think they may be headed for Walvis Bay. We need you to have Kurtzman check every ship that has come into or out of that port in the last five days, and we need to know if any of them are nuclear powered. You may also want to check all ships that have come into Charleston recently, since we have no idea whether the terrorists may already have managed to get nuclear materials inside the country. For all we know, they've been operating this way for months."

"We're actually checking out all of that as we speak," Price said. "We'll contact you as soon as we know something. In the meantime, you can take any action you feel necessary to prevent the terrorists from smuggling radioactive material out of that country."

"You can count on that," McCarter replied. "Out here."

McCarter disconnected the call. "That was Barb. She says our theory about those three being mercenaries was spot-on. She also said they had been staying in Walvis Bay."

"Go figure," James said.

Manning looked at Hawkins and held out his hand. "Twenty bucks."

"I don't have it on me right now. I must've left it in my spare radiation suit." When Manning just stared at him, Hawkins held up his hands and said, "What? I'm good for it!"

Encizo looked in the rearview mirror and said, "Don't believe him, Gary. Get an IOU."

McCarter watched as they passed a sign and said, "Keep your eyes open, mates. We're coming into Walvis Bay."

"What are we looking for?" James said.

"A big ship," McCarter replied.

CHAPTER TWENTY

Slowly and steadily, the men of Able Team and their two FBI allies approached the house with caution. Their weapons were held at the ready and they were prepared to take on whatever threat the IUA terrorists might throw at them. Carl Lyons would have preferred some other tactic to this one; even a straight fight or hard probe was much better than the time a soft probe took. Unfortunately, they had a game to play here that didn't involve turning the entire city of Charleston on its ear.

The Able Team leader couldn't even be sure that they would find what they were looking for at this house, or at any other, although he knew the odds were in their favor. Up until now, the IUA had managed to avoid Able Team and escape detection by an unwary American population. Their luck was running short now. Lyons could feel it; they had made several critical mistakes that had exposed their operation and the terrorists had to know that Able Team was on to them.

The five armed men moved in a staggered formation until they reached a point where the eight-foot-high wall bordering the property intersected with the adjoining lot. Lyons tossed the signal to Blancanales, who immediately knelt and cupped his hands to provide a foot cradle for Hermann Schwarz. Schwarz slung his weapon tightly over one shoulder so he didn't make a sound, and then stepped into Blancanales's hands.

A moment later he was up and moving over the wall.

Schwarz dropped to the ground just inside the wall and brought the muzzle of the SG-551 level with his chest. Schwarz locked the butt against his shoulder, pressed his cheek to the stock and sighted down the rail. The weapon felt balanced and comfortable to him, although it had been some time since he'd fired it, and he knew he could hold position long enough for his associates to join him.

Lyons was next, also assisted by Blancanales, and then Shanahan and Davis helped the last Able Team member over the wall. The two FBI agents then continued up the sidewalk, keeping in the shadows provided by the decorative wall that ran the entire length of the perimeter. The grounds were surprisingly expansive, much more than they had thought upon first inspection.

"Time?"

Blancanales pulled back the thin leather glove on his left hand—part of a pair he liked to wear during combat operations—and glanced at the watch he wore with the dial on the inside of his wrist. "Almost 1730 hours."

"All right, let's shake the trees and see what monkeys fall out."

The three warriors got to their feet and fanned out, Lyons moving up the right side of the wall, Blancanales going left and Schwarz heading straight up the middle. When the three had put considerable distance between themselves, they began to move toward the residence in a parallel formation. They had nearly reached the back patio when the chatter of a submachine gun reached their ears. All three men threw themselves to the dirt simultaneously, and the maelstrom of rounds chewed up the manicured lawn near Blancanales's position.

Lyons looked across the expansive back of the house in search of some sign of the shooter's position. It took him a little longer than he expected but eventually he spotted muzzle-flashes from a small rectangular window on the first floor close to the far corner of the house. Lyons knew at that distance his shotgun would probably be ineffective, so he brought the next best thing to bear: his Colt Python .357 Magnum.

Lyons aimed at a point maybe a half inch above the muzzle-flashes and triggered three successive rounds. The Python boomed with a finality designed to provide as much of a psychological effect as the 210-grain rounds provided a physical one. A moment later the chattering weapon stopped, and the three Able Team commandos took that as a cue to press forward.

Schwarz got to the deck where it rose about two feet off the ground. He kept one hand on his weapon as he put the other down to steady himself and vaulted onto the smooth, finished redwood. The deck ran nearly the entire length of the front of the two-story house. The place looked as if it had been renovated recently, and sported a much newer style than most of the other homes in the area. In fact, it looked as if most of these amenities were newer, and included a massive cedar hot tub, commercial gas grill and portable wet bar. Various chaise longues and tables with umbrellas and chairs dotted the deck.

Schwarz wound his way through the maze of furniture and had nearly reached a sliding-glass door when he heard the steady rap of another SMG. Schwarz moved for cover in time to avoid a trail of rounds that chewed up the deck less than a yard from his feet. Schwarz turned to look at a window almost directly above him. A thin, dark-haired man was leaning out of it, trying to balance himself on the window ledge while he attempted to cut Schwarz down with an Uzi SMG.

Schwarz reacted instantly. The Able Team warrior swung the muzzle of his SG-551 into play, snap-aimed down the rail and triggered a sustained burst. The report from the assault rifle was anything but dainty, its heavy-handed drumming significant enough to rattle Schwarz's teeth inside his head as the weapon chugged against his shoulder. The 5.56 mm rounds struck the terrorist gunner in the chest and smashed him against the wall frame with such force that he bounced off. His body became top-heavy enough that he fell out the window. Schwarz knew before he hit the deck that he was dead.

Schwarz then leveled the SG-551 in the direction of the sliding-glass doors and triggered a sustained, sweeping burst from the hip. The plate glass proved no match for the ferocity of the SG-551. Glass shards blew inward, glittering in the twilight of the clear Charleston sky. Schwarz stepped up to the frame of the sliding-glass door just outside the view of any potential observers indoors. He reached up to the strap of his equipment harness and came away with an AN-M14 TH3 incendiary grenade. Schwarz yanked the pin and tossed the hand bomb through the opening left by his assault rifle. The grenade exploded a moment later, spotting every flammable surface in a ten-yard radius with pellets of molten iron. Within a minute thick black smoke began to pour through what remained of the door frame.

Blancanales was on his feet as soon as Lyons took down the first shooter, and rushed the house with the MP-5 40 held at the ready. Every few seconds, the Able Team warrior would check his flank, as well as the position of his two partners. They had performed assault tactics like this time and again, but what they did on the training grounds never seemed quite the same as it did in real life. Of course, some of that might have had to do with the fact that the cadre—usually those who provided security for Stony Man Farm—were shooting at Able Team with rubber bullets and beanbag guns while the team wore personal protective equipment.

In this case, the terrorists weren't using nonlethal weapons. They were toting automatic rifles, submachine guns and who knew what else. On occasion, it was the what else that scared Blancanales the most. And maybe the terrorist who suddenly emerged from behind an exterior shed as Blancanales got close to the house subconsciously knew that. In this case, the terrorist wasn't brandishing a machine gun or a pistol. Instead, he swung a massive silver object at Blancanales, and only reflexes born from years of training saved the Able Team warrior from decapitation.

Blancanales shoulder-rolled after ducking the object that whistled so close to his skull he could feel the movement of air left in its wake. Blancanales came out of the roll on his feet and turned in time to see the terrorist charging him with nothing other than a broadsword in his hands. Blancanales knew it would be a story to tell if he managed to survive the assault. As the guy drew near, Blancanales grabbed his wrists at the same moment as he dropped onto his back and executed a judo circle thrill that launched his lithe attacker head over heels. The terrorist landed on his back with enough force to knock the sword out of his hand.

Blancanales got to his feet and charged the terrorist before the man had time to recover. As he got close, the terrorist thought Blancanales would try to grab him and he spun his leg around in an attempt to sweep Blancanales's feet out from under him. But Blancanales had other options in mind and as he drew near, he left the ground in a leaping side kick that landed on the terrorist's face. The force of the kick plus Blancanales's weight following behind it dislocated the terrorist's jaw and sent him reeling. The terrorist's body rolled several times before coming to a halt.

Blancanales didn't waste any time, catching his breath while he intertwined the man's hands with a pair of thick plastic riot cuffs. He then used a second pair to hogtie his feet so the guy couldn't escape. With that task completed, he returned to where he had dropped his weapon, retrieved it from the ground and moved off toward the house to help his two friends.

"I THOUGHT THEY were going to wait for us," Davis said.

"So did I," Shanahan snarled.

The two FBI agents had barely reached the wrought-iron gate at the end of the drive that stood wide open when first sounds of gunfire reached them. Shanahan had to wonder whether or not Irons and his two friends hadn't expected something like that. After all, he'd been very insistent that Shanahan and Davis pull down the perimeter in the event one or more of the occupants tried to escape. Shanahan hadn't been exactly keen on the idea but he realized he didn't have much room to complain since Irons had given him every opportunity to call the plays and he'd chosen to defer to them.

Well, he'd already agreed to this truce and they were after the same thing. As long as they found out where the terrorists were operating, Shanahan didn't really care who took the credit; frankly, he didn't think any of their three allies did, either. At least they had come forward and asked for help and explained the situation instead of leaving Shanahan and Davis out in the cold to fend for themselves.

So hell, he couldn't fault them too much.

Even as they reached the gate, Shanahan realized it couldn't be any picnic because they suddenly began to take fire of their own. Bullets chewed pavement off the driveway, ricocheting from the concrete with a whine as fragments slapped the gates in a metallic chorus. Shanahan shoved Davis to the side just in time to avoid being cut down. The pair of FBI agents went prone in a heartbeat and brought their weapons to bear on the trio of men rushing down the driveway.

Shanahan shouted only one warning, ordering the men to drop their weapons and surrender before he opened fire. The M-16 A-3s were standard issue for law enforcement, and supported only two firing modes: single shot and 3-round bursts. Shanahan would have preferred to have a sustained, full-auto capability. But such wasn't a luxury in today's modern law-enforcement community. The 3-round burst mode would have to do, and Shanahan and Davis made good use of the weapons all the same.

Davis got the first kill by taking one of the terrorists with a burst to the chest. The terrorist dropped his weapon and staggered backward from the impact of the high-velocity rounds that ripped through his sternum and punctured his lungs. A spray of pink, frothy sputum erupted from his mouth before the terrorist collapsed to the driveway.

Shanahan's first hit was a pair of low shots just below the knee of another terrorist gunman. The 5.56 mm rounds drilled through the man's shinbone. The terrorist's Uzi SMG clattered to the driveway as the man knelt and grabbed his shattered leg, no longer able to support his own weight. His mouth was still wide open in agony when a second burst from Shanahan's rifle passed through and blew large holes out the back of his head.

The last terrorist turned and tried to escape, not even looking in the direction of the FBI agents as he sprayed the area above their heads while running in the opposite direction. Later that night, Davis and Shanahan would argue for some time, each one trying to convince the other that it was his shots that brought the terrorist down. In either case, they knew it didn't matter as a plethora of slugs ripped through his flanks and spine and pitched him face-first onto the cold, unyielding driveway.

For a long time neither of the FBI agents moved. Up at the house they could hear what sounded like small-arms fire, followed by the whooshing thunderclap that Shanahan knew could only have come from military-grade ordnance. Tom Shanahan had served in the Marine Corps during the war in Lebanon, as well as a number of conflicts that probably weren't even on the history books. He'd been in combat enough to know the sound of grenades when he heard them.

Buddy Davis did, as well, although Shanahan couldn't be sure how he knew that. He'd been the man's partner for almost six years, and he realized in that moment that neither of them had ever talked about their military experiences. He knew Buddy Davis served; he just didn't know where or when, and he reminded himself that one of these days he would take the time to ask.

"Lord Almighty," Davis said. "It sounds like our boys up there started World War III."

"That it does," Shanahan said. "I told you those guys are a hell of a lot more than they seemed on the surface."

"Well, if I didn't believe you then, partner, I sure do believe you now."

The FBI agents scrambled to their feet and jogged up the driveway, one on either side. Keeping distance between themselves was almost second nature. Where automatic weapons were involved, men who crowded each other could both get dead with a single burst from an even marginally competent marksman. Shanahan and Davis searched the three bodies for identification.

"You find anything?" Shanahan asked.

Davis shook his head, holding the muzzle of his weapon toward the sky as he braced the stock against his side. "Nothing worth mentioning. You?"

"Zip."

Davis sighed and for just a moment, the two men exchanged looks. It seemed almost as if all the birds in the trees had abandoned their posts. They had been standing there maybe fifteen seconds when the silence was replaced by the distant wail of sirens. Shanahan had called the local police and told them they would be serving a warrant, but he hadn't gotten into any of the details. What they couldn't afford was to get locals involved in a shootout. Shanahan's ass was already riding the line on this one.

"I'll tell you what," he said to Davis. "It won't take the locals long to arrive. Why don't you go down to the end of the driveway and meet them, see if you can stall for time while I go find our friends."

"You sure it's a good idea for us to split up?" Davis asked.

"Probably not, but we don't have a lot of time left and I'm not really feeling inclined to stand around answering a bunch of uncomfortable questions for the next two hours. And I can just about guarantee Irons and his people are going to feel the same way."

"Okay, I'll do what I can."

The two men shook hands and separated, Davis heading back down the drive to the gate while Shanahan sprinted toward the house in search of their three allies.

THEIR ASSAULT on the terrorists had taken less than ten minutes.

Able Team searched the residence but didn't find any further terrorist resistors. The majority of the house was unfurnished, the rooms that did have furniture sparsely decorated. Once they had finished clearing the house, they met outside. Blancanales showed them the terrorist he had hogtied and left there. Just as Blancanales cut the plastic cuffs from the terrorist's ankles and hauled him to his feet, Tom Shanahan joined Able Team.

"Well, well, well…what do we have here?" Shanahan said. "If I don't miss my guess, it looks like another scumbag."

Schwarz pointed to the sword where the terrorist had dropped it. "Apparently, he's one of the old-fashioned types."

"Crazy son of a bitch tried to cut off my head," Blancanales added.

"A sword?" Shanahan said, eyeballing the terrorist. "You're putting us on. It's some sort of joke. A sword—" he shook his head "—is very ineffective in a gunfight, pal. Who do you think you are, Ali Baba?"

"We can get to that later," Lyons said. "You two take this guy back to the SUV and wait for us. I'll go with

Shanahan here and try to smooth any ruffled feathers the locals might have."

"You know they are probably going to cite you for disturbing the peace, don't you?" Schwarz quipped.

"Very funny. Now move out."

Schwarz and Blancanales split with the prisoner while Shanahan and Lyons headed toward the gate. They could already see the first two police squads that had arrived. It probably wouldn't be long before half the Charleston Police Department showed up. They were going to have a lot of questions, questions that Lyons didn't really want to spend time answering. Still, he had to keep up appearances as best he could. If it got too thick, he'd leave it to Shanahan's experience and simply slip away quietly. But for the moment, he felt as if he owed the two agents his support. He had promised them this wouldn't fall on their heads and he wasn't about to abandon them now.

"You think the guy we captured will tell us anything?" Shanahan asked.

"I can only hope."

Just as they had reached the gate where Buddy Davis was busy keeping the uniforms at bay, Shanahan's cell phone rang. The FBI agent withdrew the phone from his belt, looked at the digital number that scrolled across the LCD display and let out a moan.

"Oh, shit, it's my boss. This is going to be lovely." Shanahan reached into his breast pocket, withdrew a wireless earpiece and positioned it on his ear before answering the phone. "Yes, sir…Shanahan here."

The agent listened intently for a minute and Lyons studied his face with curiosity. Maybe it was the fading light, or maybe just the shadows playing tricks on his eyes, but for a brief moment he thought he saw

Shanahan's complexion pale a bit. Shanahan nodded, grunted a couple of times, nodded some more and then said goodbye. As he clicked off the phone and disconnected the headset he fixed Lyons with a grim expression.

"Our witness, the other proprietor of the marine supply shop? He died in the ICU about an hour ago."

Lyons took a ragged breath and blew it out through clenched teeth. "Damn and damn," he muttered.

Before either of them could say another word, Lyons's radio squawked for attention and he keyed up his mic. "Go."

Schwarz's voice said, "Ironman, we just got a call from big daddy. Apparently there's some sort of trouble at the hospital, something to do with Hadariik."

"What kind of trouble?"

"The kind that involves an armed gunman and a police standoff."

"And the hits just keep on coming," Lyons said.

CHAPTER TWENTY-ONE

It didn't come as a surprise to anyone in Phoenix Force when the vehicle they had been following led them through the dark, deserted streets of Walvis Bay and eventually came to a stop at Pier 5.

Anchored against the pier was a sizable commercial freighter with markings that none of the men recognized. Between them James and Encizo had the most experience with maritime operations, but they couldn't tell whether the vessel in front of them was powered by a nuclear reactor or featured some other conventional means of propulsion.

"One of the things we haven't considered and probably should is that the terrorists might be using a vessel that has a nuclear reactor aboard, but isn't necessarily powered by one," Encizo said.

McCarter looked at his friend. "You think that's a realistic possibility?"

"I wouldn't have suggested it if I didn't think it was possible."

"Well, it seems like the IUA does have a considerable amount of resources at its disposal," James said from the backseat. "But we're talking some serious cash to fund an operation like that one. And where would they have gotten the technology on such short notice? I mean, it's not like some government power is just going to hand over a nuclear reactor capable of producing weapons-grade plutonium to a terrorist organization. Even countries friendly to terrorists wouldn't be stupid enough to do something like that."

None of the men could argue with his logic. Sure, there were many countries who didn't mind harboring or financing terrorists, but they did it with the understanding that the terrorists wouldn't be operating anywhere near them. To turn over nuclear-weapons production capabilities to a radical group of terrorist extremists would have been pretty much suicide for any country because they ran the risk of having those weapons ultimately turned against them. And while the IUA had far-reaching resources, they were still young in the terrorist community and there were very few governments—even those harboring al Qaeda fugitives—willing to turn over that kind of technology to an untried and unproved terrorist cell.

"I think for the moment," McCarter finally said, "that instead of sitting around guessing, we should give Stony Man a little bit longer to see if they can determine exactly what we're up against."

A stony silence fell over the group for a span of about five minutes before T. J. Hawkins finally said, "You know something, I am really getting hungry. I could easily use a thick juicy T-bone and a long-neck bottle of Lone Star right now. How about you guys?"

"I could use a beer," James said.

"I could use a woman," Manning added.

"I could use a bed," Encizo chimed in.

"No offense, but I could use with the rest of you being silent," McCarter snapped. As if on cue, his cell phone rang.

"Aw, saved by the bell," James taunted.

McCarter produced a deep sigh as he flipped open the phone cover. "Yeah, talk to me."

"I just finished gathering those results you asked for," Aaron Kurtzman said. "You're not going to like it."

"If it will get me back into the action and out of the insane asylum with these four lunatics Hal expects me to lead, I'm all ears."

"Getting a little stir crazy?"

"Right now, I wouldn't use the word *crazy* too loudly. It might incite a riot."

Kurtzman chuckled. "I'll spread the word. So relative to the shipping traffic in Namibia, there hasn't been a single nuclear-powered commercial vessel come into or leave Walvis Bay in nearly a year."

"I hear a 'but' coming."

"You hear correctly," Kurtzman said. "Four days ago, a freighter arrived in Walvis Bay. It's a big diesel monstrosity of a thing, and according to her registration she isn't powered by a nuclear reactor and she doesn't have any such devices aboard. The thing that flagged our interest was the passenger manifest on her arrival in South Africa, particularly the names of three men on the list."

"Wait a minute, don't tell me," McCarter said. "Our mercenary pals."

"Give that man a cigar."

"That's too much to be a mere coincidence," McCarter said. "I'm betting that the IUA is planning to use that ship to smuggle the raw ore out of the country. So maybe they're not making the weapons-grade plutonium aboard the ship—maybe they're just using it to transport the stuff."

"That's exactly what they're doing." McCarter heard the incessant tapping of Kurtzman's fingers over the keyboard, a process he'd witnessed firsthand on many occasions. It always impressed the Phoenix Force leader how a big, burly guy like Kurtzman could manipulate a computer keyboard with all the grace and fluidity and gentleness of a concert pianist. "The freighter is called the *Lady of Stavanger.* According to her manifest she's scheduled to leave port at 0600 hours today, your local time."

McCarter looked at his watch. "That's less than two hours from now. They list their cargo and destination?"

Some more tapping and then Kurtzman responded, "They're traveling pretty light according to what I see here. In fact, they claimed they'll be significantly underloaded. Uh-oh…their next scheduled destination is Charleston, South Carolina."

"You got any photographs of this thing you can send us?" McCarter asked.

"I'll send it through," Kurtzman said. "Stand by."

Every member of Phoenix Force and Able Team had been issued a PDA some time back. All the mission files for any given assignment were transported to them in real time, as well as any up-to-date intelligence Kurtzman thought they might find useful. All of the information downloaded to the devices was held in a volatile memory chip. No actual data resided on the PDA, and it contained no flash memory and no hardware-based storage.

The other unique feature of the PDAs was that they were secured utilizing the latest in biotech identification systems. The PDA could only be activated by scanning the thumbprint of the owner's right hand and the pinkie of his left. If a positive identification could not be made within thirty seconds of the device being activated, the internal memory was wiped and any communications uplink with Stony Man's dedicated satellite severed. The only way the device could be reset at that point was a direct interface with a special terminal at Stony Man Farm, the only one of its kind that sat locked behind a coded access door.

Within a minute of making his request, a photograph came into focus on the screen. Fortunately the picture had been taken from the same angle—at least pretty close—to the view they now had of the freighter moored to Pier 5. McCarter looked at the picture, glanced at the freighter ahead, looked back at the PDA once more and then nodded with a grunt.

"No doubt about it, I have confirmed the target. We're here in Walvis Bay parked not fifty yards from that ship. I need to know from Hal what he wants us to do."

"Understood," Kurtzman said. "Wait and I'll get him on the horn."

"Weapons check now," McCarter told his team as he waited for Brognola.

Less than a minute passed before the Stony Man chief's voice sounded in McCarter's ears. "David, is everything okay? Report your status."

"We're five-by-five," McCarter said. "We've just confirmed the freighter we were looking for is here. It's a Norwegian ship apparently, and according to the information Aaron has, it's now scheduled to depart later this morning for the States."

"I understand the situation," Brognola said. "And I want to make sure that you understand that ship is not to leave port with the terrorists or their cargo under any circumstances. I am authorizing you here and now to do whatever is necessary to protect our borders, and we have made it quite clear to the Namibian government our intent of the same."

"You're telling me to do whatever I have to do."

"That's what I'm telling you."

It wasn't often that Brognola and McCarter had an exchange like this, but the situation was serious and things were obviously spiraling out of control for Able Team. That's where Stony Man needed to put its primary focus at the moment and David McCarter knew it. If Phoenix Force could complete this last part of its mission to neutralize the threat of nuclear materials falling in the hands of the terrorists, the prototype submarines became a secondary consideration. And Brognola was right: there was no way that ship could leave port.

"We're going to have one difficulty," McCarter said.

"What's that?" Brognola asked.

"Well, I think it's safe to assume that there are probably nonterrorist members on board that freighter. That's going to make it hard as hell to identify the bad guys."

For a long moment Brognola didn't say anything and McCarter began to wonder if they had been disconnected. "You and your bunch there are creative. You'll think of something."

McCarter couldn't repress a smile. "Oh, believe me, I already have."

THE CAPTAIN of the *Lady of Stavanger* had a name McCarter couldn't even pronounce, but his English was good enough for him to understand the situation.

"You want me to do what, sir?"

"I want you to evacuate your crew," McCarter said again. "I don't know how many ways to say it."

"And you think I should do this because there's a potential terrorist threat to my ship?"

"We don't *think* there's a terrorist threat, Captain," Encizo said. "We *know* there is."

"I don't think you grasp the situation here," McCarter said. "There is a terrorist group with a particularly nasty habit of killing whoever gets in their way, and they're not too selective about who falls into that category."

"Gentlemen, I can appreciate your concern," the captain said. "But this boat is scheduled to depart for the United States in under ninety minutes. You can't ask me to now evacuate my men."

"Captain, I imagine that right now you're presently operating with a skeleton crew as most of your men are still ashore and haven't checked in yet," Encizo said.

"Yes, but—"

"How many men are we talking about exactly?"

The captain stopped to consider the question. It didn't look as if he wanted to part with the information so easily, but the men of Phoenix Force knew he wasn't faced with many options. If he'd wanted to, the captain could have ordered all five of them off his ship in a moment, leaving the warriors with no choice but to employ more direct methods of persuasion. McCarter didn't want it to come to that, but they were running out of time.

"Maybe fifty men," the captain finally replied.

"Fifty men," McCarter said with disbelief. "That's it? You're worried about evacuating fifty men?"

"That may not seem like any big deal to you, sir," the captain huffed. "But fifty men is pretty important to keeping a ship this size running smoothly."

"Captain, let me put this to you another way," Calvin James interjected. "If you *don't* evacuate this vessel immediately, you not only risk exposing yourselves to the toxic effects of uranium poisoning, but your chances of reaching U.S. shores in one piece are pretty unlikely."

"What makes you say so?"

"Because the people we work for have a pretty close line with Washington," McCarter said. "And if the President believes that this ship may pose a threat to the American people, they will order the U.S. armed forces to blow it out of the water before you get within ten miles of Charleston."

A mix of shock and horror spread across the captain's face. He looked into the eyes of all five men, searched for the smallest hint of deception, but all he got for his trouble was a quintet of stony masks. McCarter was beginning to feel exasperated with the obstinate captain. He could empathize, sure, when five men suddenly show up on his doorstep, request permission to come aboard and then rip the carpet out from under him by suggesting he order all hands to abandon ship.

"Let's suppose I agree to this absurd request of yours, and you subsequently discover the entire thing is unfounded. Will you permit me and my men to leave?"

"Even if it isn't bogus, we'll let you shove off," James said. "All we want to do is make sure that when these terrorists come aboard and try to seize your ship, we're the only ones here waiting for them."

After a long time the captain finally acquiesced. "Very well, gentlemen. I will order my men to abandon ship. But I am staying aboard. And that is *not* negotiable."

"I think we can live with that," David McCarter said.

WHEN THE DOZEN IUA terrorists stole aboard the freighter posing as contracted hands, four of them carrying a large aluminum box on poles, the captain went out to meet them.

He insisted on doing his part to help protect the ship.

At first, McCarter had argued the point with him but eventually he realized that if he wanted the captain's cooperation he would have to demonstrate a little bit of his own. McCarter wasn't used to having someone else call the shots, but the situation was dire and he knew it would be next to impossible to eliminate the terrorist threat without the captain's full cooperation. So McCarter allowed the captain to play the role for which it seemed he had been destined.

The terrorists bought the ploy hook, line and sinker.

The terrorists proved easy pickings. When Manning took the first two carrying a cargo crate filled with U-92 ore, the Canadian sat on a perch thirty yards above the terrorist group, his MP-5 held at the ready with a sound suppressor attached. The reports from the weapon were negligible in the open sea air. He was so far above their heads and obscured by the darkness that it was impossible for the terrorists to pinpoint his location.

The first one to fall was positioned at the front right of the crate, and when the 9 mm Parabellum from Manning's MP-5 struck the terrorist in the chest, he dropped to one knee and upset the load. This unbalanced the remaining terrorists, and in that moment of confusion, the fact one of their men had been shot unbeknownst to them, Manning took the other man in front with a double tap to the chest. The impact flung the terrorist backward into the man behind him, who had been holding on to the crate from the rear. The two men tumbled together, their limbs becoming entangled, and both of them ended up on the deck of the ship.

The remaining terrorists now realized that something was terribly wrong, and they turned and tried to leave the ship. McCarter had expected this as being one of the possible reactions, and had positioned Enzizo and

Hawkins in such a way that the terrorists who retreated would step into the cross fire. The two Phoenix Force warriors opened up simultaneously with their MP-5s, laying down a hailstorm of autofire that generated complete pandemonium. A number of the terrorists tried to find cover and only succeeded in running into one another.

Hawkins got one of the men with a half dozen rounds that penetrated the rib cage, breaking bone and cartilage before passing into the lungs and turning them to jelly. A second terrorist slammed into a large metal box protruding from the deck and as his body bounced off, he staggered back into the line of fire. Hawkins finished the kill with a 3-round burst to the terrorist's head.

Three more terrorists who tried to escape Hawkins's marksmanship only found the assurance of death at the hands of Rafael Encizo. Countless missions and the combat experience of several lifetimes had forged the Cuban into a proficient warrior and single-minded weapon of war. The first terrorist took a 3-round burst in the kidneys that drilled into him with such force it blew a decent part of his liver and appendix onto the gleaming deck. The terrorist slammed face-first into the hard, polished wood that muffled his scream of death. The other two terrorists suffered similar fates when Encizo swept them with a continuous stream of 9 mm Parabellums. One folded up like an accordion and settled to the deck in a heap while the other was driven backward by the impact and flipped over the safety railing. Encizo was already tracking for additional enemy terrorists before his last target's body hit the pier below, bounced twice and rolled into the dark water where the fingers of the Atlantic received him into his final resting place.

A couple of the terrorists bounded down the ramp and tried to escape the assault, but Calvin James had that area well covered. Positioned behind a massive crate on the pier, James raised the MP-5 to his cheek, locked the butt against his shoulder and squeezed off one controlled burst after another. The two terrorists danced under the onslaught as James razed them with a merciless onslaught of slugs. One terrorist finally dropped out of range and tumbled down the gangplank while the other staggered like a drunken bum until he eventually collapsed and rolled off the side of the gangplank. The man's body smacked the edge of the pier before dropping out of sight with a splash.

The remaining terrorists realized that if they stood any chance of escaping death they would have to make a stand. A couple managed to bring an assortment of submachine guns into the fray, but in the confusion and noise—their senses polarized by the relentless firepower being directed at them—they didn't prove particularly effective against the Phoenix Force team well entrenched in their current positions.

When one of the terrorists managed to get within Encizo's A.O., Gary Manning dispatched him with the steady stream of rounds that cut through the spine from the base of his neck to the center of his back. The impact slammed him to the deck, and his submachine gun skittered from his fingers and traversed an awkward path across the slippery surface. It came to rest next to the elbow of another terrorist who had taken cover behind a stack of wooden crates stevedores had been in the process of loading when Phoenix Force pulled the plug.

The terrorist thought he saw an advantage, grabbed the second weapon and jumped to his feet. He began to sweep the muzzle in every direction, firing at anything that moved as he raced toward the gangplank. It was McCarter, who had taken a prone position across the taut canvas of a lifeboat, coupled with James's coverage of the gangplank, the terrorist hadn't accounted for. McCarter and James opened up simultaneously, and their unerring accuracy shot the terrorist's legs out from under him at the same time as a few rounds blew off the top of his head. The terrorist performed a rather animated dance before dropping to the deck.

The last terrorist decided to make a break for the bridge, but much to his chagrin, the captain was waiting for him with a Makarov pistol clutched in his fist. The terrorist looked surprised, but the captain wiped his expression clean with a couple of well-placed shots to the head. Under the circumstances, McCarter considered the near summary execution a bit of poetic justice.

CHAPTER TWENTY-TWO

By the time Able Team, Shanahan and Davis arrived at the hospital, the scene was nothing short of pure chaos.

Uniformed and plainclothes officers from Charleston were represented, along with county officials, a SWAT unit and hostage crisis negotiation team. Additionally, a huge number of staff had been evacuated in adjoining areas, and patients in various modes of dress were either standing, seated at benches or slumped in wheelchairs. The medical center wasn't exactly the largest in Charleston but it still boasted about two hundred beds and offered a variety of critical care services that included an ICU and an array of laboratory services.

Able Team tried to remain inconspicuous while Shanahan went to get the lowdown from the incident commander. He returned about ten minutes later, his face flushed with excitement and his hands shaking. Lyons recognized the signs of postcombat jitters so he didn't let it bother him too much. Neither Shanahan nor Davis struck him as the type to crack up in the middle of the shit.

"What's the story?" Blancanales asked.

"Details are sketchy," Shanahan said, "but apparently some nurse caught a guy trying to kill Hadariik in his sleep. She tried to stop him and he cut her throat. An orderly happened to be walking by and they got into a scuffle. The orderly managed to wrestle a knife or something away from him, but the assassin is still somewhere loose inside the building. From what I hear, they're about to send in a strike team."

"Who's in charge?" Lyons asked.

"They've put a guy with our office in charge of the scene, assisted by the city's hostage negotiation unit, but the SWAT commander is handling the tactical side."

"You know him?"

Shanahan nodded. "Yeah, guy by the name of Keane. I've interacted with him a few times in joint training exercises. Seems decent enough."

"Any chance he'd let us take a crack at this?" Schwarz asked.

"Based on what I've seen, I don't think the guy would turn down any help at this point in the game."

"Let's go chat with him," Lyons said. He turned to Blancanales and Schwarz and jerked his thumb at the prisoner handcuffed inside the SUV. "You two stay with chuckles here. We'll be back in a minute."

Lyons gestured for Shanahan to lead the way and within a minute they were standing quietly near Keane, waiting for him to finish a briefing by his second-in-command. When the two men had concluded, Shanahan got Keane's attention and then introduced Lyons. It took Lyons only a moment to size up this one. Keane was tall and appeared to be in pretty good shape. He had thinning hair with blue-gray eyes that seemed to look past Lyons rather than at him.

"You got a lot on your plate here, Keane, so I'll come

to the point," Lyons said. "The man you're after is no ordinary nut job."

"That right?" Keane said.

"That's right. In fact, I'm guessing he was sent here for the specific purpose of killing the FBI's prisoner, Manan Hadariik."

"And what makes you think that?"

"For one, I know a whole lot about this situation you probably don't simply because I have the security clearance that makes me privy to it," Lyons replied. "Second, Hadariik was arrested by the FBI earlier this morning in connection with the shootings that took place near the waterfront last night. Those shootings involved individuals who were in the country illegally and whose entry can be traced back to a country known to support enemies of the United States."

"I heard about that," Keane said with a nod, some of his defensiveness melting away. "Word on the wire was there might be some kind of terrorist connection there."

"I can't confirm or deny that with you." Lyons made a show of looking around, then leaned in and lowered his voice. "What I can tell you is that the situation has reached a boiling point and what we're seeing happen here and now could very well be a matter of national security."

"So what do you want out of me, Irons?"

Lyons didn't want to feed Keane a bunch of malarkey. Neither of them could afford it at the moment. "The man who was sent to kill Hadariik is probably a professional. That means as long as Hadariik's alive, that guy is going to keep on trying until one of them is dead. I don't imagine you have much experience dealing with professional terrorist assassins."

"Not really."

Lyons said, "Well, no offense, then, but my partners and I do. I know you have protocols and people to answer to, but I'm asking for a little professional courtesy on this one. Give us a chance to go inside and neutralize the situation before it gets out of hand. You can take the credit and the notoriety. When the job's done, we'll just fade away as if we were never here."

Keane looked Lyons in the eye. He could tell the SWAT officer was sizing him up, looking for some hint of deception. Lyons didn't let it get to him. Keane would be the one to take the credit, sure, but he would also take the heat if anything went wrong. After all, he had no reason to trust Lyons or to let him into the game.

"Listen, Keane, I know you could just as easily tell me to go pound sand and send in a squad of your own hard-chargers. And maybe they'd come out of this smelling good, maybe they wouldn't. But I can tell you one thing for sure, and that is that a number of very decent law-enforcement personnel have gone up against these guys in the past forty-eight hours and the only thing it bought them was a one-way trip to the coroner's freezer. I don't want to see any more dead cops today. It's just not worth it."

Keane looked at Shanahan. "You and I have known each other for a while, Tom. I think we can be straight with each other. What's your take?"

"I haven't worked with Irons and his people here very long, Nick. But I can tell you that he's never given me a reason to mistrust him, and so far everything he's told me about this situation has turned out to be one hundred percent certifiable. I don't want to see any more dead cops, either. I say give him a shot. I've seen him and his friends in action, and they are definitely badasses of the highest order."

Keane cracked a smile at that and extended his hand to Lyons. "All right, I don't have any problem stepping back and giving you a try. What do you need?"

"First off, let's get the cameras and gapers out of here. I'd prefer if our mugs weren't splashed all over the news channels tonight."

"Done. Anything else?"

Lyons shook his head. "We'll do the rest."

Shanahan and Lyons returned to where Schwarz and Blancanales were waiting expectantly. Buddy Davis had finally joined the crew after wrapping up the more pressing details with the Charleston police detectives who'd arrived at the terrorist house in the historical district. Beads of sweat clung to the massive black man's forehead and shimmered in the streetlights. The sun had long disappeared and succumbed to evening.

Blancanales observed the police as they began to disperse the wall of news media lining the barricades placed along the perimeter of the sidewalk where it met the parking lot. "What's the plan?"

"Keane's willing to lay low, give us a chance to squash this thing before it gets out of hand."

Schwarz frowned. "I'd already say we're a little late for that."

"In any case," Lyons said, not missing a beat, "it sounds like the IUA sent a pro to shut Hadariik up once and for all."

"If they keep taking such risks and exposing themselves like this," Blancanales said, "there's a better than offside chance Hadariik knows a lot more than he's let on."

"Maybe if we save his neck he'll be grateful enough to tell us the location of the construction facility," Schwarz ventured.

Lyons's expression went deadpan. "Not likely."

"What's this construction facility you guys keep talking about?"

As Able Team stripped the equipment harnesses from their bodies and loaded up on pistol ammunition, Blancanales explained, "We got some intelligence in Washington that the terrorists had built some kind of underwater facility where they could construct these prototype submarines. We believe they may be planning to use those submarines to strike at select targets along the eastern coastline."

"Only problem is, all of the terrorists we've interrogated so far have never been to this base," Schwarz offered.

"At least that's what they claim," Blancanales continued. "So we've been pulling our hair out for the past forty-eight hours trying to determine where this place might be located and how they could have built it without somebody raising suspicions."

Shanahan looked away, focusing at some indistinct spot on the pavement in front of him, his eyebrows scrunched together in thought. The look on his face was so intense that all three men of Able Team stopped to ponder his odd reaction. The FBI agent finally looked over at Davis and something occurred between them, some look that implied their thoughts were traversing a linear path and in a moment of realization had converged on each other.

"You think…" Shanahan began hesitantly.

Buddy Davis nodded slowly. "It's possible."

"What?" Lyons said. "What's possible?"

"It's a place the locals refer to as Coldwater Cove. The U.S. Navy purchased it from South Carolina about twelve or thirteen years ago. They were going to use it as a tactical location for whatever reasons—nobody really knew for sure since the whole thing was classified. But then there were all of those defense budget cuts and the government abandoned it. The area was restricted to all but high-ranking fuzzbudgets for a very long time, and I believe the rights are supposed to revert back to the state of South Carolina in another year or two."

"How come we're just hearing about this now?" Schwarz asked Blancanales and Lyons.

Lyons shrugged. "Beats me. Maybe nobody thought about it one way or another."

"Any idea how far they got on the construction?" Blancanales asked Shanahan.

"Not really. Like I said, nobody really knew anything about it. The Navy kept it all hush-hush and the like. Every agent gets briefed about it when they come to work for our field office, but since it was allegedly abandoned and it's apparently inconvenient to get to, the place has pretty much gone unnoticed."

"Faded from memory, if you please," Buddy Davis said.

"Out of sight out of mind, huh?" Blancanales said with a knowing look at Lyons. "I'd say just as soon as we settle the score here, we need to get you-know-who working the angles on that."

"Yeah," Carl Lyons said.

THE PAST FORTY-EIGHT hours had been long ones for Jack Grimaldi, so the Stony Man pilot was glad to see the SUV drive on to the tarmac of the private airfield and the men of Phoenix Force emerge.

Grimaldi did the first thing he always did; he counted faces and noted that the team looked tired and haggard. Grimaldi had heard from Price that Calvin James had taken a nasty graze from a terrorist bullet but the lanky soldier didn't appear any worse for the wear. His broad, toothy smile lacked none of the warmth for which it was known. All of the men seemed quite glad to see Grimaldi, actually, which didn't come as much of a surprise to him.

Thomas Jackson Hawkins was the first to make his way up the steps and into the cabin of the specially equipped Gulfstream C-21 and he pumped Grimaldi's hand warmly.

"I'd probably remark on what the cat dragged in, but then that would be insulting to the cat," the pilot said.

Hawkins burst into laughter. "Good to see you too, Ace."

Grimaldi nodded and stepped aside to let the Phoenix Force warrior pass. He greeted each of them with a similar wit, and tossed a formal salute when McCarter—who was last to board the aircraft—asked permission to come aboard in a tired but good-natured tone.

"How goes the war, big guy?" Grimaldi asked.

"I'll let you know when I've had some sleep." He clapped the pilot on the shoulder and said, "Get us the hell out of here, Jack. We've seen all of this place we want to for a good long while."

"Take a load off and relax," Grimaldi said with a grin. "We'll be airborne in ten mikes."

McCarter sighed in relief, the pilot's statement music to his ears, and true to Grimaldi's words they were homeward-bound before he'd barely settled into his seat. By the time they had climbed to a cruising altitude, McCarter noted that every one of his men was out cold. Hawkins was so tired he was snoring, albeit quietly, and James had lowered one of the retracting beds so he could rest his back.

McCarter wanted to sleep, felt as if he shut his eyes

he'd nap for a week straight, but when he attempted it, his mind raced through a million and one things and grew restless. It wasn't the first time something like that had happened, although it didn't occur often. This had been a demanding mission to lead and the IUA had proved themselves a formidable enemy. Still, McCarter was proud of every man on his team. They had faced enormous odds and overcome by being adaptable. The Briton had always known he served with the finest fighting force the world had ever known, and the events of the past forty-eight hours proved it beyond any doubt.

Since he couldn't sleep, McCarter studied the data recently piped to the computer systems aboard the Stony Man airborne command center. He brought himself up to speed on all of the intelligence Able Team had gathered in the past thirty-six hours and then studied the tactical schematics of the Fast-Attack Covert Operations Submarine. The brainchild of the late Dr. Philip Stout—a decorated veteran of the Navy in Korea and Vietnam and expert in naval warfare operations—the FACOS boasted an impressive array of features never conceived for an underwater craft before. At least, not quite like this.

The concept of implementing a tactical first-strike contingency with nuclear capabilities in an underwater vehicle of that size and complement would have been laughed at as ridiculous in many scientific circles. And according to the military community's response, Stout had been viewed by many of his predecessors and contemporaries as unorthodox. But a few muckety-mucks in the U.S. Navy had seen the genius of the idea and decided to fund the project.

And damn if Stout hadn't pulled it off.

Obviously members of the IUA had seen the brilliance of Stout's ideas and decided to twist them to suit more sinister purposes. Only the quick intervention of Phoenix Force had managed to avert nothing short of a full-blown radiation emergency, and now Able Team was going to need their help finding and destroying the facility before whoever was in charge of the IUA terrorists could unleash the weapons on an unsuspecting America. Not that America wasn't at least a little more awake after all the recent noise Lyons and friends had been making along the East Coast.

The thought of it brought a smile to McCarter's lips.

The Phoenix Force leader had entertained the idea of sending his men back to the Farm for a well-deserved rest, especially in light of the fact they had been coming off a two-week-long mission in Italy when Stony Man sent them to Namibia, but he couldn't leave his friends to deal with this on their own. No matter how tired they were, no matter how much they just wanted to relax and let this be somebody else's problem, McCarter knew they had a responsibility to lend a hand. He decided to contact Harold Brognola and tell him as much.

"How's your team?" Brognola asked.

McCarter turned to look at the sleeping bunch before he replied, "Getting some rest. Our trip will take quite a bit of time, so they'll be ready to go once we've slept and had some decent chow. If you can call MREs decent."

"We'll make sure to kill the fatted calf, as it were, on your return to the Farm." Brognola paused for a time, and McCarter waited because he sensed the man had something important to say. Finally, Brognola continued, "David, I know that was a pretty terrible task you had to carry out there at the mines. I'm sorry it had to be that way."

McCarter considered whether to respond and finally decided to be candid with Brognola. The two had been friends too many years to stand on ceremony. "It was as tough for you to ask us as it was for us to do it, Hal. You don't owe me any apologies and I'm pretty sure I can speak for the rest when I say that."

Brognola sighed. "Thanks for letting me off the hook."

"Forget it. So do we have a plan?"

"Able Team's still in Charleston and right now I've just been informed they have some serious trouble. One of the terrorists they captured last night, a man by the name of Manan Hadariik, apparently possesses key knowledge to the exact location of the IUA's mysterious construction facility. Able Team recently allied themselves with a couple of FBI agents who are helping them tread the waters of Charleston, literally and figuratively. We haven't heard from them since they last checked a few hours ago telling us they were going to investigate another potential lead, but we just caught a snippet of a news segment that some trouble's brewing at the hospital where Hadariik is staying."

"What sort of trouble?"

"That's unknown at this time. We haven't been able to reach any of the team. All we know is they're alive, and that's the best we can get at the moment. I'm sure they'll check in soon."

"I have to tell you, Hal, it sounds like the situation's quickly going out of control there."

"I wish I could disagree with you, but I'm afraid you're right. It's damn decent of you to offer to get involved in this."

"This is *our* mission," McCarter said. "And it's not over until it's over. We owe the IUA quite a bit for all the trouble they've stirred up, and I'm ready and willing to repay them."

"I understand," Brognola replied. "But in the spirit of being a voice of reason, just make sure you keep this about the mission and not make it personal. I know the death of Matombo wore pretty hard on you."

"Oh, we've given back plenty to Matombo. Anything we do from here out will be for the sheer fun of it."

"That's the spirit. I'll be in touch as soon as I know something about Able Team. You got an ETA?"

"I'm not exactly sure, but I can patch you up to Grimaldi. He'll probably be able to give it to you down to the second."

"You'll be going straight to Charleston, I assume."

"Other than one fuel stop, yes. I already talked to Grimaldi and he's on board with the plan."

"If the IUA manages to get those subs deployed before Able Team can find the underwater facility, it'll be solely up to you guys to neutralize them. I want you to understand in no uncertain terms that's the priority, David. I appreciate you wanting to help Able Team, but they have additional support on the ground at present. And before you get up your ire in protest, you should know that came straight from Carl."

McCarter nodded. "That sounds like him. Big, blond, bullheaded Lyons."

"That it does."

"We'll stay on mission until either the submarines are destroyed or we get the all clear from you. In either case, we're ready whenever you need us."

"Okay then…until we talk again. Take care and get some rest, McCarter. That's an order."

McCarter acknowledged the instruction before disconnecting the call. McCarter closed his eyes but he didn't really sleep. In the back of his mind he was running through the worst-case scenarios. A U.S. eastern coastline in ashes and millions of dead Americans who had been incinerated by nuclear warheads. Even a twenty-kiloton bomb would be devastating, particularly if there was more than one delivered to a single target.

Maybe it wouldn't happen; maybe they had managed to stop the terrorists from delivering the U-92 ore. And maybe, just maybe, there was still a chance Able Team could find the subs and destroy them before the IUA could hatch their plot against America. Too many maybes made for a poor bedfellow, and although he tried his hardest McCarter still couldn't sleep. And he knew why. He would not rest until the enemy had been utterly destroyed. The scorched-earth policy against America's enemies had begun.

And McCarter wouldn't relent until the policy was implemented in full.

CHAPTER TWENTY-THREE

Able Team went in hard and fast.

To give them every tactical advantage, Keane had the utility company cut the power to every nonessential area of the medical facility. Most of the critical patients were still inside but they were in secured areas under the protection of armed security officers fortified by uniformed police. Keane had wanted to send in detectives, as well, but Lyons insisted they keep the plainclothes officers out of it. They would have a hard enough time tracking down the assassin sent to terminate Hadariik and they didn't want to add any unnecessary complications. This was going to be a search-and-destroy mission, and the Able Team warriors didn't want to introduce variables they couldn't control. At least men in uniform were readily identifiable, unless the assassin was clever enough to steal one from a guard or cop and walk out under everyone's noses.

Lyons didn't think the guy was that smart.

Once they were inside and had cleared the foyer, the trio gathered near a stairwell to discuss their options.

"Okay, we have three floors that need to be searched," Lyons said. "Each of us will take one."

"And when we find him?" Blancanales asked.

"Don't engage or compromise your position unless it's absolutely necessary," Lyons replied. "You spot him, do what you can to keep him contained and call for reinforcements. I'm not looking to take this guy alive. He doesn't get any different consideration than any other hostile would."

"You're saying terminate."

Lyons nodded. "With extreme prejudice."

Without another word, the three men broke and headed for their assignments. Lyons took the topmost floor, Blancanales manned the second floor and Schwarz headed back toward the front lobby, where he would search the offices and labs on the main floor. The medical center offered pretty advanced services but it wasn't as large as most hospitals. It wouldn't take long to search the place.

It didn't.

Lyons had cleared about half of the rooms on the third floor when he spotted the IUA assassin. He might have missed him on the initial sweep, as the man was hiding in an office behind the nurses' station, had he not panicked and started shooting. Lyons ducked into a room before several rounds burned the air where he'd been standing a heartbeat before. He had to check the ingrained reaction to immediately return fire.

Lyons leaned around the corner and triggered a round from his Colt Python .357 Magnum, but he made sure the shot went well above the assassin's head. He only needed to make the show look good. The assassin responded with return fire and Lyons retreated into the room.

He keyed up his radio. "Heads up, boys. I've made

contact, third floor. I'm going to try pushing him toward the stairwell."

The other two Able Team warriors signaled their acknowledgment. The plan was to corner the assassin in a way that would remove risks to any bystanders. As long as the gunner was allowed to roam freely in populated areas, innocent lives were at risk. Most areas were under guard, but there hadn't been time or a practical way to account for every patient and every employee. There were also visitors, temporary staff and others with business in the medical center such as equipment technicians, contractors and volunteers.

As Lyons hoped, the assassin left his hiding place and headed toward the stairwell. Perfect. This would definitely lessen the risks to bystanders. Lyons broke cover and gave chase as soon as he heard the stairwell door open. When he reached the door, Lyons paused with pistol held at the ready. There was a small possibility the assassin would be lying in wait for him for the purpose of drawing him into a sucker play. Lyons didn't feel like getting his head blown off at this critical juncture; his team and his country needed him and it wouldn't do getting killed now.

Lyons edged the door open and poked his head through it, pistol leading. No shots rang out and he didn't see any movement. In fact, that bothered Lyons more than the sound of escape—it was *too* quiet. And a half second later, the warrior knew why. Lyons felt the movement of air behind him a moment before the arm snaked around his throat, and it was the only thing that saved him. If his attacker had actually managed to pull off his ruse, he would've been able to get Lyons into a choke hold that would have been difficult, if not completely impossible, to evade.

In this case, Lyons turned his head to the side so that the meaty part of the assassin's forearm lodged against the muscles in his neck rather than the soft, vulnerable area of his windpipe and esophagus. Lyons still felt a considerable amount of pain given the number of nerves in his neck, but at least he could breathe. And if he could breathe, he could fight. The only bit of misfortune, though, was that the door slammed on his wrist and ejected the pistol from his hand with enough force Lyons knew it had probably fractured his right wrist.

Lyons reached up and around and tried to grab the man's ear or the side of his neck—any vulnerable spot that might gain him the advantage—but the assassin pulled his head clear of Lyons's reach. Lyons twisted his right hip in the same direction he had turned his head, thereby putting his opponent's choke hold on shaky ground. He took a deep breath and then jumped into the air and brought all of his weight down on the man's instep. The assassin released his hold and howled, dancing backward with the sudden pain.

Lyons was on the man before he had a chance to recover. He delivered a reverse punch that connected with the assassin's jaw and sent him reeling into an equipment cart against the hallway wall, probably abandoned there during the evacuation. The assassin quickly recovered and as Lyons moved in the man produced a knife from a concealed sheath.

Lyons danced out of the way as the guy swung the knife, but it didn't take much effort since the sloppiness of the attack made it obvious to Lyons the assassin had not been well trained with bladed weapons. The man attempted another attack, this one a sweeping back slash toward Lyons's midsection, and Lyons saw his opening. As soon as he'd evaded the blade that whistled past his stomach, Lyons checked the man's forearm while simultaneously snaking a foot out, catching the assassin at a vulnerable point on the knee. Lyons heard the crackle of tearing cartilage and tendons, like the kind heard sometimes when tearing a turkey leg away from the body.

The man let out a scream and faltered, but before Lyons could deliver another blow he swung the knife again, this time nicking Lyons's shoulder. The guy then tried for an overhand smash but Lyons brought up his left forearm and executed a smashing block. He'd forgotten the previous injury from the door, and white-hot needles of pain lanced up and down his arm like a thousand fire ants. It hurt like hell, but Lyons figured better pain in his wrist than a blade buried in his chest.

The assassin took advantage of the moment to execute a sweep that caught Lyons off guard and dropped him onto the linoleum. The warrior immediately brought up his forearms as the assassin literally fell on him and tried to drop the blade into his chest. The knee injury had forced his attacker to hold his legs in an awkward position, and Lyons saw the vulnerability for what it was. He fired a knee into the man's groin, and the assassin let out another yelp as the breath seemed forced from his lungs. Lyons then slapped his hands across the guy's ears, assaulting his eardrums. The blow disoriented him for a moment, and Lyons used that time to wriggle to a point where his legs were now where his upper body had been.

The assassin realized his mistake just a millisecond before Lyons lashed out with a snap kick. The steel toe of his boot caught the assassin under the point of the chin, snapping his teeth together with enough force to crack them. He then delivered a heel kick with enough force to fracture the assassin's jaw. Lyons's last kick landed on the man's exposed solar plexus, knocking the wind out of him and cracking the lower part of the sternum.

A shot rang out.

The man stiffened, his eyes going wide with shock, before he toppled onto Lyons's legs, twitched several times and then went still. When he fell forward, Lyons was able to see the source of the gunshot. Rosario Blancanales knelt at the far end of the hallway, his SIG P-229 pistol held straight and steady, muzzle smoking. Slowly he climbed to his feet and jogged over to where Lyons still lay on the ground disentangling his feet from the lifeless body of the assassin. Blancanales helped Lyons to his feet.

"What are you doing here?" Lyons asked.

Blancanales nodded. "Glad to see you, too."

"How did you know?"

"When you radioed to say he was coming our way, I was near the stairwell so I cracked the door and waited. I didn't hear anything for a while, and when he didn't come down I radioed but you didn't reply. I knew something was wrong at that point, figured I'd better check it out. That's when I got to the stairwell landing on the third floor and found this."

He handed Lyons the .357 Magnum.

"Well," Lyons said, holstering the Python and then clamping a hand on his friend's shoulder, "I'm glad you did. But next time, follow orders and hold position."

"It's a good thing I didn't," Blancanales said with a nod at the deceased terrorist. "Otherwise you might have been his next victim."

"I was holding my own."

"Yeah, sure." Blancanales noticed Lyons cradling his wrist. "Come on, let's go tell Keane that we're clear. And then we can get a doctor to check out that wrist."

As soon as Price and Brognola received an update on Able Team's status, the pair went to work on the new intelligence.

The information from their FBI liaison of the Coldwater Cove facility proved extremely useful to Kurtzman and his team, and before long they were gathered in the operations center and looking at an overlay map with blueprints and other information regarding the facility. The raw data Kurtzman extracted from Department of Defense computers would provide the Stony Man field units with the tactical advantage they needed to launch a preemptive strike against the facility.

Brognola wished they could have had the information sooner, but he knew it wouldn't do any good to focus on the lack of information. Somehow they should have flagged it earlier, but nobody would have necessarily connected the dots. With time, a lot of projects like the underwater construction facility would have faded from memory. Who would have thought that terrorists would use such a place? In fact, who would have thought the IUA would know anything about it?

"In addition to the information we gleaned on the facility," Price said, following Kurtzman's briefing of the intelligence, "we also managed to run down the shortlist of potential suspects who might be able to pull off something like this. We cross-referenced that with subjects who might have also been able to acquire the resources to mount such an extensive operation. Only one name came back."

Kurtzman stabbed a key and the lights dimmed. The face of an older man, rather handsome with a trimmed beard and dark hair, appeared on the massive LCD panel mounted to the wall. "Meet Latif al-Din. Forty-two years old, native born and raised in Algiers. Al-Din was college educated in, of all places, Afghanistan. He was a sworn member of the Taliban regime and later was linked directly to al Qaeda through his affiliation with a number of Islamic extremist groups. Until 2006."

"What happened then?" Brognola asked.

"Nothing."

"Nothing?"

"Aaron's right," Price said. "In 2006 al-Din simply dropped off the map. His family was killed shortly after the start of the Iraq war and it was assumed that he perished along with them. The only problem with that theory is that CIA's assets inside the country at the time, who were keeping an eye on him, were never able to actually *confirm* that. Additionally, we found out he was ousted from al Qaeda but nobody seemed to know when or why. We had no details whatsoever and so, again, CIA analysts figured it was because he'd been killed."

"Then in 2007 there were rumors floating around he was actually still alive and operating underground somewhere," Kurtzman said. "Coincidentally, that's about two years after Stout began the FACOS project."

"Except you no longer think it was coincidence," Brognola said.

"That's correct," Price said. "We wanted to test out all possibilities that he had somehow managed to get inside the country. However, there were significant safeguards in place and the no-fly lists were fairly comprehensive at that point. That meant if he was in the United States, he either managed to sneak over a border or he came in disguised."

"We think it was the latter," Kurtzman said. He tapped a key and another face appeared on the screen, this of a man about al-Din's age with blond hair and a mustache. The guy was obviously on a morgue table, as he had no shirt on, his eyes were closed and there were suture lines visible on his chest.

Price said, "This is Hans Johann Vanderwine, a businessman and import broker with a Dutch trading company. Vanderwine was placed on Interpol's watch list in connection with the murder of his wife and children, and in 2007 he was spotted having entered the United States on what he called a business trip. Since he'd been in the country many times before, customs didn't give him a second look."

"How does he play in all of this?" Brognola asked.

"Vanderwine was apparently well known in the import and trading circles," Price answered. "So the fact he had committed such a heinous crime and then entered the U.S. where he could easily be caught didn't seem very likely. In addition to the fact we have extradition treaties with Holland, so it wouldn't have made much sense for him to come here."

Kurtzman nodded his agreement. "The most telling thing about it, though, Hal, is that records show Vanderwine had already exited the country just a week earlier. So it doesn't make any sense that he would return to Holland, kill his family for no apparent motive, leave a massive trail and then enter the U.S. once more just a few days later."

"How did we miss this?" Brognola asked.

"How do we miss anything like this?" Price said. "Plain sloppiness."

"So how did you connect him with al-Din?"

"Well," Kurtzman explained, "that was a little trickier but we managed to pull footage from when he entered the country at LAX. Fortunately, all footage of customs is kept and vaulted for ten years, which has been made much easier now that we have digital technology. We pulled the footage and ran facial-recognition software."

"It didn't match up with his previous entry," Price added. "So we knew it couldn't have been Vanderwine. But since there are no decent photographs to compare with al-Din, we weren't sure who it was.

"After Vanderwine was captured by police, he maintained his innocence during questioning. We pulled the footage of his interrogation and had our specialists review it. They believe he was telling the truth."

"How did he end up dead?"

"The details on that are sketchy because it happened after he was extradited back to Holland," Price replied. "Basically, he died while awaiting trial. Found hung in his cell. It was ruled suicide, but we suspect it probably wasn't, although he was being treated by a clinical psychiatrist for depression, a condition that surfaced after he was told about his wife and children being dead."

"Doesn't make much sense."

"It didn't to us, either, and we considered it extremely odd that all of this happened to occur not too long after al-Din dropped off the face of the planet. Finally, we were able to get our hooks into a retired agent who worked undercover and apparently knew al-Din fairly well. He had solid intelligence al-Din was still alive and remembered some informants saying he'd entered the country at the exact same time as this footage was taken."

"So you think we're actually looking at al-Din in that footage."

"We're convinced. There are just too many parallels we're able to draw to make this mere happenstance," Kurtzman said. "We can't *positively* identify the man in this photograph as al-Din, but we're convinced it's probably him."

"And you think he's behind this why?" Brognola asked. "What's his motivation?"

"Revenge, possibly," Price said. "And maybe it's just because he was on the outs with al Qaeda. Our CIA contact was able to fill in quite a number of details in that regard. He said al-Din was always in disagreement with the leaders on strategy and tactics. This would have given him an opportunity to step out on his own."

"So he recruits his own cell, finds investors and others to back his operations and then penetrates the U.S. with the intent to build the prototype submarines."

"Exactly. But since he has no connections on the outside willing to risk being discovered, he runs around Charleston to recruit local expertise. Now he's either ready or pretty close to implementing these weapons."

Brognola considered the theory and had to admit it seemed sound enough given the facts. "Here's the thing that doesn't make sense. We know he didn't have time or resources to get the nuclear reactors on board. Otherwise he would have no reason to risk exposure by sending a hit team to eliminate the two maritime suppliers who sold him the submarines."

Price nodded. "With you so far."

"We also know that Phoenix Force was successful in their mission to destroy the mines and to neutralize the ship that would have transported the raw ore to the U.S. With no ore, there's no plutonium. With no plutonium, there are no nuclear warheads. What's left?"

"You think we've satisfied the mission?" Kurtzman asked.

Brognola appeared to think about it. "I don't know that I'd say that. But I'm betting we've certainly lessened the time criticality. If this Latif al-Din is behind this, he's bound to hear sooner or later that the U-92 isn't coming. He'll either have to try locating another source or go with what he's got. Either way, I think it buys us a little more time."

"Well, with the information about Coldwater Cove now in our possession," Price said, "we can dispatch Able Team to that location and have them investigate. If al-Din's there, they'll know what to do. And if he's not, you're probably right that at least we bought ourselves a little more time."

"What about Phoenix Force?" Brognola asked. "What's their ETA?"

"I talked to Jack, and Aaron's been tracking them by GPS. At their current speed and including the two fuel stops they'll have to make, we expect they'll be arriving within the next twelve hours."

"That leaves only one question remaining, then," Brognola said.

"What's that?" Kurtzman asked.

"Will it be soon enough?"

It was a question for which they had no answer. All they could do was wait and hope.

CHAPTER TWENTY-FOUR

It took Able Team a little over an hour to wrap up their business with Keane, who then pulled strings with some very important people in Charleston and the grateful staff of the medical center to attend to Lyons's wounds. Fortunately, the X rays revealed only a minor crushing injury, some damage to the soft tissue, which is why it had hurt like a bitch. A wrap in a rigid soft splint did the trick in stabilizing the wrist but it significantly impaired Lyons's mobility to his gun hand.

"Try not to use that limb for at least a few days," the doctor told him as he handed Lyons a prescription bottle of anti-inflammatory pills.

"This won't put me to sleep, will it?"

"No, might increase your appetite. But otherwise it shouldn't affect your metabolism one way or another."

Lyons popped one dry, pocketed the pills and then tossed the doctor a salute and got out of there quick. He still didn't like hospitals, although he was grateful for the treatment and attention he'd gotten. Particularly from the pretty brunette nurse and redheaded X-ray lab technician. Hey, he might have been injured but he was still a red-blooded American guy who could appreciate the same things appreciated by most red-blooded American guys.

When he was back on the street with his friends, Lyons realized it must have been something Blancanales and Schwarz read in his face. "What?"

"Took good care of you, did they?" Schwarz teased.

Lyons wasn't going to give him that kind of ammo. "I'd say the care was adequate."

"Uh-huh," Blancanales said, nudging his friend. "I saw them. If you'd call that merely adequate, you should have had your eyes checked while you were in there."

Shanahan was there, as well, but obviously he hadn't picked up on the reason for the two men ribbing their friend. Oh, what difference did it make anyway? Lyons had learned long ago he couldn't really hide anything from his friends who were so observant it was almost creepy.

Davis had already departed the scene with their prisoner and taken him to the local jail to be held until he could be transferred to the Homeland Security detention facility outside of Washington.

"You talk to the head Fed?" Lyons asked.

"Yeah, and it looks like the information Shanahan here gave us was right on the money," Blancanales said. He nodded toward Schwarz and said, "Why don't you show him?"

Schwarz whipped out the PDA and handed it to Lyons. "Take a look at this."

"Okay," Lyons said as he stared at the grainy image of a blue screen with a series of white lines. "But what am I supposed to be looking at?"

"That there is a blueprint of the Coldwater Cove construction project that once belonged to the special-warfare branch of the U.S. Department of the Navy, my friend," Schwarz said. "They had completed a significant part of the infrastructure before the project got canned. The contractor who did the job never got the go-ahead to disassemble any of the completed frameworks, so allegedly it's all still there."

"Is it enough to act as a dry dock for the IUA?"

"*More* than enough."

"The place was abandoned years ago, just like Shanahan said," Blancanales added. "It is possible that if they managed to get this far with the construction, the IUA could easily use it to manufacture at least several of the FACOS prototypes with room to spare."

"That's good enough for me," Lyons said. He turned to Shanahan. "Now all we need to know is the best way into that place."

Shanahan rubbed his eyes, trying to clear the weariness that had set in. Lyons knew he and Davis had been up all night and all of this day. Add to that the natural fatigue of combat, the continuous rush of adrenaline followed by complete exhaustion, and it wasn't a stretch to see why the guy would be on the edge of collapse at this point. Lyons could understand it because he'd been there, but he had also grown used to these long bouts through missions with little to no sleep.

Shanahan seemed to shake it off and finally said, "There's one way I know of and that's by boat. But like I said before, that area's restricted to any boat traffic by the Navy, and the U.S. Coast Guard patrols the area on a regular basis."

"I'm sure we could get past that restriction easy enough," Blancanales said with a shrug.

"We'll have to if it's our only option," Lyons said. "Any idea where we can secure a boat on short notice?"

Shanahan nodded. "The Bureau maintains a couple. One of them is even equipped with a deck-mounted gun."

"Impressive," Schwarz cooed.

"Yeah, we had one installed with a .50-caliber due to the increased violence by drug-runners. After two agents got killed trying to intercept a major cocaine shipment out of Cuba, the deputy director got authorization to acquire one in surplus from the Coast Guard, with the caveat that we only use it against equipment such as boats and engines."

"We wouldn't use it against personnel unless they gave us a reason," Blancanales said.

"Or they were *wearing* equipment," Lyons added. "How soon do you think you could get it?"

"I'll make the call right away," Shanahan said, whipping out his cell phone. After hitting the speed dial, he said, "But we have a crew that maintains the boat, and they'll have to come along."

Lyons shook his head. "Sorry, Shanahan, but that's no dice. I was pushing the envelope bringing you and Davis into this. We can't compromise our security any more."

"It violates procedure," Shanahan said. "If the boat crew is dispatched, there's no way we're going to get authorization to use their vessel. The crew is specially trained to handle that thing, and there's no way in hell they'll just lend it out to me. I got clout, but I ain't got that much clout."

Lyons took out his own cell phone. "You take care of the boat. I'll take care of the clout."

LATIF AL-DIN COULD NOT believe his ears when the news arrived about another failed attempt to eliminate the liability posed by Manan Hadariik.

To make matters worse, he'd learned through his secondary contacts that the Americans had somehow managed to intercept the crew delivering the second batch of U-92 ore, and that there had been no contact from their mining operation over the past twelve hours. They were supposed to have checked in via the special radio transmitters that used the radio waves to send an encoded signal buried with those signals transmitted by radio stations within Namibia.

That could only mean that the facility had either lost its communication capabilities with the last sandstorm reported to have gone through the area, or they had been compromised in some way. When al-Din considered the fact the transport team had been intercepted, it only stood to reason that the mine had been shut down for good, as well.

They had made a tactical judgment; that's all there really was to it. Al-Din had slowly watched this operation begin to unravel. These American agents were tenacious and fierce; al-Din would give them that. He could hardly believe that his very best jihad warriors had been put down so easily by the Americans, and now these bastards that fought like devils straight from hell were probably planning to assault the facility next.

After advising his spy to leave the country by whatever means possible, al-Din stormed off in search of Hezrai. He knew he could not stay behind any longer—Hezrai would have to lead the assault from here out. Al-Din knew that if one of his underlings were captured it wouldn't necessarily mean an end to the Intiqam-ut-Allah, but if they somehow managed to penetrate the facility and al-Din was still here, there was a remote chance he could be either killed or taken prisoner.

If that happened, it would spell certain doom for all

of them and their plans here would be for nothing. No, they would have to launch the submarines in very short order for whatever shape they were in. Fortunately, they had managed to produce enough weapons-grade plutonium to deliver four missiles, each with about an eight-kiloton payload. It wouldn't be as spectacular as six submarines with two missiles per craft, each capable of delivering a 100-ton or better return. Nonetheless, the death toll would still be several thousand or more per device.

It took al-Din a while but he eventually managed to locate Hezrai.

The leader of the security force was bent over a diagram with the work master, the two studying some important piece of information. Al-Din called to Hezrai, who joined him on the catwalk overlooking the construction facility out of earshot of the men. Al-Din briefed him on the recent news and the look on his face was aghast. For a moment, Hezrai stood there with head bowed, probably waiting for the worst to come by al-Din's hand. After all, he had been warned that if he failed al-Din again there would be a price to pay—an ultimate price that Hezrai seemed ready to accept.

By this point, though, al-Din was numb and would not have taken any satisfaction from killing Hezrai. In fact, he would derive more from knowing there existed a strong possibility Hezrai would fall at the hand of the Americans much more than by his own. It also gave him a significant amount of satisfaction to know that before long he would be away from this place for good. For the past two years he had lived here day and night, and now it was time to leave and go to his secure facility and wait to see if his plan would be even partially successful.

Al-Din's announcement of his departure did not seem to bring relief to Hezrai.

"I am troubled by the fact that you will not be here to celebrate our victory," Hezrai said.

"You know why I must leave. In the unlikely event that you are not successful and the Americans discover this base, which we both know has become more likely in the past few hours, there must be someone to carry us forward. I am the natural choice to lead us to the next mission."

"I understand."

"I have complete confidence that you will carry out our mission here without fail. There is no way the Americans could respond to us when we are so close."

"You speak words of greater truth than you may know. The weapons are secured aboard two of the vessels as you ordered."

"And the remainder?"

"Since it now seems unlikely that they will ever launch, or even be effective if they did, I have wired them with explosives. They will provide a significant diversion and repel any invasion force long enough for us to launch the remaining two."

"What about the warheads?"

"Primed and ready. We have tested the launch sequences of all four and they will deploy to their designated targets."

"What about antimissile systems?"

"The Americans have considered a first-strike scenario utilizing conventional underwater crafts such as fully equipped nuclear submarines. But a six-man submarine carrying such a small nuclear payload is not a contingency for which I believe they have trained or are prepared."

"And it is based on this that you think their efforts will be in vain?"

"I believe it is a strong possibility, yes."

"Then I shall leave you with complete confidence." The two men embraced in ceremonial fashion, and then al-Din said, "It seems I have misjudged you again, Hezrai. It is obvious that you are dedicated to our cause. That you are willing to risk your life for it is compelling enough proof to me of that."

"I wish you well, Latif."

"And you."

Al-Din spun on his heel and headed for the stairwell that would take him to the surface station and ultimately provide his exit. At the top he knew his private security force, a force he'd been training for this very day, awaited him in an armored vehicle. They would whisk him away to his secondary base of operations, a safe haven in an abandoned building in the heart of a modern commercial district in uptown Charleston. There he would await his chance to leave the country. It was no longer safe to stay in America; he had other obligations needing his attention and in places he would be much safer.

While he would have preferred his mission to bear out more success, he could not ask for more than this. This had been his greatest accomplishment, even if it hadn't turned out exactly as he planned. This was one of those times where his critical mistake in killing the American scientist had utterly backfired on him. Still, he could not let that affect him now, not in such a critical time where every single decision could lead him closer to escape or to mayhem. There were no hard-and-fast rules for this game.

TRUE TO HIS WORD, Lyons called Stony Man and within an hour Shanahan had an authorization from his SAIC to take the boat. The U.S. Coast Guard had also been notified and planned to provide whatever backup they would need. While Lyons had been getting checked out, Schwarz and Blancanales cleaned their weapons and performed an inventory on ammunition. Lyons had opted to trade out his RS-202 shotgun for a more practical assault weapon, an M-16 A-3/M-203. Schwarz and Blancanales decided to stick with the same weapons they had used on the assault against the house, respectively.

Lyons had agreed to let Shanahan tag along but only as a pilot for the boat. Once they reached the facility, Shanahan would wait on the perimeter and man the .50-caliber machine gun while Able Team went in and took care of business. With any luck, they'd be able to keep the submarines inside the facility, never exposing them to the light of day.

"Any idea what kinds of numbers we're going to see?" Schwarz asked.

He had to shout to be heard over the noisy boat motor and wind as they made their way along the shoreline and in the direction of Coldwater Cove. During transit, Schwarz had agreed to man the machine gun—they didn't want to run into trouble and let the terrorists catch them unawares. It was going to be hard enough. In some respects, this was where the tactics of Able Team differed in so many respects from Shanahan's.

To law enforcement, and especially an old veteran of the FBI like Shanahan, things should have been handled more like a procedural police operation where they followed the playbook letter for letter. But to Able Team, it was just another form of urban warfare, plain and simple. This had become a fire mission, a search-and-destroy of the highest order. Their enemy was determined but had poorly predicted one thing—the resilience of the Able Team warriors.

While most would have given up, turned tail and run or simply thrown up their hands with exasperation, the men of Able Team stood for something higher. Much higher. A dedication to duty and a fierce resolve against which no terrorist had been able to stand before, and probably never would again. So much had changed in the past decade for each of these men, both personally and professionally. They had suffered unbelievable adversity, tackled the odds and faced down the enemy without flinching.

Now, at long last, their persistence had paid off once more and they were about to enter what could well become either their greatest victory or something as simple as a watery tomb.

Lyons had no illusions about what they faced, and neither did any of the men aboard the boat with him. No, it was entirely possible that one or more of them—hell, maybe *all* of them—would perish this night. And then maybe, just maybe, there was a chance they would survive. Lyons couldn't be sure they were right about the base being at Coldwater Cove, but he figured it was too important not to check out at this point. So now they were here on this boat, freezing their collective nuts off and about to perhaps go up against the meanest terrorist group the world had ever known.

"Hey!"

Lyons shook his head to clear the cobwebs. "What?"

"How many?" Schwarz asked.

Lyons shrugged. "Maybe twenty, thirty. Hell, I don't know. Maybe a hundred."

"Well, however many," Schwarz said as he double-checked the action on his SSG-551, "I'll be ready for them."

Lyons nodded and cradled the M-16 A-3 a bit tighter to his body. Somehow, he drew a little warmth from the weapon, in spite of the cold metal that only got colder under the chilly breezes. The cold felt good against Lyons's skin, removing the sweat from his forehead and rejuvenating him. He was beginning to feel the strain on his body and he knew he had to clear his mind of the distractions. A distracted combatant equaled a dead one, and he knew they couldn't afford to take anything for granted.

"Irons!" Shanahan shouted.

The Able Team warrior turned and watched as Shanahan pointed toward the starboard part of the boat. "We're coming up on Coldwater Cove now!"

Lyons nodded, tapped Blancanales to signal he should keep his eyes open and then climbed down from the elevated observation post and took up a position that would afford him some protection. As they got closer to where Shanahan pointed, none of the men saw a thing.

Had they missed the entrance? Or was Shanahan simply not remembering it correctly. Then suddenly the boat slowed and slewed to the right so fast that it nearly tossed Lyons over the railing. Fortunately he caught his balance and managed to recover. It had been a while since he'd gotten his sea legs under him. The boat traversed a narrow corridor of water, the hills shooting up on either to form natural walls.

Then Lyons saw it. Light. Faint at first, but steadily growing as they got closer and closer. Lyons locked the stock of the M-16 A-3 against his shoulder and hunkered a little more behind the relative safety of the boat. Not that the fiberglass skin would withstand a bullet for very long, but it might provide adequate cover enough for Lyons to stand his ground during the initial assault. Then again, he didn't see much reason to worry on one front, since Able Team had surprise on their side.

And Carl Lyons meant to use that in every way possible.

CHAPTER TWENTY-FIVE

Hezrai had never known a bigger coward than Latif al-Din.

For the past two years he'd been forced to act subservient to the man, pretend to be his friend and a member of the Intiqam-ut-Allah, all in the name of loyalty to al Qaeda. Well, he hoped this latest demonstration would prove to them that al-Din deserved nothing but death and that would promote Hezrai to a leadership position.

After all, it was Hezrai who had done all of the real work. It was Hezrai who had overseen the work crews, Hezrai who had managed the money and affairs of al-Din behind his back, Hezrai who had spied on al-Din for his master, all the while pretending to be a servant and soldier in the service of the cause. When al Qaeda had first approached him, mere hours before al-Din made contact for the first time, Hezrai had almost refused. But then better sense had taken hold and Hezrai realized he would probably only be a middle-ranker at best if he'd decided not to help them.

His place had not yet been secured, but Hezrai knew now—with him poised to launch the attack and al-Din on the run—his fortunes were about to change.

As soon as Hezrai received word the submarines had been pressure tested successfully, Hezrai briefed the crews and then assigned them to their respective craft. They would only be able to launch two submarines, this much was true, but the missiles would yield much more than eight kilotons each. This was something Hezrai had chosen to keep from al-Din, since he would then realize too late once the missile was launched.

The original targets had been Boston, New York, Washington and Miami. But Hezrai felt that Miami was too far and that Charleston would make a more effective demonstration. It was something he had not chosen to reveal to al-Din, since it wouldn't do much good. As long as he got out of the area in time with his men, Latif al-Din could burn for all he cared. It would also destroy any evidence of this facility or the fact they had ever been here. That would prevent the Americans from tracking them.

Hezrai watched as the area around the submarines filled with water now that the inlets had been opened. It didn't take more than a few minutes before they were completely submerged. Once they had received the signal, the subs dropped completely from view and were knifing through the murky water, fading over distance until he could no longer detect them. So at long last they were about to see the fruition of their labors. The submarine launching against Charleston and Washington would take about an hour and a half to reach its destination, the other submarine more like three.

Hezrai knew he wouldn't have time to pack much, and in fact he had prepared a bag for this very purpose. The remainder of the staff had orders to evacuate the base as soon as possible, leaving explosives in place to blow on the remaining submarines they had been unable to complete due to al-Din's premature strike against Stout. That was what had precipitated this whole thing, and Hezrai had known even when al-Din gave that order, it was a mistake.

But the leadership in al Qaeda advised he go along willingly with it, probably unwilling to give up their only asset inside of al-Din's organization. That had always been part of the problem, as Hezrai saw it. They had always seemed jealous of al-Din's accomplishments and successes, perhaps even afraid, and Hezrai began to wonder how they would feel about him once he'd completed this mission. It struck Hezrai as almost ironic that this wasn't even his mission; this had been the mission of Latif al-Din, a man embittered by the murder of his family and utterly convinced this would buy his satisfaction.

Now, Hezrai was here once again completing al-Din's wishes with no real thought to his own ambitions and desires. If it had not been a way to elevate his status in al Qaeda, Hezrai sincerely doubted he'd be doing it. In fact, he probably would have killed al-Din long ago and this would all be over by now. Hezrai missed his own country and could not wait to return to Algiers.

The steady drone in his ears, the increasing buzz of what could only have been an outboard engine, drew Hezrai's attention. Standing on the catwalk that overlooked the six slots where just a quartet of the subs remained, Hezrai turned his eyes in the direction from which the sound seemed to emanate. Through the haze he could suddenly see a searchlight sweep the water beyond the inlet valves and a moment later the outline of a fairly large boat took shape.

The boat proved small, a patrol boat of some kind but nothing so large as a cutter or other naval vessel, and

Hezrai at first wondered if someone just happened to stumble into the place. It took only another moment to realize the grave error in that assumption when lights started to wink from the approaching boat. It only took Hezrai a moment to ascertain those lights were muzzle-flashes, and he suddenly perceived the faint echo of metal on metal.

The occupants in the boat were firing automatic weapons at them.

"We're under attack!" Hezrai shouted at the men clustered below him. "Get to your defensive positions!"

Hezrai then clawed for his pistol and brought it into play. He sighted on the boat and began to trigger one round after another, intent on taking at least one of the enemies with him. He managed to get off several rounds before he felt the burning, tearing sensation in his stomach just a millisecond before something lifted him off his feet.

Hezrai never felt his body tumble and bounce down the hard metal framing that surrounded the catwalk—never took note of the bloody streak his body left along one of the precious subs in which he had put such faith. That's because his mind had succumbed to the inky blackness of death in the same way his body succumbed to the black, swirling water of Coldwater Cove.

IT ALMOST SEEMED as if someone had tripped a switch because all three of the Able Team warriors, without any sort of prearranged signal, opened up on the facility simultaneously. The heavy reports from the .50-caliber machine gun drowned out those made by Schwarz's SSG-551 or Lyons's M-16 A-3. Their 5.56 mm high-velocity slugs matched ferocity as the pair complemented Blancanales's steady maelstrom from the Browning.

Lyons took out the first terrorist, however, one of the bursts flipping the man over the railing and dumping him into the murky waters. Lyons grinned to himself and swung the muzzle in the direction of another terrorist who was sprinting across some sort of runner that ran parallel with a metal catwalk spanning what Lyons assumed to be the main dry dock area. He triggered his weapon again, but this time the terrorist managed to evade the shots by diving behind the cover of a large fifty-five-gallon drum.

Schwarz got the next one with a 2-round burst that punched through a terrorist's chest. The impact spun him into a nearby metal beam and he bounced off before tumbling into the water. It was the first time they were close enough that Schwarz could tell the terrorist had fallen into the water in one of the docking slots, and that he noticed the bristling antenna protruding from the sail of one of the subs.

The submarines weren't small but they weren't overly massive, either. They were designed for short-range reconnaissance and strike, not prolonged missions, and for a moment Schwarz had to wonder—now that he had seen them and had an actual context from which to postulate his theories—if the subs had been designed to come back at all. He pushed the gruesome thought from his mind, realizing that America did not treat her armed forces like that. Suicide missions were the lot of men like Schwarz and his colleagues, not servicemen and women of the country.

Schwarz flinched reflexively as he heard a couple of rounds skid off the metal top rail of the boat. It took him a little time to locate the source of the firing, but when he did, Schwarz neatly dispatched the terrorist with a 3-round burst to the stomach.

Shanahan had slowed the boat considerably and now they were on top of the terrorist operation. Lyons immediately noticed six slots and only four boats present. For a second, he wondered if two of them were already away but he knew there wasn't much point in thinking about it. They couldn't worry about that this moment. He needed to concentrate on one thing at a time and that included the subs that were present and the several dozen terrorists now shooting at them from various locations throughout the facility.

In one sense, the terrorists had the advantage because not only were they on higher ground, but also they had adequate cover from which to fire. A plethora of rounds struck their boat and skidded across the deck, and at one point it got so thick that Schwarz had to abandon his post and dive to the deck to prevent being cut to ribbons.

During a lull in the firing, Blancanales played the part of "good trooper" and manned the machine gun once more. The rock of the boat as Blancanales commenced firing seemed almost soothing to all the men aboard.

Lyons didn't want a repeat performance of getting pinned down by so many terrorists at one time so he gestured for Schwarz's attention and indicated he should follow. As soon as Shanahan nosed the boat around so the side rail was against the metal overhang of an inlet valve, Lyons and Schwarz exited the boat by jumping onto the exterior of the inlet valve and then dropping the eight feet or so to the top of one of the subs.

A pair of terrorists who were concealed broke their cover and fired salvos in their direction. Lyons got one with a burst he triggered from the hip, the rounds coring through the man's pelvis and gut before they dumped him onto his back. The second terrorist seemed more fearless than the other, madly charging Schwarz with a scream and his rifle blazing—the rounds buzzed dangerously close past Schwarz but still wide of the mark.

The Able Team commando aimed the weapon from his shoulder, sighted carefully at the charging terrorist and squeezed the trigger. Several rounds crashed through the terrorist's shoulder and ripped his arm from its socket with penetrating force. The man twisted to his left and spun directly into the line of fire such that Schwarz's next several rounds ripped through his ribs and hip. The terrorist's spin continued until he lost his footing on the edge of the narrow walkway along the top of the submarine, fell off and slid down the side to crash into the water with a giant splash.

Complete pandemonium had now engulfed the facility. The cacophony of reports from more than two dozen automatic rifles and SMGs nearly deafened the occupants as they reverberated inside the cavernous structure. More terrorists exposed themselves, each trying to gain a more advantageous position from which to assault the Able Team trio, but every time they did they were either cut down by Schwarz or succumbed to the blanketing fire provided courtesy of Blancanales and the Browning .50-caliber machine gun.

As SOON AS he'd positioned the boat in such a way as to unload two of the occupants, Tom Shanahan grabbed his M-16 A-3 rifle and began to do what he could to help engage the enemy, keeping them at bay. The vociferous noise of battle ground against his nerves, but Shanahan found himself quickly becoming accustomed to it. He couldn't say this was the kind of lifestyle he would have preferred every day on the job, but at the moment he knew that was just the way things had to be.

In one respect, he wished that Buddy Davis had been

there with him. The camaraderie and efficiency among his three allies was obvious; they were used to one another and they moved and fought with the confidence and skill of a well-oiled machine. Shanahan was an outsider and he knew it, although these men had seemed extremely grateful for his help and insight. At one point, one of the trio had told Shanahan that without the information he and Davis had provided, they might never have found this underwater base.

At first, Shanahan hadn't wanted to believe any of it. The thought of this terrorist group calling itself the IUA operating with such impunity inside the country had seemed frightening enough, but now to come against them firsthand, to find out all of it was true? Well, that seemed almost too much to comprehend. Shanahan had to wonder how it could have gotten this far. Maybe he would ask his new friends once they got through it. But for the moment, he needed to put all of his focus on the mission in front of them.

It was a battleground, a true one like those in war, and Shanahan knew this could be it.

The will to survive, to see his wife again and hug his kids, was enough to keep him sharp and alert. That mentality saved him when he saw a terrorist pop from cover and try to take advantage of his position to flank Shanahan. The FBI agent spotted him, however, swung the muzzle of his M-16 A-3 in the terrorist's direction and squeezed the trigger twice, delivering a pair of 3-round bursts at the enemy. The first set was close but no cigar. The second trio landed on the money, punching holes in the man's gut and folding him over to the point he flipped over the railing of the catwalk and landed noisily on one of the subs.

Shanahan's next 3-round burst caught another terrorist gunner in the stomach. The 5.56 mm slugs ripped open the tender flesh and perforated his intestines. Blood poured from the wounds and the terrorist's rifle clattered to the deck of the submarine he'd been standing on. Holding his stomach and screaming, the terrorist dropped to his knees and looked up. The light slowly faded from his eyes, and eventually the terrorist fell face-first to the deck with a barely audible thud.

Shanahan would never forget the look in those eyes for as long as he lived.

THREE TERRORISTS TRIED to move as a single unit and board their boat, but Blancanales was ready for them. They had thought by approaching on the flank through the use of a small utility boat used to service the subs that Blancanales wouldn't be able to take them. They were wrong. As soon as Schwarz observed their approach, he shouted a warning at Blancanales, who swung the machine gun in their direction.

The boom-boom-boom of the heavy-caliber weapon sounded as ominous as the damage it rendered to its targets. The terrorists were surprised, having believed that Blancanales couldn't swing the gun on them at that angle. The weapon spit .50-caliber rounds at their position and immediately began to rip massive holes in the hull of their flimsy craft. One of the terrorists caught a couple of rounds in the chest and tumbled backward, entangling the feet of one of his comrades.

The man tried to free his legs but he wasn't fast enough, and a few .50-caliber skull busters blew his head off his shoulders. Blood spurted from the top of the headless corpse as the body twitched and tumbled over the side. The last man saw his friends and boat were being decimated at an unprecedented rate, and he obviously decided to abandon ship while he still had the chance. The terrorist smartly abandoned his weapon before diving over the side. A moment later, the boat began to come apart and Blancanales made sure to put enough rounds through the bottom it wouldn't be used again.

Lyons and Schwarz rose from cover and rushed down the top of the sub, careful not to lose their footing on the damp, slick surface. They reached a ladder well at the end of the boat that extended to the catwalk. Lyons provided cover while Schwarz was the first to climb to the catwalk. He then crouched and covered both sides while Lyons advanced up the ladder. Once together, the pair advanced in the direction of what looked like a small operations area while Blancanales covered their movements with the .50-caliber machine gun.

As they neared the end, a quartet of terrorists burst from hiding and leveled their weapons in Schwarz's and Lyons's direction. The pair dived for cover, Lyons cursing himself for bunching up on his partner's backside instead of keeping back some. It was Blancanales who provided their salvation as he opened up on the four terrorists with the machine gun. Heavy-caliber slugs punched through the group as if they weren't there and they tumbled into one another under the brutal force of the weapon.

One terrorist, similar to his partner in the boat, was literally decapitated by a pair of .50-caliber rounds. A second terrorist took four slugs to the back that blew out large parts of his spine and he pitched off the catwalk. His body sailed as straight as a missile into the murky black water below and was immediately sucked between the swirling water that provided natural suction due to the formation of the caves.

As the last terrorist dropped, Schwarz looked behind

him and said, "Maybe going this way wasn't such a good idea."

Lyons shook his head slowly and the pair climbed wearily to their feet. They were no longer under assault by the remaining terrorists, who seemed to have abandoned their posts and fled the area. The two Able Team warriors were about to advance when Schwarz suddenly looked down at one of the subs and grabbed Lyons's arm to get his attention. He pointed at a line of what looked like thin gray strips along the side of one of the boats.

"What is that?" Lyons asked, squinting.

"Can't be sure from here," Schwarz said. "But if I had to guess I'd say it was plastic explosive of some kind. Maybe C-4."

The two exchanged a glance, both coming to the same horrific conclusion at the same moment. They looked around and took notice that the place was now quiet and deserted, and nobody had stuck around to shoot at them. Then another moment elapsed before they could hear Blancanales shouting at them from the boat, beckoning them furiously to get back as quickly as possible. The only word they could make out through the tremendous echoes in the cavernous facility bordered on something like "Hurry."

The two raced back to the ladder and slid down it, neither bothering to descend rung by rung. They half ran, half slipped their way along a sub—one that was probably wired to go just like the others—not risking even so much as a look behind them until they reached the boat. Schwarz climbed aboard first and Lyons followed a moment later. Once they were aboard, Shanahan maneuvered the boat away from the complex and raced for the exit tunnel at top speed.

They barely made the corner before the explosives

blew and a massive wave of heat could be felt by all the men, even at that distance.

"What the hell—?" Blancanales rasped.

"They had the place wired to blow!" Schwarz said. "You mean, you didn't know?"

Blancanales shook his head. "No, I was only telling you to get back here because we got information that two submarines were spotted making full speed away from Charleston. We must have just missed them."

Lyons looked at Schwarz and said, "If you hadn't seen those… Well, we would've—"

"I'd just prefer not to think about that if you don't mind," Schwarz said.

Lyons looked at Blancanales. "So there are still two boats unaccounted for?"

"Yeah, a Coast Guard cutter spotted them on sonar. I guess they've been told to intercept and destroy if either refused to heave to. And I also understand the President has alerted the Navy."

"Damn! That's all we need right now."

"Well, it looks like the IUA at least saved us some time by doing for us what we would have probably done ourselves by blowing up those other subs."

"Maybe," Lyons replied. "But if those two remaining subs are loaded with warheads, this isn't over."

Not by a long shot.

CHAPTER TWENTY-SIX

When the call came from Stony Man that the IUA had managed to launch two submarines, a cold pang of fear clawed at the guts of every man in Phoenix Force.

They were still more than an hour from the eastern coastal regions and without any sort of real equipment to pursue the submarines even if they could reach their location on time. McCarter didn't mind admitting that he still hadn't formed a solid plan on how to take down the terrorists. They had plenty of weapons and ammunition, a fully stocked armory aboard the C-21, in fact, but no equipment for amphibious operations.

"You won't have to worry about that," Price said over the secure satellite uplink. The LCD monitor displayed her and Brognola at seats within the operations center. "The subs were spotted by sonar equipment aboard a U.S. Coast Guard cutter. The cutter is monitoring their progress but has been ordered not to engage and notified that under no circumstances are they to intervene."

"Any idea where they're headed, Barb?" Manning asked, the concern apparent in his voice.

"Not yet, but we do know they've split. One is heading north up the coast and the other is heading due east out to sea. We're guessing that the northbound submarine is probably going to deploy missiles at targets in New England."

"That would make sense," McCarter said. "Only places like Boston or New York, maybe even Atlantic City, would be considered worthwhile targets. The terrorists would want to inflict as much damage as possible and kill as many people as possible. Densely populated cities are much more viable targets than rural areas or small towns."

"Acknowledged," Brognola said. "But we also have to consider the alternatives. They could be aiming for any number of military targets. Our intelligence says those missiles have a very short range. They had to be compact in order to launch them from the FACOS prototypes, so that severely limits their fuel capacities and affects their range."

"What about using countermissile defense systems, Hal?" Hawkins asked. "Couldn't the Air Force or Navy just blow these things out of the sky?"

"If we were equipped with ground-fighting artillery such as the Patriot missile guidance systems, yes," Brognola said. "Unfortunately, that isn't standard fare along U.S. shores. We just never even looked at a contingency of this kind. Our antimissile systems are scaled around the idea of defending against globalized first-strike capabilities by foreign powers. We've always expected nuclear missiles to be ICBMs coming from locations we monitor around the clock."

"This is what made the FACOS such a perfect weapon," Price added. "And a *dangerous* one. The idea of sneaking right up to an enemy's shore and being able to deliver tactical strike teams or a nuclear payload was always considered nothing short of absurd."

"Well, obviously the IUA picked up on that," James said.

"So do you have any particular game plan for us?" McCarter asked.

"Able Team has advised they can catch the submarine headed due east out of Charleston. They're fairly confident they can intercept before the sub reaches international waters. At that point, it gets a little more difficult because we then have legitimate shipping traffic to worry about. However, we have notified certain parties of a potential threat and that we are investigating. We're asking commercial vessels to slow or even hold position for the next two hours until we can verify one way or another that both subs have been neutralized."

"What about the other?" McCarter asked.

"That's where you come in," Price said. "We've dispatched a Navy destroyer to lay in a pursuit course. The U.S.S. *Harpoon* is her name and she's commanded by Captain David Stevanojich. He's an Iraq War veteran and top-rated commander, highly decorated. He was specifically selected for this mission. You will land at Dulles and immediately depart via a chopper sent by the destroyer to pick you up."

"Stevanojich has been notified that you are en route," Brognola said. "He's been told nothing other than you're a special strike team of Navy SEALs. He knows most of those men but I don't think he'll question you. Try to do your best to look the part. If he suspects you aren't exactly as you claim, well, let's just say that could lead to a whole bunch of uncomfortable questions."

"We'll be on our best SEAL behavior," McCarter replied with a grin.

Hawkins made a seal bark sound and clapped his arms together, which evoked a punch in the arm from Calvin James.

Brognola shook his head. "I see your team has gotten some rest."

"A little too much, I think," Price added, but she grinned.

"No, they're this way all the time," McCarter said, rolling his eyes. "Doesn't matter how much sleep they've had."

"Well, we're glad to have you back in time to help out," Brognola said. "And I know Able Team feels the same. Lyons asked me to pass on his thanks for your help."

"Don't mention it," McCarter said. "We'll be in touch as soon as we've neutralized the target."

McCarter signed off and then the team went into high gear. They began pulling on fresh black combat fatigues like those the SEALs were known to wear. They also went with a complement of MP-5s—standard primary weapon of issue for SEAL operations—along with M-67 fragmentation grenades and military load-bearing harnesses. Each man carried a Ka-bar fighting knife, and Manning brought a satchel of underwater demo equipment.

"Where are we going to deploy from?" Hawkins asked McCarter. "The destroyer?"

McCarter shook his head. "I believe we'll come in direct via the chopper. We'll do this straight up, air-assault style. That's what most everyone will expect."

"David's right," James said. Everyone would defer to his judgment since James knew the SEAL methods and operating procedures. "When we get to the *Harpoon,* we'll track the submarine until they have to surface. That's when we hit them."

"We're going to try to board?"

"If all goes the way we plan," Manning said, patting the satchel filled with demolitions, "we won't have to board."

"If at all possible," McCarter added, "we're going to attempt to take her intact so that we can have a specialist secure the nuclear payloads. But if it goes hard or they resist, we'll send the thing to the bottom of the bloody Atlantic and the terrorists with it."

"Yeah, don't worry about it, Hawk," Encizo said. "It'll be as easy as falling off a bull."

ABLE TEAM BUZZED the water just above the location pinpointed by the U.S. Coast Guard. To be realistic, Lyons wasn't sure what more they could do until the cutter arrived with depth charges. They could see the Coast Guard vessel approaching rapidly in the distance, lights flashing as it sped toward the target. Somewhere in the dark choppy waters below was the submarine. Nothing on board the FBI boat was advanced enough for Schwarz to use to track the exact location, so they could only guess. If they weren't directly over it, however, they were darn close because Kurtzman had been feeding the cutter intelligence directly to Able Team's PDAs.

When the cutter arrived, Lyons climbed aboard and spoke with her captain, a guy whose nametag read Cpt. N. Pryor. "Permission to come aboard, Captain."

The captain nodded and tossed him a salute, which Lyons decided to return as a sign of respect more than anything else. "My name is Irons. You've been told of our mission?"

"I have, sir."

"Captain, I'll say up front that this is my mission but

it's your boat so I'm going to let you run it. There's a submarine somewhere around here that wants to wreak havoc against our cities. I won't mince words—let me tell you straight that this submarine may be equipped with weapons-grade nuclear materials."

"I wasn't informed…" Pryor began hesitantly.

"I'm sure you weren't and I'm equally sure this comes as a shock. But the fact is, that's where we're at and under no circumstances can we let this thing launch any weapons at American shores, nuclear or otherwise. So whatever you were told, you can be sure here and now that you have whatever authority you need to assist us to stop this. No need to check back with anybody because we don't have that time. We understand each other?"

"Yes, sir," Pryor said.

"Okay, let's go hunting. Do you have anything on board that might be able to neutralize a submarine?"

"In fact, we're carrying depth charges and a K-gun."

"Really? That's not something I would have normally thought would be standard equipment aboard a Coast Guard cutter."

"It isn't, but when we went to an elevated alert status yesterday we were given orders to equip our systems with these antiques. So your news about the submarine doesn't surprise me. But…missiles? Nuclear warheads?"

"Like I said, you should know what's at stake if you're going to be involved," Lyons said. He looked around to make sure none of the cutter crew was within earshot and added, "But under no circumstances are you to ever discuss that with anyone now or in the future. We do the mission and then we're done. No reports, no war stories, *nada.* I assume you can keep quiet."

"But my superiors—"

"Will be instructed not to ask questions. Don't ask, don't tell…that's the deal. Understand?"

"I do."

"Now, if you don't mind, my friends and I would love to see you in action."

The captain nodded and then turned and ordered his men to general quarters while Lyons helped Schwarz and Blancanales aboard. Lyons flashed a signal to Shanahan that he could return to Charleston, which they knew he would do gladly since the boat was running dangerously low on fuel and he'd probably be riding on fumes by the time he hit port.

The trio then accompanied the captain to the cramped bridge, where the radio officer was tracking the submarine by sonar. They weren't far off the mark, just a couple of miles, and it didn't take long to catch up with the sub. As soon as they were in range, Lyons turned the operation over to Pryor, who immediately issued orders to begin the leading process. In this case, they would attempt to get the submarine to surface by dropping depth charges just ahead of the craft. The resulting disturbance was designed to provide a psychological effect and, while not taking the submarine apart at the seams, it would sure as hell make the crew think they were doomed.

Lyons could not imagine a more terrifying scenario except maybe burning to death. To think about being trapped in an underwater tomb, sitting on the bottom of the floor of the Atlantic Ocean as small stress fractures let in water and the oxygen slowly seeped out was not something a normal person looked forward to—even a terrorist would find that disconcerting. Although Lyons could think of worse ways to go than smothering to death or drowning, a certain amount of time inside the submarine would be enough to grind on anybody's nerves.

Once the cutter was in position, Pryor gave the order to drop the first charge. Although they didn't carry depth charges as standard equipment, the crew seemed no less efficient in using them. They rolled the first charge into place, closed the cradle around it and then stabbed a switch. The K-gun sounded off with a bang and dropped the charge into the ocean. The cutter was moving at a steady eight knots and within no time at all they had dropped the first three.

"Depth of target?" Pryor questioned the sonar man from his seat on the bridge.

"I make target currently at seventy feet."

"Distance of charges?"

"Charges will reach intercept distance of one-five feet within ten, that is one-zero, seconds."

"Stand by to detonate," the captain ordered.

"Aye, sir."

All three of the Able Team warriors felt almost worthless as they watched the U.S. Coast Guard go to work. Well, this was their specialty and Lyons knew Able Team had to be content to leave it to them. The time would come soon enough for that sub to surface. According to their design schematics, the submarines could not fire unless they surfaced. They were simply too small to pump water fast enough to maintain ballast while firing missiles. Lyons hoped this team was good enough to call the bluff and bring the submarine to the surface; otherwise, it would sink to the bottom of the Atlantic and become little more than a watery grave for however many terrorists were on board.

"Blow the charge!" Pryor said.

For a minute or two there wasn't a thing to indicate that the depth charge had even blown. Then a flurry of bubbling water appeared a hundred feet astern. Pryor gave the order for the next charge to be blown, and the fire-control officer nodded as he stabbed the button. After the third one was blown, Lyons considered the depth charges they were using. They were designed for much larger subs than this one and Lyons began to wonder if anyone had accounted for the fact these FACOS prototypes were much smaller. Hell, this project had been classified, and to his knowledge neither Pryor nor any of his people really knew what they were dealing with.

Lyons whispered his concerns to Schwarz and Blancanales.

Blancanales nodded his agreement and approached Pryor, who was now searching aft with a pair of binoculars. "Pardon me for interrupting, Captain."

Pryor looked at Blancanales. "Yes, sir. What is it?"

"Well, my friends and I were just discussing the possibility that you may not have been given the proper tactical information regarding this submarine."

"What information is that?"

"This sub is not just any normal submarine. At least not in the, um, conventional sense. These subs are special tactical versions that are considerably smaller than a normal submarine."

"Well, I appreciate the heads-up, Mr. Rose, but we were given some facts about this sub when I asked why they were loading us up with training depth charges."

"Training depth charges?" Blancanales repeated, arching an eyebrow and looking at Schwarz and Lyons, who shrugged simultaneously.

"Yes." Pryor put the binoculars to his eyes and continued, "As the name implies, those submarines are not your standard depth charge. They have only about one-eighth the normal yield and are utilized for training exercises by the Navy."

"I see, heh. Well, then, I guess—"

"Skipper!" the sonar man called. "I have target now showing a depth of fifty-seven feet and climbing. She's surfacing, sir!"

"Acknowledged, Sterns. Good work!" Pryor turned to the fire-control officer, who doubled as his XO. "Lansing, issue small-arms to all crew and prepare a boarding party."

"Stand down there a minute, Lansing," Lyons said.

"Mr. Irons," the captain said.

The bridge went dead quiet and for one second all eyes fell on the Able Team leader. In a moment, he knew he'd made a big mistake. If he'd wanted to do this a different way, the proper thing would have been to pull Pryor aside and talk to him one-on-one. In this case, the breach of etiquette wasn't lost on anyone and in spite of Pryor's orders he couldn't allow it to just go by. He'd lose the respect of his men almost instantly.

Lyons put up his hands. "My apologies, Captain Pryor. I was out of line. This is your boat and I promised you could run it."

Pryor's lip twitched but he seemed to accept Lyons's apology graciously enough. He returned his attention to Lansing. "Lansing, I believe I gave you an order."

"Aye, sir!" Lansing saluted and made his way off the bridge.

Pryor looked back at Lyons. "Mr. Irons, can I see you a minute?"

Lyons and Pryor went outside the bridge and Pryor wasted no time getting to business. "Mr. Irons, with all due respect to your position, you have to understand that I can't and won't run my ship that way. Being a captain *depends* on commanding the respect of every man aboard."

"I understand, sir," Lyons said. "And I am truly sorry I stepped on your toes. It wasn't intentional. But you have to understand that what you're about to undertake isn't really within your area of expertise. This is what my men and I do. You're about to go up against an armed group of terrorists and you're not really trained for that. We are. So I'm asking you to let us handle this from here. If it'll make you feel better, we'll take the backup gladly."

Pryor gave it a moment, watching Lyons for a time, and then finally nodded before stepping back inside the enclosed bridge area.

Lyons signaled for Blancanales and Schwarz to join him, and together the three Able Team commandos climbed down to the foredeck and prepared for their assault on the submarine. Pryor had ordered the cutter to run an intercept course for where they had pinpointed the submarine would surface. Several tense minutes passed as the cutter slowed to a near standstill and Lyons, Blancanales and Schwarz waited at the front of the craft with weapons held at the ready.

The sail broke the water first and for a moment, as the water rushed down its sides, it seemed as if the crew aboard the cutter could hear no other sound. Then the stillness passed and it began to come back. The lap of water against the side of the cutter as it chugged closer toward the sub; the steady, rhythmic motion made by the Atlantic currents; the squawk of an occasional sea-faring bird as it passed overhead. In that same moment, something rose suddenly and ominously from the deck of the sub as it seemed like the top, forward deck of the sub retracted on itself.

"They're going to launch that thing," Blancanales observed in a hoarse voice.

Lyons turned and called to Pryor, "You got any heavy weapons aboard?"

"You better believe it," Pryor replied.

"Then you'd better use them quick."

"Fire-control officer…" was all the Able Team trio heard as Pryor ducked inside the bridge and a moment later four gun batteries opened simultaneously.

They were only 30 mm electric chain guns but they were more than adequate for the job. Sparks ricocheted off the deck as the cutter found its range and zeroed on the targets, and then suddenly they were punching through the thin metal skins of the missiles, which were now angled out of the sub like some great harpoons. There was a sputtering fire from one of the missiles but then it flamed out. The other one fired fully but merely succeeded in sending the deck awash in brilliant flame as the fuel spilled from the holes punched through the missile was ignited.

After a time, the firing ceased and another period of silence followed. Then a hatch opened in the sail and the first terrorist emerged waving a massive white flag. He was followed by a second and a third, and then eventually a total of six men appeared on the still smoldering deck with arms held high in the air. How their shoes weren't melting to the thing was anybody's guess.

Lyons felt a genuine pang of regret. "Oh, man! I'm disappointed now. I *hate* it when terrorists surrender!"

Blancanales looked with mock disbelief at his friend a moment and replied, "Ironman, you definitely need a vacation."

CHAPTER TWENTY-SEVEN

When Phoenix Force stepped off the chopper and onto the deck U.S.S. *Harpoon,* they were greeted with enthusiasm and shouts of adulation by everyone from Captain David Stevanojich to the cooks.

McCarter would have preferred a little less attention but he realized that Navy SEALs had somewhat of a reputation as being the toughest special operations units in the U.S. military's arsenal. Then again, the Army felt that way about Delta Force and Special Forces, and the USAF about its combat air patrol units, and so forth. In the end, what neither the men aboard the ship nor many others who had encountered Phoenix Force realized was that they had set eyes on the most experienced and elite fighting force in the world.

Phoenix Force had become America's foreign legion for Stony Man, a five-man team of combat specialists like something out of the old espionage novels of World War II. In truth, they were nothing short of legendary in their own right. Most of the time, it was their ability to stay out of the public eye and the limelight that had proved to be their greatest weapon, and this kind of dog-and-pony show made every man on the team uncomfortable.

McCarter decided not to let the attention bother him, instead choosing to focus on the mission at hand. By all practical purposes, McCarter would have been a captain, being head of a SEAL team, so in essence he held the same rank as Stevanojich. However, deference was usually granted to the captain of a vessel over that of a special warfare officer so McCarter decided to salute first when greeted by Stevanojich.

"Permission to come aboard?" McCarter said in a monotone.

"Permission granted, Captain," Stevanojich said, immediately returning the salute.

"I've been informed you were already briefed on the situation," McCarter said.

"I have been briefed and you can expect my full cooperation."

"Can you give me a status?"

"Follow me to the bridge, if you would, gentlemen," Stevanojich said.

"My men need to get prepped for the operation, Captain," McCarter said quickly. "But I'll be happy to accompany you."

Stevanojich nodded in understanding and the pair made their way to the bridge. The area was brightly lit as the sun climbed steadily into the sky. The light glittered like diamonds on the blue water of the Atlantic and a chill breeze ran through the room that was open to the air at the moment. Men bustled in and out, some carrying sheets of paper that they handed diligently to officers who conducted quiet conferences or reviewed and signed before dismissing the men who brought them with snappy salutes.

Stevanojich led McCarter to a map of the area. "This

is our present position. The target we're tracking for you is approximately one nautical mile ahead of us."

"At our present speed, how long until we overtake her?" McCarter asked.

The captain turned to one of his other officers and looked askance.

The guy immediately stepped forward, pulling a radio headset from his ear and said quietly, "ETA to target is approximately ten minutes, sir."

"Thank you, XO." Stevanojich looked at McCarter with the same expectant glance as he had his officer.

"You understand that our orders are to first attempt to take the vessel intact," McCarter said.

"I was told that much, yes," he said. "What I wasn't told is why."

McCarter looked around at the half dozen men in the room and then cocked his head with a hesitant glance.

Stevanojich turned and barked, "Clear the bridge."

Everybody vacated the bridge without question.

When they were alone, McCarter said, "It's believed there may be nuclear missiles aboard this vessel, and that it is being controlled by terrorists. My men and I have been ordered to coordinate with you to try to coerce the vessel into surfacing."

"Coerce how?"

"However you think it best," McCarter said. "Your mission is to get that tug up here where we can deal with it. Once you've done that, we can take it from there. I just got word on my way here that the second submarine a couple miles off the coast of Charleston has just surrendered to another team, and that they were forced to surface after depth charges were dropped on them. We're hoping this will go just as smoothly but we're going to need your expertise to make that happen."

Stevanojich scratched his chin thoughtfully. "Well, depth charges might be possible, although I'd prefer to utilize a homing torpedo."

"If that's what you think is the best solution, I have no objections. Just as long as you do enough damage to force them to the surface and not so much that they end up in the bottom of the ocean."

"That's why I suggest the homing torpedo," Stevanojich said. "For one, depth charges aren't as practical at these depths as the ones deployed by your other crew. We're out much farther from shore. Additionally, we can blow a homing torpedo with tremendous precision, which means it only takes one. Dropping standard depth charges via a K-gun would probably take more charges and much longer."

"Sounds like we can leave this in your capable hands, Captain," McCarter said with a grin.

The two men saluted and then McCarter wheeled and left the bridge. As he descended the steps he saw the other officers converge on the command center once more, and in the sun he could see Stevanojich's animated silhouette as he gave orders to prepare the assault. McCarter reached the gunship and immediately began to double-check his equipment while the pilots prepared to get the chopper airborne once more.

"We have a green light, mates," McCarter told the rest of the Phoenix Force warriors. "They're going to get that thing to the surface. As soon as they do, we'll move in."

The men all grunted their assent and then within five minutes they had clearance to take off. McCarter donned a headset so he could communicate with the chopper pilots while also monitoring the situation aboard the bridge. The traffic increased between the chopper and the bridge, the pilots maintaining a step-by-step communication on the status of the shipwide operations. Most of the initial chatter was just a lot of preparations, the position of various units and so forth. At one point, a pair of F/A-18 pilots indicated they were in position to provide antisubmarine backup if the primary mission failed.

McCarter wasn't surprised by it. He'd been told upon landing at Dulles that the Navy had also deployed the U.S.S. *Dwight D. Eisenhower* to the area just as additional support. To the general crews of the ships lending support, only the captains of the vessel knew this was a live operation. The remaining staff thought they were simply participating in a training exercise, and if anybody questioned it, they would be able to answer very truthfully in that regard. McCarter felt better in a way, knowing they had that kind of backup. According to James, who had been on *"Ike"* a couple of times, the carrier boasted a combat wing of nearly sixty aircraft.

McCarter keyed up his radio. "Team Two to Command."

Stevanojich's voice came back almost instantly. "Command to Team Two, go ahead."

"Team Two is in position. Call the ball. I repeat, you may call the ball."

A minute later McCarter could hear another controller's voice indicate the homing torpedo was away. A total of twenty seconds elapsed. Thirty. At one full minute, McCarter started to get nervous. They had been nearly ready to overtake the submarine when the chopper left the flight deck—supposedly that's what had been reported by Stevanojich's officers anyway— yet there was still no confirmation on the success or failure of the torpedo. McCarter waited another thirty seconds and then as he reached for the transmit key he heard Stevanojich's voice echoing in his ears.

"Command to Team Two. Command to Team Two."

"Team Two," McCarter replied. "Go, Command."

"The hammer is down and you are a go. Repeat— the hammer is down and you are a go!"

One look out the window was all McCarter needed to realize the destroyer captain's word was nothing short of gospel. The regular outline of the submarine sail broke the surface quickly, and the remainder of the submarine followed with such speed and force that it actually rocked when it completed surfacing. McCarter rapped the pilot on the shoulder and pointed in the direction of the boat. The pilot nodded and immediately banked the chopper in that direction. They made two full circles before the pilot swung the chopper in directly over the mast.

McCarter gave his men a thumb-up sign and they shuffled to the open door of the Sikorsky Sea King. James was the first out, rappelling down the nylon rope with the skill of the practiced professional. Hawkins followed a moment later, and when he hit the deck he crouched and covered the sail with his MP-5 while James served as belay man while the remainder of the team hit the deck.

They had barely finished gathering on the deck when the hatch on the sail flipped open and a terrorist popped his head out. The man immediately produced an assault rifle and pointed it in their direction. Before he could get off a shot, however, Hawkins opened up with a full salvo from the MP-5. A score of 9 mm Parabellums rocketed on course, some of them striking the side of the sail as Hawkins got his range before they struck the terrorist. His head blew apart under the impact of the burst and he dropped from sight.

There was a hiss and suddenly the deck seemed to drop away from the feet of a couple of the Phoenix Force team. Manning and James nearly tumbled into the gaping maw but McCarter and Encizo managed to haul their friends to safety before they tumbled into the gears and infrastructure of the missile launchers.

McCarter gestured for Manning to go to work on the missiles with the demolitions gear while the remainder of the team entered the submarine to neutralize the terrorist aggressors. McCarter had heard the terrorists immediately surrendered to Lyons and his team without incident, but apparently this crew didn't intend to be so amicable. A second terrorist leaped into view even as the Phoenix Force warriors were making their ascent up either side of the sail. The terrorist gunner didn't see the two pairs climbing the sail, spying only Manning, who had his back to the terrorist. The guy obviously thought he saw an easy target and slowly raised his AK-74S assault rifle to his shoulder with the intent of shooting Manning dead.

The terrorist would never know what hit him.

McCarter and James saw what was happening as they came over the top rail, which ran along the edge of the sail. They triggered their weapons at the same moment, causing the terrorist to dance under a merciless stream of rounds. The terrorist's corpse finally pitched forward and fell over the side of the sail, hitting the deck a moment later with a grotesque thud.

James didn't hesitate to jump into the hatchway and proceed down the railing in spite of the fact he knew the terrorists could be waiting for him. The remainder of the team followed, and three more terrorists inside tried to pin them down. In the confines of that space the reports from so many weapons being fired at one time threatened to deafen all of the occupants. Although it was nothing in contrast to the heavy blast that turned the front end of the sub into little more than scrap metal.

The aftereffects of the blast concussed the terrorists in the sub with such force that it ruptured their eardrums, causing them to bleed from their ears. One terrorist was so close the force of the explosion popped one eyeball from his socket. Fortunately, the four men of Phoenix Force were far enough from the area to experience only mild disorientation and ringing of the ears that lasted a few minutes.

Within a quarter hour, they were back on the deck of the sub with terrorists in custody and watching the U.S.S. *Harpoon* approach while a pair of choppers circled overhead.

CHAPTER TWENTY-EIGHT

It was Carl Lyons's turn to be surprised when he got the call from Tom Shanahan, who asked, "You planning to help us finish wrapping up this case or not?"

"What are you talking about?" Lyons asked.

That's when Shanahan explained that there was still one open residence in Charleston that hadn't been looked at.

"I took the liberty of putting a couple of my associates on the last place on your map, just to keep an eye on it when we got diverted to the medical center. I got a call a few minutes ago from the stakeout squad and they tell me there have been some interesting comings and goings there in the past few hours. At least one group of Arab males was seen arriving by vehicle and going inside the house."

"But if we've taken down the terrorist base and the submarines," Lyons said, "that means this is either a remnant force or the leader of the operation decided to cut his losses."

"Well, I was about to put together a task force and get a warrant, but I thought I'd call and offer you a piece of the action before I did."

Lyons chuckled. "Getting to like skipping all the red tape?"

Shanahan's reply was sheepish. "I guess you could say it's a nice change of pace."

"Give me the address and one hour."

"That means you're in?"

"Wouldn't miss it."

THE MEN OF Able Team were reunited one more time with Shanahan and Davis, and this time Lyons decided to let the FBI agents call the shots.

"The plan's simple," Shanahan said. "No more of those soft probes or whatever you call them. This is going to be a blitz."

Schwarz grinned. "You know, we know another guy who says that all the—"

"Uh, probably should skip that," Blancanales said.

"Okay," Schwarz said in a disappointed tone.

The five men stormed the house with a vengeful fury, following behind Shanahan, who drove his sedan straight through the front door in a blaze of glory. The occupants came out in full force themselves, although they weren't ready for such an unorthodox entry.

Shanahan came clear of the car with an M-16 A-3 held at the ready. With a little of Schwarz's wizardry, the weapon had been converted to full-auto and Shanahan made immediate use of this new feature. The FBI agent sprayed the living room with a firestorm of 5.56 mm rounds. Two terrorists caught the first of Shanahan's fusillades to the gut, a number of rounds cutting them across the midsection and shredding their intestines.

Buddy Davis joined the concert a moment later with several bursts from his own weapon, also modified for full-auto. One terrorist got a round that drilled through his lip and punched out the back of his skull in a gory mess that sprayed one of his comrades nearby. The second man was blinded by the spray in his eyes for only a moment, but that moment proved fatal when Davis followed up with two rounds to the chest. The impact sent him crashing onto a coffee table and drove shards of wood and glass into the terrorist's back.

Able Team made its approach from the back to prevent any terrorists from escaping. Schwarz and Blancanales took windows while Lyons came through a door. They didn't have to worry about taking fire from above since this was an expansive ranch style. Two terrorists who had been sitting in a room adjoining the kitchen, television blaring, emerged with SMGs drawn only to come face-to-face with Blancanales. The Able Team warrior raised his MP-5 40 and triggered a sustained burst. The .40 S&W slugs struck one terrorist in the chest and blew a hole in his heart before exiting his back. The second terrorist took a pair of rounds to the head that fractured every tooth in his mouth on impact before lodging in his brain. The terrorist crumpled to the kitchen floor, his head skidding through a puddle of his own blood.

Another terrorist burst from the door of a bathroom in a half mode of dress, his weapon in acquisition and catching Blancanales off guard. The terrorist's head burst apart before he could trigger a single round and a booming echo rolled through the kitchen. Blancanales whirled to see Lyons standing on the other side of the room with the muzzle of his Colt Python smoking, leveled in that general direction.

Both men whirled at the sound of a trio of terrorists who appeared at the end of a far hallway, cramped in the narrow confines but SMGs blazing all the same. As they raised their weapons to return fire, Schwarz took them with a flanking maneuver from his SSG-551, cutting through their ranks with a merciless onslaught of high-velocity slugs. The terrorists danced and jerked under the impact, and Lyons and Blancanales joined the concert a moment later just for good measure. Blood and bits of flesh washed the walls surrounding the terrorists and they toppled to the carpet one on the other, creating a pile that was nearly impassable.

There was the slam of a door behind them and Lyons took off after the fleeing terrorist, shouting at his comrades to continue clearing the house.

As they watched him go, Schwarz joined his friend and said, "He's so impetuous."

Blancanales looked at him, stunned.

"What? I think it's kind of manly." Schwarz shrugged. "Gives me shivers."

"You worry me," Blancanales replied.

LATIF AL-DIN BURST from a side entrance and raced toward the rear of the house. He heard the clatter of footfalls behind him and knew one of the Americans was pursuing him. Al-Din could not understand how they had found him so quickly. Somehow this location had been compromised—someone or something had given it away. Maybe more of Hezrai's sloppiness, or maybe Hadariik had talked. Yeah, that was probably it. He had given that young man everything, a cause for which to fight and a purpose in life.

This was the gratitude.

The submarines had failed, as well, more incompetence from the likes of Hezrai. Yesterday, al-Din had been the head of the most powerful terrorist cell ever to operate inside America. Today, he was running for his life. And it didn't make any sense why he should run; he wouldn't get away and he knew it.

Al-Din stopped running, turned and waited for his pursuer to catch up. He raised the pistol in the direction of the footfalls and a moment later a big, muscular American appeared. He had blond hair and blue eyes, a truly Aryan look, and al-Din smiled at the pleasure it would bring him. Here he would be killing a true American, a model of Americanism, maybe even a symbol of what it meant to be American.

Except when he squeezed the trigger the American didn't die—he didn't fall, didn't even flinch. That's when Latif al-Din realized it was over. The American hadn't died because al-Din had missed. Had he missed on purpose? It didn't really matter because the next—and last—thing he saw was the American raise a big stainless pistol and a flash burst from the muzzle.

And then Latif al-Din saw nothing.

THE WEARY FACES of the eight warriors ranged around the table of the War Room at Stony Man Farm looked on as Harold Brognola made his announcement.

"With al-Din dead and the facility destroyed, the remainder of the IUA has scattered."

"Any chance they could make a comeback?" Hawkins asked.

"We think their remaining numbers are negligible," Price replied.

"It doesn't seem likely," Manning added helpfully. "Start-up groups like this don't tend to survive unless the leadership remains intact. Al-Din's dead and we don't have any evidence that they have enough resources left to reorganize."

"Well, if they do make an encore appearance at least we'll be better prepared for them," Lyons said.

"Hear, hear!" McCarter said.

"You men did a fine job," Brognola said. "As usual. And you earned a bit of R & R."

"What about Hadariik?" Blancanales asked. "What's going to happen to him?"

"He'll go into federal protection somewhere once we've finished debriefing him," Price said. "He possesses considerable information on the membership inside of the IUA. He'll come in quite useful for some time."

"And Tom Shanahan?" Lyons said.

"He's been promoted to SAIC and transferred to Homeland Security, with Buddy Davis acting as his right hand," Price said.

"It's well deserved," Lyons remarked. "He's a good man."

"Well, I'd say that since things are quiet on the home front and we're done with our little soiree, some fishing is in order," Schwarz said.

"What fishing?" James cracked. "You're just going to take off for three days and come back to tell us *another* story about how the big one got away."

"Again," Blancanales added, holding his hands up and apart with a look of mock surprise.

Schwarz shook his head and replied, "Now that's just wrong."

Don Pendleton's Mack Bolan

Blood Play

Russian criminals infiltrate New Mexico's casinos to play for the highest stakes: nukes!

The Russian *mafiya* is out to take control of a Native American nuclear-waste plant in order to manufacture nuclear warheads in America's own backyard. Mack Bolan and Stony Man must deal with kidnapping, murder, classified secrets and a killing spree that won't end until Bolan claims victory— or forfeits his final fight to the death.

*Available July
wherever books are sold.*